"SOME OF THE FINEST IMAGINATIVE
ACTION THIS SIDE OF THE MISTY
MOUNTAINS."— *The Columbus Dispatch*

The Captain raised his voice so all could hear,
"Some of the rumors are true: There is trouble
brewing up North. High King Aurion prepares
for war with Modru!" A collective gasp of dismay welled up from the assembled Warrows.
"There's a great wall of darkness stalking down
the land from the North, like a great black
shadow. And inside the darkness is bitter cold
and the sun shines not. And there be fell creatures within that blackness, Rucks and such, a
gathering of his Horde. Some skirmishes with
the Enemy's forces already have occurred."

Shouts broke out among the Warrows. *Black
Shadows? Modru's Horde? Legends come to
Life?*

"Why now?" a small voice asked, puzzled.
"After four thousands years, why does Modru
threaten now?"

Book One of the Iron Tower Trilogy

THE DARK TIDE

DENNIS L. McKIERNAN

A SIGNET BOOK

NEW AMERICAN LIBRARY

A DIVISION OF PENGUIN BOOKS USA INC.

SIGNET TRADEMARK REG. U.S. PAT. OFF. AND FOREIGN COUNTRIES
REGISTERED TRADEMARK—MARCA REGISTRADA
HECHO EN DRESDEN, TN, U.S.A.

SIGNET, SIGNET CLASSIC, MENTOR, ONYX, PLUME, MERIDIAN
and NAL BOOKS are published by New American Library, a division of Penguin Books USA Inc., 1633 Broadway, New York, New York 10019

First Signet Printing, August, 1985

9   10   11   12   13   14   15   16   17

PRINTED IN THE UNITED STATES OF AMERICA

To my own Merrilee:
Martha Lee

And to Laurelin:
Tina

And the ichor and the thees and thous
are respectfully dedicated to
Ursula K. Le Guin

Contents

FOREWORD

Do you ever yearn for a particular kind of story and simply can't come by it? Perchance you read one once, and keep looking for another like it, but it just isn't to be found. And so, every now and again, it may be that you reread the only one you have and keep wishing for . . . more.

For me, there are many stories or series of tales like that, written by fine authors: Joy Chant, Ursula LeGuin, J. R. R. Tolkien, Patricia McKillip, Katherine Kurtz, to name a few of my favorites. And when a new work of theirs shows up on the shelves, I can't wait to get my hands on it to devour it in its entirety. Unfortunately, some of my favorite writers—such as Tolkien—have sailed upon the Darkling Sea, and no more will new gramaryes with those particular spellbinders' special enchantments come our way.

Yet, the type of tale that captures my heart and soul is hard to come by—not as rare as unicorns, perhaps, but still uncommon. And it's a long sigh between. My unoccupied hands keep straying among the special books on my shelf, fumbling for one that perhaps, by some miracle, I've overlooked. And I haunt the book stores, seeking new tales, or sequels, or prequels. Yet they seldom come, and I am often disappointed.

For years I have followed that pattern—and still do—questing for the works of others. But those quests only occasionally bear the rare, sweet fruit.

In 1981 I thought to try my hand at this *alchemy*, to tell a tale of my own choosing, and this is it. Oh, I don't believe I've matched the magnificent prose of the others, my favorites, for their glamours are their own and unique; yet I have told the tale I set out to tell, and perhaps the spell I cast will bind you.

Make no mistake, this book is written for those who love the Realms of Chant, the Deryni of Kurtz, McKillip's Riddles, Middle-earth of Tolkien, Le-Guin's Earthsea, and the kingdoms, peoples, and special wizardry of the many others whom I've not mentioned but whose spells exist nonetheless. And if you don't like their *magical* worlds, chances are you won't like *The Iron Tower* either—but then again, I could be wrong. On the other hand, if you enjoy a high Quest and the Wizards, Harpers, Dragons, Hobbits, Riddlemasters, Enchantresses, and all the rest that goes with it, then odds are you'll find you like the story of Tuck and Danner and Patrel and Merrilee, the Warrows of this tale.

I hope you enjoy it.

Dennis L. McKiernan
Westerville, Ohio—1983

JOURNAL NOTES

Note 1:
The source of this tale is a tattered copy of *The Raven Book*, an incredibly fortunate find dating from the time before The Separation.

Note 2:
The Great War of the Ban ended the Second Era (2E) of Mithgar. The Third Era (3E) began on the following Year's Start Day. The Third Era, too, eventually came to an end, and so started the Fourth Era (4E). The tale recorded here began in November of 4E2018. Although this adventure occurs four millennia after the Ban War, the roots of the quest lie directly in the events of that earlier time.

Note 3:
There are many instances in this tale where, in the press of the moment, the Dwarves, Elves, Men, and Warrows spoke in their own native tongues; yet, to avoid the awkwardness of burdensome translations, where necessary I have rendered their words in Pellarion, the Common Tongue of Mithgar. However, some words do not lend themselves to trans-

lation, and these I've left unchanged; yet other words may look to be in error, but are indeed correct. (For example, DelfLord is but a single word, though a capital *L* nestles among its letters. Also note that waggon, traveller, and several other similar words are written in the Pendwyrian form of Pellarion and are not misspelled.)

Note 4:
The "formal" speech spoken at the High King's court is similar in many respects to Old High German. In those cases where court speech appeared in *The Raven Book*, first I translated the words into Pellarion, and then, in the objective and nominative cases of the pronoun "you," I respectively substituted "thee" and "thou" to indicate that the formal court speech is being used. Again, to avoid over-burdening the reader, I have resisted inserting into the court speech additional archaic terms such as hast, wilt, durst, prithee, and the like.

"And that is what Evil does: forces us all down dark pathways we otherwise would not have trod."

Rael of Arden
January 10, 4E2019

CHAPTER 1

THE WELL-ATTENDED PARTING

With a final burst of speed, the young buccan Warrow raced through ankle-deep snow, his black hair flying out behind. In one hand he carried a bow already nocked with an arrow, and he sprinted toward a fallen log, clots of snow flinging out behind his flying boots; yet little or no sound did he make, for he was one of the Wee Folk. Swiftly he reached the log and silently dropped to one knee, quickly drawing the bow to the full and loosing the arrow with a humming twang of bowstring. Even before the deadly missile had sped to the target, another arrow was released, and another, another, and another—in all, five arrows were shot in rapid succession, hissing through the air, striking home with deadly accuracy.

"Whang! Right square in the center, Tuck!" cried Old Barlo as the last arrow thudded into the mark. "That's four for five, and you would'er got the other, too, if you'd'er held a bit." Old Barlo, a granther Warrow, stood up to his full three feet two inches of height and turned and cocked a baleful emerald-green eye upon the other young buccen gathered on the snowy slopes behind. "Now I'm telling all you rattlepates: draw fast, and loose quick, but no quicker as what you can fly it straight. The arrow as strays might well'er been throwed away, for all the good it does." Barlo turned back to Tuck. "Fetch up your arrows, lad, and sit and catch your breath. Who's next now? Well, step up here, slowcoach Tarpy."

Tuckerby Underbank slipped his chilled hands back into his mittens and quickly retrieved his five arrows from the tattered, black, Wolf silhouette on the haycock. With his breath blowing whitely in the cold air, Tuck trotted back through the snow to the watching group of archers at the edge of End Field, where he sat down on a fallen log, standing his bow against a nearby barren tree.

As Tuck watched little Tarpy sprint toward the target to fly arrows at the string-circle mark, the young buccan sitting beside him—Danner Bramblethorn as it was—leaned over and spoke: "Four out of five, indeed, Tuck," Danner said, exasperated. "Why, your first arrow nicked the ring. But Barlo Stingy won't give you credit for it, mark my words."

"Oh, Old Barlo's right, you know," replied Tuck. "I hurried the shot. It was out. He called it true. But you ought to know he's fair, Danner. You're the best shot here, and he says so. You're too hard on him. He's not a *stingy*, he just expects us to get it right—every time."

"Humph!" grunted Danner, looking unconvinced.

Tuck and Danner fell silent and watched Old Barlo instruct Tarpy, and they carefully listened to every word. It was important that they as well as the other hardy youth of Woody Hollow become expert with the bow. Ever since the word had come from the far borders of Northdell that Wolves were about— in autumn no less—many young buccen (that time of male Warrow-hood between the end of childhood at twenty and the coming of age at thirty), in fact most young buccen of the Boskydells, had been or would be in training.

Even before the onset of winter, which had struck early and hard this year, killing most of the late crops, wild Wolves had been seen roaming in large packs up north; and strange Men, too, were spied in the reaches across the borders beyond the Thornwall. And it was rumored that occasionally a Warrow or two—or even an entire family—would mysteriously disappear; but where they went, or just what happened to them, no one seemed to know. And some folks said they'd heard an awful Evil was way up north in the Wastes of Gron. Why, things hadn't been this bad since the passing of the flaming Dragon Star with its long, blazing tail silently cleaving the heavens, what with the crop failures, cattle and sheep dying, and the plagues that it had brought on. But that was five years ago and past, and this winter and Wolves and strange happenings was now.

And down at the One-Eyed Crow, not only was there talk of the trouble in Northdell, but also of the Big Men far north at Challerain Keep, mustering it seems for War. At the moment, holding forth to a most attentive Warrow audience was Will Longtoes, the Second-Deputy Constable of Eastdell, who, because of his dealings with the *authorities*—namely various Eastdell Mayors and the Chief Constable in Centerdell—appeared to know more than most about the strange doings abroad:

"Now I heard this from young Toby Holder who got it in Stonehill—them Holders have been trading with Stonehillers ever since the Bosky was founded, they came from up there in the Weiunwood in the first place, they say—anyway, the word has come to Stonehill to gather waggons, hundreds of waggons, and send 'em up to the Keep."

Hundreds of waggons? Up to the Keep? Warrows looked at each other in puzzlement. "Whatever for, Will?" asked someone in the crowd. "What can they want with hundreds of waggons?"

"Move people south, I shouldn't wonder, out of harm's way," answered Will.

What? Move 'em south? With wild Wolves running loose and all?

Will held up his hands, and the babble died down. "Toby said rumor has it that, up to the Keep, King Aurion is gathering his Men for War. Toby said the word is that the Big Folks are going to send their Women and youngers and elders west to Wellen and south to Gûnar and Valon, and even to Pellar." As Will took a long pull from his mug of ale, many in his audience nodded at his words, for what he said seemed to fit in with what folks had heard before.

"But what about the Wolves, Will?" asked Teddy Cloverhay of Willowdell, who was up in Woody Hollow delivering a waggon load of grain. "I mean, wull, ain't the Big Folks afraid that the Wolf packs will jump their travelling parties, it being winter and all, and the packs roaming the countryside?"

A general murmur of agreement came from the listening crowd, and Teddy repeated his question: "What about the Wolves?"

"Wolves there may be, Teddy," answered Will, "but Toby says the Big Folks are preparing for War, and that means they're going to be sending some kith away to safe havens, Wolves or not." Will took another pull on his ale. "Anyways, I reckon that the Wolves won't tackle a large group of travellers, the Wolf being what he is, preying on the weak and defenseless and all."

"Wull," responded Teddy, "there ain't many as is weaker than a younger, or some old gaffer, or even a Woman. Seems to me as they wouldn't send them kind of folks out west or south to fend against Wolves."

Again there was a general murmur of agreement, and Feeny Proudhand, the Budgens wheelwright, said, "Teddy is as right as rain. Folks just don't send their kin out agin Wolves; not even the Big Folks would do that. It sounds like *Word from the Beyond*, if you asks me."

Many in the crowd in the One-Eyed Crow nodded their agreement, for people in the Boskydells tend to be suspicious of any news coming to them from beyond the Spindlethorn Barrier, from Foreign Parts as it were. Thus the saying *Word from the Beyond* meant that *any* information from beyond the borders, from Outside, was highly suspect and not to be trusted until confirmed; certainly such news was not *Sevendell Certain*. In this case, the *Word from the Beyond* had in fact come from beyond the Thornwall—from Stonehill, to be exact.

"Be that as it may, Feeny," shot back Will, fixing

the wheelwright with a gimlet eye, "the Holders are to be trusted, and if young Toby says he saw the Stonehillers gathering waggons to send up to the Keep, and preparing for a stream of Big Folk heading to the south, down the Post Road, then *I* for one believe him."

"He *saw* them?" asked Feeny. "Well, that's different. If Toby says he actually *saw* them, then I believe it, too." Feeny took a pull from his own mug, then said, "I suppose it's the Evil up north."

"That's what they say," spoke up Nob Haywood, a local storekeeper. "Only I talked to Toby, too, and he'd heard that the Big Folks are saying that it's Modru's doings!"

Ooohh! said some in the crowd, for Modru of Gron strode through many a legend, and he was always painted the blackest evil.

"They say he's come back to his cold iron fortress way up north," continued Nob, "though what he's doing there, well, I'm sure I don't know."

"Oi then, that explains the winter and the Wolves and everything!" exclaimed Gaffer Tom, thumping the iron ferrule of his gnarled walking stick to the floor. "The old tales say he's Master of the Cold, and Wolves do his bidding, too. Now everybody here knows it started snowing in September, even before the scything, and certainly before the apple harvest. And the snow's been on the ground ever since, with more coming all the time. And I says and everybody knows that ain't altogether natural. Besides, even before the white cold came, there appeared them Wolf packs, up Northdell way for now, but like as not they'll be near Woody Hollow soon. Oh, it's Evil Modru's doings, all right, mark my words. We all know about him and his mastery of the cold and the Wolves."

A hubbub of surprise mingled with fear rose up in the room, for with these words Gaffer Tom had reminded them all of the cradle-tales of their youth. And the Gaffer had voiced their deepest fears, for if it truly was Modru returned, then it was a dire prospect all of Mithgar faced.

"Not Wolves, Gaffer," said Bingo Peacher, a hunter of renown, sitting in a shadowed corner with his back to the wall. "Modru, he don't command wild Wolves. Nobody commands Wolves. Ar, maybe now and again there are tales of Wolves helping the Elves, but even the Elves don't *tell* 'em what to do, they *asks* them to help. Oh, Wolves is dangerous, right enough, and you've got ter give 'em wide berth, and they'll do the same for you unless they're starving— then look out. Ar, I don't doubt that Modru is behind all this cold weather, and that's what's driven decent Wolves south where their food has got to, or where they can raid some hard-working farmer's flocks, but that don't mean that Modru gives Wolves their orders. Wild Wolves is too independent and don't bow down to no one, not even Modru. Oh no, Gaffer, it ain't the Wolves that Modru commands; it's *Vulgs*!"

Vulgs? cried a few startled voices here and there, and the faces of most of the listeners turned pale at the thought of these evil creatures. Vulgs: Wolf-like in appearance, but larger; vile servants of dark forces; savage fiends of the night; unable to withstand the clear light of the Sun; evil ravers slaughtering with no purpose of their own except to slay.

Grim fear washed over the crowd at the One-Eyed Crow.

"Here now!" cried Will Longtoes, sharply. "There ain't no cause to believe them old dammen's tales. They're just stories to tell youngers to get 'em to behave. Besides, even if they were true, well, you all knows that Modru and Vulgs can't face the daylight: they suffer the Ban! And Adon's Ban has held true from the end of the Second Era till now—*more than four thousand years!* So stop all this prattle about Modru comin' to get us." Will had put up his best show of confidence, but the Second-Deputy Constable of Eastdell neither looked nor sounded sure of himself, for Gaffer Tom's and Bingo's words had shaken him, too. Many was the time as a youngling he'd been told that Modru and his Vulgs would get him if he didn't mind his manners; and, too, he recalled the fearful saying: *Vulg's black bite slays at night.*

"Think what you will," replied Gaffer Tom, pointing his cane at Will, "but many an old dammen's tale grows from the root of truth. Like as not the early winter here in the Bosky has brought the Wolves, and maybe even some Vulgs, too. And like as not they are the cause of the *Disappearances*. Who's to say it *ain't* Modru's doings?"

As the Gaffer's cane thumped back to the floor for emphasis, nearly all the folks in the Crow nodded in agreement, for Gaffer Tom's words rang true.

"Well, early winter or not," replied Will, stubbornly, "I just don't think you ought'er go around scaring folks, what with your talk about a hearthtale bogeyman, or Vulgs. And as to the Wolves, we all know that the Gammer began organizing the

Wolf Patrols up in Northdell, 'cause they're the first
ones as is had to deal with them. And the Gammer
has asked Captain Alver down to Reedyville to take
over and lead the Thornwalkers. What's more, archers are being trained, and Wolf Patrols organized,
and Beyonder Guards set. All I can say is Wolves
and any other threat will soon fear Warrows, right
enough."

The folks in the crowd murmured their endorse-
ment of Will's last statement about old Gammer
Alderbuc, past Captain of the Thornwalkers; and
many in the crowd had praised Gammer's hand-
picked successor, Captain Alver of Reedyville; and
all were confident in the abilities of the Thornwalkers, for many of those there in the Crow had
been 'Walkers themselves in their young-buccan
days. And although these facts concerning the
Thornwalkers were well known throughout the
Boskydells, still the crowd in the One-Eyed Crow
had listened to Will's words as intently as they would
have were they hearing them for the first time, for
Warrows like to mull things over and slowly shape
their opinions.

As to the Thornwalkers, ordinarily they were but
a handful of Warrows who casually patrolled the
borders of the Boskydells; and, like the Constables
and Postal Messengers, in times of peace they served
less as Boskydell officials and more as reporters and
gossips who kept the outlying Bosky folks up on the
Seven Dells news. But in times of trouble—such as
this time was—the force was enlarged and "Walking" began in earnest. For, although the Land was
protected from Intruders by a formidable barrier
of thorns—Spindlethorns—growing in the river val-

leys around the Land, still those who were determined enough or those who were of a sufficiently
evil intent could slowly force their way through the
Thornwall. Hence, the patrols and guards kept close
watch on the Boskydell boundaries, "Walking the
Thorns" as it were, or standing Beyonder Guard,
making certain that only those Outsiders with le-
gitimate business entered the Bosky. And so the
Spindlethorn patrols, or Thornwalkers as they were
called, were especially important now, what with
Wolves crossing into the Land and strange Folk
prowling about. Why, indeed, that was the reason
Old Barlo was training a group of archers: to add
to the Thornwalker ranks.

"Wull, all as I can say," replied Gaffer Tom from
his customary chair in the One-Eyed Crow, "is that
the 'Walkers is got a fight on their hands if we're
dealing with Modru's Vulgs. Them archers had better learn to shoot true."

And shoot true they did, for not only was Old
Barlo a good teacher, but Warrows, once they set
their minds to it, learn quickly. Over the past six
weeks, Old Barlo had had them shooting in the bright
of day and in the dark of night, in calm still air and
through gusting winds, through blowing dim snow
and across blinding white, from far and from near,
at still targets and at moving ones, on level ground
and uphill and down, in open fields and in close
brambly woods. And now they were learning to shoot
accurately while breathless and panting after
sprinting silently for a good distance. And the young
buccen Warrows had learned well, for the shafts
now sped true to the target, most to strike in or

near the small circle. But of all of Barlo's students, two stood out: Danner was tops, with Tuck a close second.

"All right, lads, gather 'round," cried Old Barlo, as Hob Banderel, the final shooter, came puffing back from collecting his arrows. "I've got something ter say." As soon as the students were assembled around him, Old Barlo continued: "There's them as says there's strange doings up north, and them as says trouble's due. Well, I don't pretend to ken the which of it, but you all know Captain Alver asked me to train as good a group of bow-buccen as I could, and you was selected to be my first class." A low murmur broke out among the students. "Quiet, you rattlejaws!" As silence again reigned, Barlo went on: "You all know that more Thornwalkers is needed in the Wolf Patrols and for Beyonder Guard, them as can shoot straight and quick. Well, you're it!" Barlo looked around at the blank faces staring at him. "What I'm trying to say is that you're done. Finished. I can't teach you no more. You've learned all I can show you. No more school! Class is dismissed! You've all graduated!"

A great yell of gladness burst forth from the young buccen, and some threw their hats in the air while others joyously riddled the Wolf silhouette with swift-flying arrows.

"Did you hear that, Danner?" bubbled Tuck, jittering with excitement. "We're done. School's out. We're Thornwalkers—well, almost."

"Of course I heard it," gruffed Danner, "I'm not deaf, you know. All I can say is, it's about time."

"Hold it down!" shouted Old Barlo above the babble, as he took a scroll from his quiver and began untying the green ribbon bound around it. "I've got more ter say!" Slowly the hubbub died, and all eyes turned once more to the teacher. "Wagtongues!" he snorted, but smiled. "Captain Alver has sent word," Old Barlo waved the parchment for all to see, "that Thornwalker guides are to come and take each and every one of you to your companies. You've got one more week to home, then it's off to the borders you'll go, to your 'Walker duty."

To the borders? One more week and away? A thick pall of silence blanketed all of the students, and Tuck felt as if he'd been struck hard in the pit of his stomach. *One week? Leave home? Leave Woody Hollow? Why of course, you ninnyhammer,* he thought, *you've got to leave home if you're joining the Thornwalkers.* But, well, it was just that it was so sudden: one short week. Besides, he had only thought about *becoming* a Thornwalker, and he'd not really envisioned what that meant in the end, leaving his comfortable home and all. Tuck's spirit rallied slightly as he thought, *Oh well, after all, a fellow's got to leave the nest sometime or other.* Tuck turned and looked to Danner for reassurance, but all he saw was another stricken Warrow face.

Tuck became aware that Old Barlo was calling out assignments, posting Warrows to the Eastdell First, and the Eastdell Second, and to other companies of the Thornwalker Guard; and then his name was being shouted. "Wha—what?" he asked, his head snapping up, recovering a bit from his benumbed state. "What did you say?"

"I said," growled Old Barlo, stabbing his forefinger at the parchment, "by Captain Alver's order,

you and Danner and Tarpy and Hob are posted to
the Eastdell Fourth. Them's the ones what are up
to the north, between the Battle Downs and Northwood along the Spindle River, up to Spindle Ford.
The Eastdell Fourth. Have you got that?"

Tuck nodded dumbly and edged over to Danner
as Old Barlo resumed calling out assignments to
the other Warrows. "The Eastdell Fourth, Danner,"
said Tuck. "Ford Spindle. That's on the road to
Challerain Keep, King Aurion's summer throne."

"Like as not we won't be seeing any King on any
kind of throne, much less the High King himself.
And we won't be doing too much Wolf patrolling
either, if we're stuck at the ford," grumped Danner,
disappointed. "I was looking forward to feathering
a couple of those brutes."

As Danner and Tuck chatted, two other Warrows
made their way through the crowd and joined them:
Hob Banderel and Tarpy Wiggins. Of that four-
some, Danner was tallest, standing three feet seven,
with Hob and Tuck one inch shorter and Tarpy but
an inch over three feet. Except for their height, as
with all Warrows, their most striking feature was
their great, strange, sparkling eyes, tilted much the
same as Elves', but of jewellike hues—Tuck's a sapphirine blue, Tarpy's and Hob's a pale emerald green,
and Danner's, the third and last color of Warrow
eyes, amber gold. Like Elves, too, their ears were
pointed, though hidden much of the time by their
hair; for, as is common among the buccen, they each
had locks cropped at the shoulder, ranging in shade
from Tuck's black to Hob's light ginger, with Danner and Tarpy both being chestnut-maned. Unlike
their elders, they each were young-buccan slim, not

yet having settled down to hearth and home and
four meals a day, or, on feast days, five. (But, as the
elders tell it, "Warrows are small, and small things
take a heap of food to keep 'em going. Look at your
birds, and mice, and look especially at shrews: they're
all busy gulping down food most of the time that
they're awake. So us Wee Folk need at least four
meals a day just to keep a body alive!")

"Well, Tuck," said Hob, "it's the Eastdell Fourth
for us all."

"Four always was my lucky number," chimed in
Tarpy. "Fourth time's the charm, they say."

"No, Tarpy," put in Danner, "*third* time's the
charm. Fourth time is *harm*."

"Are you sure?" asked the small Warrow, fretting.
"Oh my, I hope that's not an omen."

"Don't let it bother you, Tarpy," said Tuck, aiming a frown at Danner. "It's just an old saying. I'm
sure the Eastdell Fourth will be good luck to us
all."

"Well, I think it will be the best Thornwalker
company of them all," smiled Hob, "now that we're
in it, that is."

At that moment, Old Barlo again called for quiet,
interrupting the babble among the graduates. "Well,
lads, you're about to shoulder an important duty.
One week from now you'll be on your way, and I
wish I was going with you, but I've got to stay behind to get another group ready. Besides, the 'Walkers needs them as is spry, which I ain't anymore.
So it's up to you, Thornwalker Warrows, and a finer
bunch I've never seen!"

A cheer broke out, and there were scattered shouts
of *Hooray for Old Barlo!*

"There's just a couple of more things I've got to say," continued Old Barlo when quiet returned. "We meet in the Commons at sunrise next Wednesday, and you'll be off. Pack your knapsacks well; take those things we talked about: your bows, plenty of arrows, warm boots and dry stockings, down clothes, your Thornwalker-grey cloaks, and so on. The 'Walker guides will bring food, and ponies for them as needs 'em for the faraway trips." Old Barlo paused, looking over his charges, and before their very eyes he seemed to grow older and sadder. "Take this week to say goodbye to your friends and family, and any damman you may have about," he said quietly, "for like as not it'll be next spring or later before you'll be to home again."

Once more Tuck felt as if he'd been kicked in the stomach. *Next spring? Why, he wouldn't even be home for Yule, or Year's End, or . . . or . . .*

"Cheer up, lads!" Old Barlo said heartily, " 'cause now it's time for your graduation present. We're off to the One-Eyed Crow, where I'll set up a round of ale for each and every one!"

Again there was a cheer, and this time all the young buccen shouted *Hooray for Old Barlo!* three times. And they tramped away, singing rowdy verses of *The Jolly Warrow* as they marched down from Hollow End toward the One-Eyed Crow.

The week was one of poignant sadness for Tuck; he spent the time, as many of his comrades did, saying goodbye. It was a goodbye not only to his friends and acquaintances, but also to the familiar places he'd frequented throughout his young life in and around Woody Hollow: the Dingle-rill, now

rimed with ice; Bringo's Stable, with its frisky ponies; Dossey's Orchard, where many a stray apple
had come into Tuck's possession; Catchet's Market,
full of the smells of cheese and bread and open
boxes of fruit and hickory-cured bacon hanging from
overhead beams; Gorbury's mill, grumbling with
the groan of axles and the burr of wooden-toothed
gears and the heavy grind of slow-turning water-
driven millstones; the Rillbridge, under which was
some of the best jiggle-bait fishing in the Boskydells; Sugarcreek Falls, where Tuck's cousins from
Eastpoint had taught him to swim; and the High
Hill on the Westway Trace, from which all of Woody
Hollow could be seen. These places, and more, Tuck
visited, moving quietly through the snow to stop at
each and fill his being with its essence, and then
after saying goodbye he would sadly trudge on.

But the place to which Tuck turned the most was
The Root, his home, with its warm, cozy burrow
rooms, the smell of his mother's cooking, and all
the familiar objects that it seemed he'd never really
looked at before. And to his mother's surprise he
actually straightened his cubby; and without bidding from his father, he split a cord or two of wood,
laying in a good supply outside the burrow kitchen
door before he was to be off. Each evening he sat
before the fireplace, having a pipe with his sire,
Burt, a stonecutter and mason, while his dam, Tulip, sewed. And they quietly talked about the days
that had been, and the days that were, and the days
that were yet to come.

Tuck spent some time with Merrilee Holt, maiden
Warrow, dammsel of Bringo Holt, the farrier, and
his wife, Bessie, who lived four burrows to the east.

Merrilee and Tuck had chummed together since childhood, even though she *was* four years younger. Yet in these last days, Tuck saw for the first time just how black her hair was, and how blue her eyes, and how gracefully she moved; and he marvelled, for it seemed to him that he should have *noticed* these things before. Why, back when he had first begun Thornwalker archery training, and she had insisted that he teach her, too, he should have seen these things about her—but he hadn't. Instead, they'd laughed at her struggle to pull an arrow to the fullest. But even when she became skilled, using Tuck's old stripling bow, still at the time he'd seen only her accuracy and not her grace. And why was it only in this last week that he realized that she alone really understood him?

"You know that I'll not be here for your age-name birthday," Tuck said on the last wintery forenoon as they tramped through the snow on the Commons, trudging toward the Rillbridge. "I'm disappointed that I'll miss your party when you officially become a young damman."

"I'll miss you, too, Tuck," answered Merrilee, sadly.

"Well, be that as it may," said Tuck, "here, I've a present for you. Early it is, yet likely I'll still be at the Spindle Ford when you pass from your maiden years." Tuck handed her a small packet, and inside was a gilded comb.

"Oh Tuck, what a wonderful gift," beamed Merrilee. "Why, I'll think of you every day—every time I use it." Carefully Merrilee put the gift away in a large coat pocket, saving the paper and ribbon, too. They both stopped and leaned over the rail of the Rillbridge, listening to the churn of the millrace and watching the bubbles of air darting under the ice, seeking escape but being carried along by the fast-flowing stream.

"What are you thinking, Tuck?" asked Merrilee, as the bubbles swirled by below.

"Oh, just that some people go through life like those bubbles down there, caught in a rush of events that push them thither and yon, never able to break free to choose what they would. I was also thinking that many of us are blind until we've but a short time left to see," he answered, then looked up and saw that Merrilee's eyes had misted over, but she smiled at him.

The week had fled swiftly, and now it had come to the last hours of the last day. Once more Tuck found himself with his parents before the fire at The Root.

"Merrilee and I went down to the Rillsteps today," Tuck said, blowing a smoke ring toward the flames, watching it rend as the hot draft caught it and whirled it upward. "Thought I'd give them one last look before leaving. Danner was there, and we talked about the times we'd played King of the Rillrock. He always used to win, you know. No one could dislodge him from that center stone, Rillrock. He'd just knock us kersplash right into the Dinglerill, shouting, 'King of the Rillrock! King of the Rillrock! Danner Bramblethorn is the King of the Rillrock!' "

"His sire was like that, too," said Tulip, looking up from her stitchery. "We used to think that he was *glued* to that rock. Many a time your own dad was tumbled into the Rill by Hanlo Bramblethorn."

"Hmph," grunted Burt Underbank, pausing in his whittling, inspecting the edge of his knife, "that's right. He did. Fought like a cornered badger, he did. Against all comers and all odds. Harrump! Took us all down a peg or two. Seemed to think that rock was his own personal property instead of part of the east public footway across the Dingle-rill. From what I hear, Danner's even better at it than Hanlo was."

"What makes Danner that way, Dad?" asked Tuck. "I mean, it seems he's always got to be the best at what he takes up. Why is he that way?"

"Like sire, like bucco, I always say, Tuck," answered Burt.

"No, Dad, I mean, what makes people the way they are? What makes me," Tuck paused, then found the word he was searching for, "easygoing, while Danner is, uh . . ." Tuck couldn't seem to come up with the appropriate word.

"Pugnacious," said Tuck's mother.

"More like quarrelsome," said his father, "if he's anything like Hanlo was."

"Well, all I know is that he always wants to be King of the Rillrock at anything he does," said Tuck, puffing another smoke ring at the hearth.

"I think people are born to their nature," said Mrs. Underbank.

"I think it's the way they're raised," said Tuck's sire.

They sat and gazed at the fire for moments as the flames twined and writhed and danced, casting flickering shadows throughout the parlor of The Root. Burt threw another log on the pyre. They watched as sparks flew up the chimney, and the

flaming wood popped and cracked as it blazed up.
Then the flames settled back, and once more the
quiet was broken only by the faint creak of Tuck's
rocker, the snick and slice of Burt's knife against
the whittling stick, and the pop and whisper of Tulip's needle, puncturing cloth and pulling bright
floss through taut linen stretched drumhead tight
within the embroidery hoop.

"I saw two more strangers today," said Burt after
a moment. "More Thornwalkers, I think. Went riding down to the stable, each leading a string of
ponies. That's seven, no, eight so far." Burt stopped
his whittling and leaned forward to tap the dottle
from his pipe against the hearth. Then he settled
back, stuffing the warm clay into a pocket of his
unbuttoned vest. "You all set, Tuck?" he asked for
perhaps the tenth time that day and the fiftieth time
that week. "Tomorrow's the day."

"Yes. I'm ready," answered Tuck, quietly.

The sound of Tulip's sewing stopped, and she sat
in her chair by the soft light of the warm yellow
lamp and looked down toward the needlework in
her lap. But she stitched not, for she could no longer
see what to do through her quiet tears.

Dawn found grey-cloaked Tuck wandering through
a milling, chattering crowd in the Woody Hollow
Commons. It seemed as if the entire population of
the town had turned out in spite of the cold to see
the Thornwalkers off. A lot of folks had come up
from Budgens, too, for a few of their buccoes had
been trained in Old Barlo's class and would be off
to Thornwalker duties this day, also.

Tarpy and Hob had managed to find Tuck, and

now they were looking for Danner. But before they could find him, Geront Gabben, the Woody Hollow Mayor, standing up on the Commons' platform, rang the fire gong for quiet. As soon as he got it, he sallied forth into a speech of indeterminate length.

"My friends, on this most auspicious of occasions," he began, and such a beginning should have tipped off most of the Warrows that Geront was in a talkative mood. But perhaps because this was a farewell parting for the Thornwalker young buccen, the Warrow citizenry only thought that this was a "fare-you-well" speech, and Warrows do love speeches—short ones, that is. And so, some in the crowd cried out, *Tell it to 'em!* and *Hear! Hear!* and Mayor Gabben, encouraged, pressed on. Tuck listened intently for a while, but finally his attention began to stray. It seemed that the Mayor couldn't decide whether this was a sad and solemn occasion or a happy, ribbon-cutting ceremony as he swung back and forth between the two and droned on and on. But when folks in the crowd began to call out, *What's your point, Geront?* and *Let's get on with it!* and other not so subtle notices of restlessness—to the extent that the Mayor began to feel somewhat chivvied—Geront, puffing and fuming, rambled his speech down to an unsatisfactory ending; and at last he introduced Old Barlo, which brought on such a loud and prolonged cheer of relief that it left Geront with the grand delusion that in some mysterious fashion his speech had been a smashing success after all.

Old Barlo mounted the platform and got right to the matter at hand. "Folks, it's time these here brave lads," *Yay!*—he was interrupted by a lengthy cheer—

"time these brave lads were on their way. There's no call to delay them further, 'cause the Thornwalkers (*Hooray!*), the Thornwalkers has got crossings to guard (*Rah!*), borders to protect (*Rah!*), and Wolves to repel." *Hip! Hip! Hoorah!* Barlo waited for the cheering to subside, and, casting a gimlet eye at Geront, he continued. "And they can't do them duties if they've got ter stand around here listening to speech making and cheering crowds!" *Rah! Rah! Old Barlo!* Then Barlo pointed to the first Warrow in a line of eight strangers standing quietly to one side, all dressed in Thornwalker-grey cloaks. "Them as is assigned to the Eastdell First, there's your guide." The first Warrow raised his hand. Barlo then pointed to the second grey-cloaked 'Walker. "Eastdell Second," Barlo called out, and that Warrow held up a hand. "Eastdell Third," came the next cry, as Barlo continued down the line.

When Eastdell Fourth was called, Old Barlo pointed to an emerald-eyed Warrow with fair hair who was holding a string of seven ponies—five riding and two pack ponies, their coats heavy with winter shag. Tuck, Hob, and Tarpy made their way to the guide, and from the far side of the Commons came Danner. With a deep bow, Tuck introduced himself and named his companions.

"Patrel Rushlock at your service," spoke the guide with an infectious grin and a sweeping bow of his own. Patrel was small—even shorter than Tarpy, who, for the first time ever, felt as if he simply *towered* over another young buccan, though he was but one inch different. Yet, somehow—perhaps because of his bearing—Patrel seemed neither diminished nor overshadowed by the four taller, Woody Hollow buccen.

"Let's fix your knapsacks to this pack pony," said Patrel, getting right to the matter at hand, "then each of you pick out one of the riding mounts for your own. The one with the white face is mine. But heed this: keep your bows and quivers. We may need them before we come to Ford Spindle," he said ominously, momentarily frowning, but then his face brightened and the wide grin returned. "If you have a flute or pipe, or any other tune maker, keep it, too, and we'll have a ditty or three to cheer us along the way." Tuck then saw that a six-stringed lute was strapped across Patrel's shoulders to hang at his back.

Shortly, they, as well as the Thornwalkers of the other Eastdell companies, were ready to leave. All turned to say that one last goodbye to young dammen and maidens, sires and dams, brothers and sisters, grandams and granthers, aunts and uncles and other relatives, friends and neighbors, and additional assorted buccen and dammen who had come to see them off and who were collected in knots and rings and clumps, Warrows with stricken and worried and crying faces, and cheery and smiling ones, and proud and stern and grim looks, also.

"Harrump! Take care of yourself, lad," said Burt to his only bucco, "and watch out for the wild Wolves. Make 'em fear the sight of an Underbank—harrump!—or any other Warrow, for that matter."

"I will, Dad," answered Tuck, and quickly he embraced his sire, then turned to his dam.

"Wear your warm clothes, keep your feet dry," said Tulip as she clasped Tuck to her. "Eat well, and, and . . ." but she could say no more through her tears. She held on tightly and softly cried until Burt gently disengaged her embrace from Tuck, and Tuck quickly swung astride the dappled grey he had chosen as his mount.

A friend gave him a pouch of Downdell leaf, "The best there is"; another friend handed him a new white-clay pipe, "Smoke it well"; while a third gave him a small tin box with flint and steel and shavings of touchwood, "Keep your tinder dry."

Merrilee Holt, who had shyly hung back, squared her shoulders, stepped forward, and held an elden silver locket up to Tuck. "Would you wear my— favor?" the Warrow maiden asked. Speechless with surprise, Tuck nodded dumbly, and he leaned down for Merrilee to slip it over his head. As she did so, she whispered in his ear, "Take care, my buccaran," and kissed him on the lips, to the raucous whoops of some of the striplings nearby. But Merrilee simply stepped back to the crowd, her eyes glitter-bright with tears.

"Hey, Tucker," spoke up his cousin Willy, stepping to the pony's side and holding up a new, blank diary and a pencil, "keep a journal, hey? Then when you get back you can read to us of all your adventures, hey?"

"All right, Willy," said Tuck, stuffing the gift into his jerkin along with the leaf and pipe and tinderbox. "Thanks. I'll try." Then Tuck smiled, raised his hand, waved to all those who had come to see him off, looked again at his parents with their arms about one another, and last of all looked at Merrilee, who brightly smiled back. At a nod from Patrel, Tuck and his companions, who also were finished with their farewells, urged the ponies forward. They wove through the waving crowd and out of the Commons, riding toward the North Trace up through the Dinglewood, aiming for Spindle Ford.

As the ponies trotted away from the heart of Woody Hollow, the five riders—Tuck, Danner, Hob, Tarpy, and Patrel—could hear Woody Hollow Mayor Geront Gabben leading the townfolk in a rousing cheer: *Hip, hip, hooray! Hip, hip, hooray! Hip, hip, hooray!* And someone began ringing the fire gong.

The Sun crept upward in the morning sky as they rode farther and farther from Woody Hollow. The sounds of the cheering crowd and clanging gong slowly faded away to disappear altogether in the snow-blanketed quiet of the Dinglewood, and all became silent except for the creak of leather saddles and harness, the muted sounds of pony hooves stepping in the snow, and an occasional muffled snuffle from one, or perhaps four, of the riders.

CHAPTER 2

RETREAT TO
ROOKS' ROOST

The bright light of the mounting Sun fell aslant 'cross the white, glistening snow. From the glitter, tiny evanescent shards of sparkling color winged to the eye, as if reflected from diminutive fragments of shattered jewels nestled among the fallen flakes. The cold crystalline air was calm, and in all the wide Dinglewood nothing seemed to be astir except for a jostling flock of noisy ravens squabbling over a meager breakfast up among the barren trees on Hawthorn Hill. Down below, wending slowly along the North Trace were five Warrows astride five ponies, leading two more of the animals laden with gear.

Patrel, riding in the lead, turned and looked over his shoulder at the glum faces of the four young buccen behind. For the past six miles no one had said even a single word; and for a group of Warrows to remain silent for two solid hours, well, that's no mean feat. Deciding that this dolorous mood had lasted overlong, Patrel shucked his mittens and unslung his lute; he plucked a few strings, strummed a chord or so, and tweaked a tuning key or two this way and that.

"Hey," said Tarpy, his utterance breaking the muteness to fall upon startled ears, "give us a happy tune; we need it." And Tarpy clucked his pony forward till he rode beside Patrel. At Patrel's nod, Tarpy called to the others: "Hoy, you grumlings, clap your heels to those ponies and gather 'round."

Tuck, riding last and leading the pack ponies, was jerked out of his gloomy thoughts by Tarpy's call. Clicking his tongue, he urged the grey forward. "Come on, Danner," he said as he drew even with the young buccan, "let's go."

"What for?" asked Danner, mumpishly. "He's just going to twang that stringed gourd of his, and I don't feel at all like a song."

"Perhaps that's just exactly what we do need," answered Tuck. "Even if it's just a song, still we'll cheer up a bit, I'll wager. And right now I could do with a bit of cheering up, and so could you—so could we all."

"Oh, all right," grumped Danner, agreeing more to keep Tuck quiet than for any other reason, and he kicked up his pony. In moments, Tuck, Danner, Hob, and Tarpy were all riding grouped around Patrel. "All right, lads," grinned the small Thornwalker, looking aflank, "it's time you learned what the Thornwalkers are all about." Patrel plucked a chord or two, checking a last time the tune of the lute, and then his fingers began dancing over the strings as he sang a lively, simple, Warrowish tune.

> *We are Thornwalkers,*
>   *Thornwalkers are we;*
> *We walk around the miles of bounds*
>   *To keep the Bosky free*

Of Wolves and Vulgs and great wild dogs
And other enemy;
We are Thornwalkers,
Thornwalkers are we.

We are Thornwalkers,
Thornwalkers are we;
We've trod the Thorns from night to morn
Through Bosky history.
Our ears can hear, and never fear,
For keenly do we see;
We are Thornwalkers,
Thornwalkers are we.

Patrel began the third verse, and this time Tarpy and Hob joined in, thinly singing the refrain: *We are Thornwalkers, Thornwalkers are we.*

We are Thornwalkers,
Thornwalkers are we;
The Seven Dells, well I can tell,
All of them we do see,
To north and east and south and west,
Wherever they may be;
We are Thornwalkers,
Thornwalkers are we.

"Come on, you sickly sparrows," urged Patrel, pausing, "you can chirp louder than that." And with a wide smile, he struck up the tune again and sang another verse. This time four other voices picked up the lilt of the rustic song, and even though they sang *tum-tiddle-tum* in the places where they could not guess the words, still their timber strengthened.

We are Thornwalkers,
  Thornwalkers are we;
We walk along the Spindlethorn
  Wherever it may be,
Through fens and fields and woods and hills
  'Long rivers bound for sea;
We are Thornwalkers,
  Thornwalkers are we.

On the last verse, all the Warrows were grinning broadly and singing lustily, and to Tuck's surprise Danner's voice was the heartiest of all.

We are Thornwalkers,
  Thornwalkers are we;
And finer scads of sturdy lads
  No one will ever see;
We guard and ward and work so hard
  To keep the Bosky free;
We are Thornwalkers,
  Thornwalkers are we—Yo ho!
We are Thornwalkers,
  Thornwalkers are we—Hey!

And with this last *Hey!* Patrel planged his lute with a loud discordant *twang!* and all the Warrows broke into guffawing laughs. The somber mood was gone.

"So that's what we Thornwalkers do, hey?" asked Hob, merrily. "Guarding and warding. It sounds as if we'll be busy."

"Oh no," grumped Danner, "not if we're stuck at Spindle Ford. I expect it means we'll spend a lot of time sitting around waiting for something to happen, but it never will."

"Well that suits me just fine," chimed up Tarpy. "I'd rather sit around a warm campfire, sharing a pipe or song or tale, than to be out in the cold looking for Wolves and Vulgs and great wild dogs."

"And the other enemy," added Tuck. "Don't forget the *other enemy* the song spoke of—*Wolves and Vulgs and great wild dogs and other enemy*." Tuck turned to Patrel, "What does the song mean—*other enemy?* Where did the song come from in the first place? I've never heard it before, and I think I'd better write it down in my new diary—my cousin Willy will really like it. Besides, a song that good deserves to be spread about, and, well, it seems to me as if we should have heard it before."

"Oh . . . ahem . . . well," stammered Patrel, somewhat flustered and flushed, fumbling embarrassedly as he refastened the strap to sling the lute across his back once more. "I'm pleased you liked it. And you haven't heard it before because it's new. I mean, well, I made it up myself as I rode down to collect you four."

"Made it up yourself?" burst out Tarpy. "I say! I thought only minstrels and harpers did that sort of thing. You aren't a minstrel now, are you?"

"My Aunt Oot used to make up songs now and again," interrupted Hob, "mostly in the kitchen. Songs about food and cooking. Rather pleasant. Nothing jolly like yours, though."

"Tell us about the words, Patrel," said Tuck. "I mean, tell us how you came up with your song."

"There's not that much to say," answered Patrel. "You all know that the Thornwalkers help to protect the Bosky—a big responsibility that is, too, for it's a wide Land. Seven Dells: North, South, East, West, Center, Up, and Down. Ringed 'round by the Great Spindlethorn Barrier. Bounded by two rivers, the Wenden and Spindle, and by the Northwood and the Updunes."

"What is this," grumbled Danner, "a geography lesson?"

"No," laughed Patrel. "Well, perhaps a touch of both geography and history."

"Come on, Danner, let Patrel speak," said Tarpy, his Warrowish nature astir to listen to things he already knew. "Besides, I've always wanted to learn where harpers get their tunes."

"Argh!" growled Danner, but he fell silent.

"But, Tarpy, I don't know where harpers get their tunes," protested Patrel. "I only know where mine come from. It's very simple. The mission of the Thornwalkers is to patrol the Dells and the Spindlethorn Barrier, to guard against unsavory Beyonders coming into the Bosky for ill purposes, and to repel Wolves, or great wild dogs."

"What about the Vulgs?" asked Hob.

"Yar! And the *other enemy*," snorted Danner, sarcastically. "I'll give you an *other enemy!*" He leaned over toward Hob and made a face. "Boo!"

"Danner!" burst out Tuck, exasperated. "If you don't wish to listen, then ride on ahead."

"Just who do you think you're ordering about?" bristled Danner. "I—"

"Hold it!" shouted Patrel, his own fiery temper rising. Then, as he got control of himself: "Let's not get to squabbling among ourselves." He turned to Danner. "Just what point are you trying to make?"

"Well," grouched Danner, "just what *other enemy* could be a threat to the Bosky?"

"How about Vulgs?" shot back Hob.

"And Rūcks, Hlōks, and Ogrus," chimed in Tarpy.

"Ghûls," added Tuck.

Danner looked disgusted. "You left out Cold-drakes! And Modru! And bloody Gyphon himself!" he snapped. "And it seems you've also forgotten High Adon's Ban! And that's why there isn't any *other enemy*: the Ban!"

Amid the burst of babble that followed, Patrel's clear voice cut through, bidding silence, and when it reigned: "Danner's got a good point there. Now hush and let him speak."

Danner looked somewhat flustered as all Warrow eyes fastened in silence upon him, but he was not speechless: "Well, you all know what the old tales say." Danner's voice took on the rhythm of a chant, as if he were reciting a well-learned school lesson. "When Gyphon challenged Adon for control of the Spheres, War broke out in the three Planes: Upper, Middle, and Lower. Here in Mithgar the struggle was mighty, for Modru, Gyphon's servant, was supreme and his Horde was nearly without number. Yet the Grand Alliance opposed them, not realizing that the outcome here in the midworld would tip the balance of power in the Upper and Lower Planes, too.

"And so it was that the Grand Alliance of Men, Elves, Dwarves, Utruni, Wizards, and Warrows fought on the side of Adon in the Great War against Gyphon, Modru, Vûlks, Ghûls, Hlōks, Ogrus, Rūcks, Vulgs . . . and some Dragons.

"Here, in the Middle Plane, by an unexpected stroke the Alliance won; Modru lost. And so it was that Adon won and Gyphon lost on all three Planes. As forfeit, Adon banished from the light of day, on pain of death, all the Folk who aided Gyphon in this Great War. From those of the Dragons who opposed Him, Adon took their fire, and now they are Cold-drakes and also suffer the Ban.

"And it is said that Adon's Ban *shall rule for as long as night follows day, and day follows night*.

"He banished Gyphon, too, 'beyond the Spheres,' though no one I've asked knows where that is.

"Modru himself fled through the night from the Wastes of Gron to the far frozen land beyond. The tales tell that he lives there because in the winter the nights are long, very long, and the Sun, his bane, is feeble for six months each year. Yet in the summer Modru must hide away, for then the days are long and the Sun rides high, and the Withering Death is ever at hand."

Danner then paused, looking at the others, and his voice took on a pedantic tone. "So you see, *that's* why the Bosky has little to fear from *other enemy*: His Ban would slay them!" Danner looked at the other Warrows, challenge in his eye, but no one there gainsaid him, and the ponies wended slowly northward.

"Ah, Danner, you are right," said Patrel after a bit. "Yet remember this: Adon's Covenant kills only if they get caught in the Sun, but not at night. And other Thornwalkers have reported fleeting glimpses from afar of great black beasts, like Wolves, but dire, running through the dark."

"Vulgs," breathed Hob.

"Perhaps," answered Patrel. "If so, then they must lie up in the cracks and splits of the land when the

Sun is on high, and thus the Ban strikes them not
As for Rūcks, Hlōks, and Ogrus, or Vûlks and Ghûls
or Cold-drakes, I think none are here in the Bosky
though they, too, could escape the Sun in the same
manner. Yet we are a far distance from the moun
tains they haunt: the Grimwall, the Rigga, and the
Gronfangs."

"But Vulgs run fast and far, they say," said Tarpy
"and perhaps they've run all the way to the Bos
kydells."

"Yes, but what has driven them to come to the
Bosky now?" asked Tuck. "It's been a long span
since the end of the Great War. Why have they come
at this time? And to the Bosky?"

"If!" exclaimed Danner, compelling their atten
tion. "If it's Vulgs and not Wolves. Who's to say i
wasn't Wolves, or even wild dogs, seen from afa
by the Thornwalkers, instead of Vulgs? Look, the
Ban has held good for two whole Eras. Why shoulc
Vulgs show up now?"

"Ah! There's the rub," responded Tuck. "Why
indeed, now?"

The ponies plodded forward, and the Warrows
rode on in silence for a bit, pondering the puzzle
"The only thing that comes to mind," continuec
Tuck, "is that it is said Gyphon, just as He wa
vanishing, swore a bitter vow to Adon, claimin;
that He would be back."

" *'Even now,'* " Danner quoted, his voice sepul
chral, " *'Even now I have set into motion events you
cannot stop. I shall return! I shall conquer! I shal
rule!'* That's what the old tales say Gyphon last spa
at Adon, then He was gone, beyond the Spheres
banished. But He was wrong, for He hasn't re

turned. In four thousand years He hasn't returned. That's how long they say it has been. And for those same four thousand years, no Rūck, no Vûlk, ah, fie! Nothing! Nothing suffering the Ban has threatened the Bosky! Ever!''

Again silence descended upon them, and each rode immersed in his own thoughts. Finally, Patrel spoke: "Maybe so, Danner. Maybe you are right. But they say Vulgs now push through the Spindlethorns. And no one says why."

Northward they wended throughout the day, at times riding, at other times walking and leading the ponies, sometimes stopping to eat, or to take care of other needs, or to feed grain to the mounts, or to break through the ice on a woodland stream to refresh their canteens and to give the ponies a drink.

The large, thickset trees of the Dinglewood bordered close upon the trail, their grey bark and stark branches casting a somber pall upon the North Trace. A pall, too, seemed to have dropped over the Warrows, and little else was said that day as they pressed on through the silence of the barren forest. The Sun slowly crossed the cold sky, and its rays did little to warm the travellers. When the orb sank below the western horizon, darkness found the five young buccen huddled around a campfire on the far edge of the Dinglewood, some thirty miles north of Woody Hollow.

They drew lots to see in what order the watch would be kept, with Tuck pulling the mid-of-night turn. As all prepared to bed down, except Hob, who had the first watch, Patrel said, "Tomorrow night we all sleep in a hayloft—Arlo Huggs' hayloft. I stopped at his place on the way to Woody Hollow. He has a farm along Two Fords Road, about twenty-five miles north of here. Arlo said he'd be glad to put us up in his loft, and his wife, Willa, said she would feed us a hot meal, too." This last brought drowsy approval from all but Hob, who merely smiled as he threw another limb on the fire and began his tour.

It was midwatch when Tuck was awakened by a prod from Danner. "It's your turn, Tuck," said Danner, gruffly.

Tuck threw some branches on the fire and gathered more wood from the pile to have at hand to ward away the cold. Danner was still sitting on a log near the blaze, glowering mumpishly at the flames.

"Get some sleep, Danner," sighed Tuck. "Perhaps you'll not be so grumpy if you get enough rest."

"What do you mean, grumpy?" flared Danner, glaring at Tuck.

"You've got to admit, you were somewhat of a grouch today," answered Tuck, distressed, wondering how this conversation had gotten off on the wrong foot.

"Look, Tuck," shot back Danner, "my philosophy is this: I'm like a mirror—I only give back what I get."

They sat without speaking a moment, as the fire popped and cracked. "Well, Danner, I think you ought to consider this: you either can be like a mirror or like a window; but remember, only the window lets light in." Tuck then stood and began his rounds, and Danner took to his bedroll, a thoughtful look on his face.

After a turn around the camp, Tuck came back to the log, and by the moonlight and firelight he began recording in his new diary the day's events in terse sentences or cryptic notes, except for Patrel's song, which he wrote out in full. He would jot down a few words, then tour the perimeter, returning to write some more. And that is how he passed his watch, writing in his journal, as the Moon slid westward to be hidden by clouds moving to the east. It was a diary he planned to keep up throughout the next few months—the record of his travels.

The next morning dawned to falling snow. After a light breakfast of dried venison and bread, and grain for the ponies, the five broke camp and headed once more to the north. A breeze blew from the west, carrying eddying flakes aslant across their path, and they rode with their cloaks wrapped tightly around them and their hoods up. Through the falling snow they went, and their mode of travel was much the same as the previous day's, only now they trekked 'cross open land, having left the Dinglewood behind. The North Trace continued to carry them toward Two Fords Road, but the route was becoming harder to follow as the thickening snow obscured the path. Hence, slowed by the storm, it was not until midafternoon that they finally struck the main artery toward Spindle Ford.

"I sure am looking forward to that hot meal and hayloft you spoke of last night," said Tarpy to Patrel as the Warrows slogged through the snow, now calf-deep, leading the ponies and giving the animals a respite.

"Ha! Me too!" answered Patrel. "I hope Willa won't mind if we are a bit late, and keeps the meal hot. I judge we'll get to Arlo's well after dark."

"Blasted storm," carped Danner, then fell silent as they trudged on.

Patrel's words proved to be accurate, for it was three hours into the night when they came at last to the edge of Arlo's farm. The wind had risen, and a mournful wail could be heard as it keened through a nearby stand of timber. With their backs to the gust, the five Warrows turned down the lane leading to the Huggs' stone field house.

"Hold!" said Patrel above the wind moan, his voice tight with apprehension. "Something is wrong."

"What?" asked Hob. "What's the matter?"

"There's no light in the house." Patrel reached for his bow. "Ready your weapons."

"What?" asked Danner, unbelieving. "Bows?" Then he saw Patrel was serious and, shaking his head, followed suit.

"Maybe they've just gone to bed," spoke up Tarpy, but took up his bow just the same.

"No. There should be a light. They were expecting us," answered Patrel. "Take care. Let's go."

Arrows nocked, they proceeded toward the dark house, on foot, leading the ponies. Off to the side, the barn loomed like some great dark beast. Now they could hear an ominous banging above the moan, as from a loose shutter blowing in the wind. Closer they came, and now they could see that the windows of the house seemed open, for curtains were blowing in and out. Tuck's heart was pounding, and his lungs were heaving in ragged gasps. He felt as if he could not get a firm grip on his bow. It took all of his courage to force one foot ahead of the

other. Motioning Tuck and Danner to the left and
Tarpy and Hob to the right, Patrel stepped toward
the porch. As he put his foot on the top step the
door burst open with a *Blam*!

Tuck's heart gave a great lurch, thudding in his
mouth, and he realized that he had a deadly aim
centered on the doorway's gaping blackness. The
bow was fully drawn, and Tuck could feel the fletching of the arrow against his right cheek as he held
steady, ready to release. And for the life of him, Tuck
could not recall taking the pull. *And nothing came
through the doorway.* Just as abruptly, *Wham*! the
door slammed to. *Whack*! It whipped open again
and *Blam*! shut once more as the wind swirled again.

"Lor!" said Tarpy, relaxing his pull a bit, as they
all did, "I thought—"

"Hsst!" Patrel cut off Tarpy's words and motioned them to go forth.

Tuck and Danner went around to the left of the
house and Tarpy and Hob to the right, while Patrel
stepped through the front door. As they went along
the side of the house, Tuck saw that the curtains
were indeed whipping and flapping in and out of
the windows, for the glass was shattered. *Bang! Blam!*
They could hear the front door slamming to and
fro. On they went, coming to the kitchen door, splintered from its hinges and hanging awry. Into the
house they went just as Patrel, already in the kitchen,
managed to light a lamp. *Whack! Slam!*

The glow revealed a shambles: overturned chairs,
a shattered table, broken crockery, an upside-down
bench, smashed glass—ruin. Snow blew in through
the broken door and past torn curtains across the
sills of the shattered windows. Tarpy and Hob at

last entered and looked about as the wind moaned and gnawed at the destruction. "We took a quick check of the barn," said Hob. "Empty. No livestock. It's gone." *Thwack! Whack!*

"What's happened here?" asked Tarpy, as Danner lit another lamp.

"I don't know, yet," answered Patrel. *Blam! Whack!* "Hob, will you latch that infernal front door? Tarpy, pull the shutters to. Although the glass is broken, they will keep most of the snow out. Danner, use your light to help Tarpy. Tuck, add the light of another lamp or candle to mine. We'll see what we can make of this."

As Tuck found one more lamp and lit it, Patrel propped the kitchen door in its jamb, for the most part sealing out the wind and snow. They then opened what turned out to be the pantry door; Patrel took a quick look inside. "Nothing. No one," he said to Tuck. "Let's look—"

"Ai-oi!" came a call from another room, and Patrel and Tuck rushed to find Danner kneeling with his lamp, Tarpy and Hob peering over his shoulder in the fluttering light.

"What is it?" asked Tuck, and then he saw—blood. A lot of blood. And in the center, a huge paw print.

"Wolves," hissed Tarpy.

"No," said Danner, grimly. "Vulgs!" And off in the distance, mingled with the moan of the wind, came a single, horrid, prolonged, savage wail.

"The Vulgs smashed through the windows and doors," said Patrel when they all had gathered again in the kitchen following a thorough search. "See, the broken glass flew inward, as if the evil creatures hurtled through."

"Yar, and the kitchen door," put in Danner, gesturing at the panel propped in the opening. "Remember, it was broken inward, too."

"What about Farmer Arlo and his wife? Where are they?" asked Tarpy, his eyes wide and glittering in the lamplight. "We've looked everywhere."

"It's another *Disappearance*," whispered Hob, and Tuck felt his heart plummet.

"No, Hob, say instead a Vulg slaughter," said Patrel, his voice grim as he peered at the stricken faces of the others, his own a sickly, ashen grey. "This time it's not just a mysterious disappearance. This time all the evidence cries out wanton murder, Vulg butchery."

"If it's murder," asked Tarpy, tears brimming, one hand with a sweeping gesture indicating the vacant shambles they stood amid, "then where is . . . where are . . ."

"The bodies," spoke Danner, harshly, his jaw clenched in anger. "What did the bloody Vulgs do with the bodies?"

"I don't know," answered Patrel. "All the other disappearances I've heard about left no traces of any kind. Just this one. It's as if . . ."

"As if Farmer Arlo put up a fight, and the others didn't," put in Tuck. "The others must've had no warning. Arlo managed to bolt the doors, but the Vulgs prevailed."

"Arlo and Willa are probably out there somewhere," gritted Danner, "covered by the snow." The sound of Tarpy's soft weeping was lost in the moan of the wind, and Tuck bleakly peered without seeing through the kitchen window shutters out into the dark night.

"Well," asked Hob, after a long moment, "what do we do? Search for them? Though I don't see how we can find them in the snow in the night."

"Let's go after the Vulgs," demanded Danner, raising up his bow, his knuckles white with anger.

"No," said Patrel. "Neither search nor hunt. We've already looked over the immediate grounds with no results, and the Vulgs are beyond our vengeance by now. No, here we stay and rest, and tomorrow we press on to Spindle Ford, warning the countryside as we go."

"Faugh!" snorted Danner, raising his bow. "I say let's get the brutes!"

"Danner," Patrel's voice had an angry bite to it, "until we get to Spindle Ford, you are in my command. I'll not have you out chasing around in a blizzard at night looking for Vulgs long gone. I say we stay here, and what I say goes."

"Oh no," said Tarpy, peering around desperately. "Not here. I can't stay here. Not in this wrack. Not when there's blood on the floor in there. Not in this house."

"How 'bout the hayloft?" asked Hob, throwing an arm around Tarpy's shoulders and cocking an eye at Patrel, who nodded. "Yes, we'll stay there," continued Hob. "Besides, we've got to get the ponies into shelter and fed and watered." He took up a lamp. "Come on. Let's see to the ponies."

And so they all went, Hob in the lead with Tarpy

shivering beside him, Danner and Patrel glaring at
one another, and Tuck bringing up the rear.

They kept the same order of watch as they had the
previous night, and though Tuck didn't see how he
was going to get any sleep, it seemed as if he had just
lain down when Danner shook him awake. "Time to
get up," said Danner. "Bring your blanket; it's cold."
He climbed back down to the floor of the barn.

Tuck struggled down the ladder from the loft,
blanket over one shoulder. As he stepped from the
bottom rung, he saw that Danner was refilling one
of the lamps with oil and trimming the wick with
his knife. "Need any help?" Tuck yawned. At Danner's negative shake of his head, Tuck asked, "Any
sound of Vulgs?"

"No," replied Danner. "The wind died about an
hour ago, and the snow's stopped, too. And there's
been no sound of Vulgs, Wolves, or anything else
from out there. Blast! I've pinked my thumb." Danner sucked on his thumb and spat, while Tuck finished trimming the lamp wick. "We should be out
there, you know," grumbled Danner between sucks,
"hunting Vulgs."

"Come now, Danner," replied Tuck, lighting the
new lamp and extinguishing the old, "you heard
Patrel. We can't go blundering around at night in
the dark looking for Vulgs."

"Well let me leave you with this thought, Tuck,"
shot back Danner. "Night is the only time you *can*
hunt those slavering brutes." And Danner disappeared up the ladder into the hayloft.

Why, thought Tuck, *he's right! The Ban! They won't
be about in the daytime.*

Later, during his watch, Tuck scribbled in his diary as the last entry for the day: *How true will be our aim in the dark?*

Morning discovered the Warrows back on Two Fords Road, travelling north toward the Spindle Ford. At first light they had taken one last look about the Huggs' farm, but they found no sign of Arlo or Willa. Patrel had then tacked a note to the front door warning any who came to the stone field house about the Vulgs. Then the young buccen had mounted up and ridden away.

Two miles north, they came to another farm and spoke to the crofter there. Dread filled the eyes of the family upon hearing of the Vulgs and the fate of the Huggs. The tenant, Harlan Broxeley, sent his sons upon ponies to warn the nearby steading holders, with Patrel's request to "pass it on." Patrel and the others were loath to leave the family alone, but Mr. Broxeley said, "Don't you fret none. Now that we are warned, me and my buccoes can hold 'em off till dayrise. Then the Sun'll stop 'em. Besides, we ain't the only family near about, and you five can't protect us all. You've got to get this word to the Thornwalkers so as they can do something about it." With that and a warm breakfast, the five young buccen went on northward, bearing the news toward Spindle Ford and the Eastdell Fourth.

All day they rode north, stopping three more times to start the word spreading. Dusk found them eight miles south of the ford. "Let us press on and get to the ford tonight," said Patrel, grimly. "I'd rather we were not camped out in the open." So onward they went, as darkness fell and the Moon rose to paint black shadows streaming away into the night.

Through the enshadowed land they rode. A mile passed, and then another. Of a sudden, Tuck's pony snorted and shied, tossing its head. Tuck looked sharply into the blackness but saw nothing, and the other ponies seemed calm enough. Onward they rode, Tuck's own senses now alert. "What's that up ahead?" asked Tuck, pointing to a tall spire looming up through the darkness and into the moonlight.

"It's the Rooks' Roost," answered Patrel, on Tuck's left, "a great pile of stone that happens to be where Two Fords Road and the Upland Way come together. It means, when we get there, we'll be just five miles from the Thornwalker camp at the ford."

Toward the junction they rode. The Upland Way was a main route running aslant across the Boskydells, joining the Land of Rian in the north to that of Wellen in the west. Two Fords Road ran north and south—up from the Bosky village of Rood and north to the Spindle River. It was called Two Fords Road because it crossed the Dingle-rill at the West Ford and passed into Rian at the Spindle Ford.

As they came closer to the Rooks' Roost, by the bright moonlight Tuck could see that it was higher than he first had thought, rising perhaps fifty feet into the air, a great jumble of rocks and boulders placed there in ancient times by an unknown hand to stand ominously in the night. As the ponies plodded onward, Tuck felt as if this looming pile somehow boded doom.

Without warning, again the grey pony shied, scudding to the left. "Hey! Steady," commanded Tuck, looking to the others, but now their ponies, too, were skittish. *What's happening?* he asked himself, and then he gasped in shocked fear: off to the east a great black shape slunk through the shadows, keeping pace with the Warrows. "Vulg!" he cried to the others, his voice tight with dread. "In the field to our right! Just beyond arrow range!"

"Stay close!" shouted Patrel. "Keep riding!"

Danner, in the rear with the frightened pack ponies trailing him, grimly called out, "Two more behind us! No, three!"

"Left! Look left!" came Tarpy's startled voice. "Lor! Another one!"

The Vulgs trotted without effort. Their evil yellow eyes gleamed like hot coals when the Moon caught them just so, and slavering red tongues lolled over wicked fangs set in crushing jaws. Hideous power bunched and rippled under coarse black fur as the beasts slid through the shadows.

"Cor! Let's ride for it!" shouted Hob, clapping his heels to his pony. But Patrel reached over and grabbed the pony's bit strap.

"Whoa! Hold it! Don't panic. Stick together. When I give the word we ride for the Rooks' Roost. As long as they stay their distance, we'll just keep trotting for our goal. We've got less than a quarter mile to go." Patrel nocked an arrow, but as if that somehow were a signal, with blurring speed the Vulgs closed in. "Fly!" cried Patrel. "To the Rooks' Roost! Ride for your lives!"

With shouts and cries, the young buccen all clapped their heels to the ponies' flanks, but the steeds needed no urging, for they had taken full flight. Yet the hideous great Vulgs closed the distance with horrid quickness. Tuck wanted to cry out in fear; instead, he leaned forward and urged the grey onward. To-

ward the rock pike they raced, yet faster ran the
Vulgs. Tuck could hear Danner shouting a challenge
of some sort as the ground flew by. The Vulgs drew
abreast, and Tuck could hear guttural snarling and
see the gleam of fangs. They were now less than a
furlong from the Rooks' Roost, closing the distance
rapidly. Tuck thought of winging an arrow at the
beasts but knew that his aim would be unsteady
from the back of a running pony: *The arrow as strays
might well'er been throwed away*, he seemed to hear
Old Barlo's voice cry, and so he held his shot. Yet
a Vulg closed in and slashed at his pony's hind-
quarters; Tuck clubbed at it with his bow, and the
brute shied back as the pony plunged on.

Tuck looked ahead just in time to see Hob's steed
go tumbling down, screaming, hamstrung by the
Vulgs, but Hob was thrown free. Tuck tried to turn
his pony but was past the fallen Warrow ere he
could do so. He heard Danner yell and looked back
to see Hob on his feet with a Vulg slashing at him
just as Danner rode by and reached out an arm.
Hob caught at it and swung up and onto the pony
behind the other buccan. Yet the Vulg snarled in
rage and leapt at the twain, and Hob screamed horribly as the cruel fangs rent the Warrow's side and
leg, though still he kicked out and the Vulg fell back.
Danner's pony bolted forward at an even faster clip,
in spite of bearing double, and temporarily gained
a pace on the Vulg. Yet the slavering creature once
more closed the gap, and with a great snarl and
jaws wide it leapt at the two. *Hsss, thwock!* An arrow sprang full from the beast's left eye, and with
a sodden thud it fell dead to the earth! Tarpy had

gained the Rooks' Roost and had let fly with the shot of his life!

Tuck thundered up and leapt off to follow right behind Patrel as they scrambled onto the lower tier of stone to join Tarpy, and he turned to see Danner and Hob come at last. On, too, came the dire Vulgs, but Patrel let fly and struck one a glancing blow on a foreleg, and its yipping howl caused the others to sheer off the attack.

As their mount skidded to a stop, Danner and Hob jumped off. But with a moan, Hob collapsed unconscious to the snow, a dark stain spreading from under him. Down leapt the others to aid, but Danner hoisted Hob across his shoulders. "Climb!" he snarled, and started forward.

Tarpy ran and snatched up Danner's bow and quiver. "What about the ponies?"

With his free hand, Danner shoved Tarpy toward the rocks. "Climb, you fool, they're after Waerlings, not horselings!" But Danner was only partly right, for as the buccen scrambled up the rocks of the Rooks' Roost, the frightened ponies scaddled off into the night. Yet two ran right into the jaws of the evil Vulgs, and their shrill death cries sounded like the screams of dammen. And the blood of the Warrows ran chill.

It took all the energy of the other four to lift Hob's dead weight up to the top of the Rooks' Roost, but at last they were there. The Vulgs loped around the base of the jumble but did not attempt to climb it. And the Moon shone brightly down upon the land.

"He's still alive," said Tuck, raising his head from Hob's breast. "We've got to do something to stop this bleeding." But in his mind whispered words from the old hearthtale: *Vulg's black bite slays at night.*

"Make a tourniquet for his leg," said Patrel, "and press a bandage to his side." And so Tuck and Tarpy tended to Hob as Danner stared in hatred down at the Vulgs.

"Look at them," he spat, "just sitting there now, as if they were hatching a vile plan, or waiting for something to happen, three evil brutes."

"Three!" exclaimed Patrel. "There should be four! Where's—" They heard the click of claws scrabbling up the stone on the opposite side. " 'Ware!" shouted Patrel and rushed over in time to see a great Vulg leaping up through the shadowed stones toward the crest. As Patrel drew an arrow full to the head, he heard Danner cry, "Here come the others!" for the remaining three beasts were streaking for the mound.

With malevolence in its yellow eyes, the lone Vulg swarmed up the stone. Patrel loosed the bolt to hiss through the air, but with a twist the Vulg leapt sideways, and the shaft but struck it in the loose fur above the shoulders. Howling and snapping at the quarrel, the Vulg fell scrambling down the side of the pile, while the other three again veered off the attack, bounding down from the stones and beyond arrow range.

Patrel and Danner watched as the four Vulgs collected together. The fifth one—the one slain by Tarpy's shaft through the eye—lay like a black blot in the snow. So, too, did the three slain ponies: Hob's steed, a pack pony, and one other mount—Tarpy's. Of the other four steeds, there was no sign. "We're in a tight fix here," said Patrel, watching the Vulgs.

"I just hope our arrows last till dawn." Danner merely grunted.

Tuck and Tarpy had returned to Hob, laying their bows aside. "Maybe this will staunch the flow," fretted Tuck as he tourniqueted Hob's leg. "We need something to press against his side."

"Here, take my jerkin," said Tarpy, peeling off his quilted jacket and stripping his shirt. "Cor! It's cold," he shivered, and quickly redonned his wrap.

Tuck folded the jerkin and pressed it to the wound in Hob's side. The young buccan moaned and opened his eyes; pain crossed his features. "Hullo, Tuck," he gritted, "I've made a mess of it, haven't I?"

"Oh no, Hob," answered Tuck, smiling. "Sure, you've got a bit of a scratch, but that's not what I'd call making a mess of it."

"Where are the Vulgs? Did we get any?" Hob tried to struggle up, his breath hissing through pain-clenched teeth. "Is everyone all right?"

"Coo now, Hob," Tuck gently pressed him back. "Stay down, lad. Everyone's fine. Tarpy, here, feathered one of the brutes—the one that scratched you. That's one Vulg that'll never bother anyone again."

"Tarpy?" The small Warrow knelt by Hob's side, and the wounded buccan squeezed Tarpy's hand. "Fine shot, Tarpy. I thought I saw one of 'em drop just before I faded out." Another wash of pain moved across Hob's features, and but for his ragged breathing he was silent a long moment. "Where are we? And where are the Vulgs?"

"We're on top of the Rooks' Roost," answered Tarpy, "and a great heavy thing you were to lug up here, too. All the rest of us had to climb while you, bucco, got a free ride."

"Sorry to be such a lazybones. But the Vulgs, what about the Vulgs?" whispered Hob, his voice sinking low.

"Ah, Hob, don't you worry your head about them," answered Tuck. "They're below where they'll stay." Hob closed his eyes and made no response.

Tuck pressed his cheek to Hob's forehead. "He's burning up, Tarpy, as if fevered."

"Or poisoned," added Tarpy.

Slowly the night crept by. One hour and then another passed with no movement either by Vulg or Warrow. In an effort to save Hob's leg, every so often Tuck would loosen the tourniquet to let circulation into the limb. Yet there seemed to be a fearful loss of blood whenever this was done, and so Tuck was both loath to do it and loath not to. He was just preparing to loosen the tourniquet again when Danner cried, "Here they come! All four!"

Tuck snatched up his bow and joined the other three to look down and see the Vulgs streaking toward the mound. Up they leapt, toward the line of archers.

"Take this, night-spawn!" grated Danner. *Thuunn!* went his bowstring as he loosed the arrow. *Hsss!* It sped toward the lead Vulg scrabbling up the rocks. *Thock!* The shaft drove full into the creature's breast, piercing straight to the heart. The beast fell dead in a black heap. Howling in fear and frustration, the others fled downward.

Tuck watched until they again were back out on the land away from the Roost. Then he turned and cried in dismay, "Hob!" The wounded Warrow was on his feet, swaying, trying to answer the call to arms. Tuck sprang toward him, but ere he could reach the buccan, Hob fell with a sodden thud. "Oh Lor, his wounds are gushing," sobbed Tuck, tightening the tourniquet and pressing Tarpy's jerkin back to Hob's side.

"Tuck, it's so cold . . . so cold," said Hob, his teeth chattering. Tuck shed his own cloak and spread it over the buccan, but it seemed to do little good.

The silver Moon sailed across the silent heavens, and the bright stars glimmered in the cold sky. Three Vulgs stalked around the base of the dark spire while the Warrows atop watched grimly. And there was nothing that they could do to staunch the wounds of evil Vulg bite, and Hob's life slowly leaked away among the cold, dark rocks. In less than an hour he was dead.

Just before the dawn came, the Moon set, and the three Vulgs fled in the waning night. At day's first light, a dark reeking vapor coiled up from the bodies of the two slain Vulgs as Adon's Ban struck even the corpses of the creatures, and two withered dry husks were left behind, to crumble at the wind's first touch.

Atop the Rooks' Roost, Tuck and Danner, Patrel and Tarpy all wept as they gathered stones for Hob's cairn. They washed him with snow and combed his hair and composed his hands across his breast. His Thornwalker cloak was drawn about him, and his bow was retrieved and laid beside him. And then they slowly and carefully built the cairn over him. And when it was done, in a clear voice that rose into the sky, Patrel sang this verse.

The Shadow Tide doth run
  O'er boundless Darkling Sea
'Neath skies of Silver Suns
  That beckon endlessly.

Reach out thy ship's wings wide,
  Ride on the gentle wind,
Sail with the Shadow Tide
  To shoreless Time's own end.

Alone thou sailed away
  Upon the Darkling Sea,
Yet there shall come a day
  When I will sail with thee.

All then wept long for the young buccan with whom they would never Walk the Thorns. But at length the tears faded to silence, and weary, drawn faces gazed into the bleak morning. Yet a fell look of dark resolve slowly came over Tuck's features, and he wiped away a final tear and knelt upon one knee and placed his hand upon the cairn and said unto the grey, unyielding stone, "Hob, by all that I am, the Evil that did this shall answer to your memory." And so swore them all.

At last the Warrows stood and took up their bows. With a last sweeping look around, their eyes briefly lingering upon the barrow, they climbed down from the Rooks' Roost—known ever after as Hob's Cairn—and, shouldering the backpacks retrieved from one of the slain ponies, on foot they set off northward for Spindle Ford.

CHAPTER 3

SPINDLE FORD

Just before noon, cold and weary, Tuck, Danner, Tarpy, and Patrel trudged into the Thornwalker encampment set in the fringes of the Spindlethorn Barrier at Spindle Ford. *Hai roi! Patrel! Ho! Where's your ponies? Welcome back!* and other cries were called out as the four came among the tents and lean-tos and made for the headquarters building, one of only two permanent structures there, made of hewn, notched logs, stone, and sod. The other building was a goodly sized storehouse. The welcoming cries quickly faded as the realization that something was amiss came to those encamped, for Patrel's smile was absent, and the four strode grimly onward without returning as much as a nod. *Hey! Something's afoot!* A substantial following was tagging along by the time Patrel and the others stepped through the rough-cut door and into the headquarters.

The interior was but a single room that somehow seemed too large for the building that contained it. The floor was made of thick, sawn planks, and a stone fireplace stood at the far wall. There, two

Warrows dressed in Thornwalker grey relaxed in wicker chairs while having a pipe together. One looked to be in his prime buccan years; the other was old, a granther. Both glanced up from their deep discussion as the four entered. Recognition flooded the face of the younger of the two, and he leapt to his feet. "Patrel! Welcome back. These are the recruits, I take it. Ho, but wait, I see only three. Where's the fourth?"

"Dead. Vulg slain." Patrel's voice was flat and bitter.

"What? Vulg?" The old buccan snapped, thumping his cane to the floor and rising. "Did I hear you say Vulg? Are you certain?"

"Yes sir," answered Patrel. "We were set upon by five at the Rooks' Roost, where our companion, Hob Banderel, was slain. But that's not all: it looks as if the brutes got Arlo Huggs and his wife, Willa, too."

At Patrel's words, the elder buccan's face fell, and he sank back into his chair. His voice was grim: "Then it is true: Vulgs roam the Bosky. What fell news. I had hoped it were not so."

Silence reigned for a moment, then the elder looked up and gestured with a gnarled hand. "Patrel, you and your three friends come and sit by the fire. Tell us your tale, for it is important. Have you eaten? And introduce us. This here is Captain Darby, Chief of the Eastdell Fourth, and I'm Gammer Alderbuc, from up Northdell way." Hasty introductions of Tuck, Danner, and Tarpy were made.

As the three young buccen bowed, they saw before them Captain Darby—square-built, slightly shorter than Tuck, with hair nearly as black, though his eyes were a dark blue. He had about him an air of command. Yet, as arresting as Captain Darby's appearance was, Gammer Alderbuc's was even more so, and the eyes of the trio were irresistibly drawn to him. Old he was, a granther, yet his gaze was steady and clear, peering from pale amber eyes 'neath shaggy white brows that matched his hair. He could not have been any taller than Patrel's diminutive three feet, but he was not bent with age, and though he bore a cane, he seemed hale. This was the Warrow who had first taken action to muster the Thornwalkers and to organize the Wolf Patrols when Northdell crofters began losing sheep and other livestock because the unnatural winter cold had driven Wolves into the Boskydells. At the time, he had been the honorary First Captain of the Thornwalkers, but he had stepped aside, declaring that it was a task for a younger buccan, Captain Alver of Reedyville in Downdell. And so it was that Captain Alver assumed command of all the Boskydell Thornwalkers.

At the bidding of Captain Darby, the four young buccen shed their backpacks, cloaks, and down jackets and drew near the fire in wicker chairs. Patrel began telling their tale in short, terse sentences, starting with the events at the Huggs' farmstead and moving on to the attack of the Vulgs at the Rooks' Roost, his voice hesitating only when he told of Hob's death. Tears brimmed in Tuck's eyes.

The tale done, Patrel's voice fell quiet, and no one spoke for a moment while all reflected upon what had been said. At last Captain Darby broke the silence. "When you four came through the door," his eyes touched each of them, "I thought, *Ah, here is*

Patrel and the recruits, but I was wrong, for you are not raw recruits. Instead, you are now four blooded warriors, Thornwalkers all, who have met a foul enemy and given good account of yourselves—at high cost, to be sure, yet it is a price that sometimes must be paid whenever emissaries of fear are challenged. I am proud of you all."

"Hear, hear," said the Gammer, thumping the floor with his cane.

At that moment, hot food, sent for earlier by Captain Darby, arrived. Adjourning to the table, the four gratefully dug in. It was the first meal they'd had since the previous afternoon, their pack pony, the one with the provisions, having fled from the Vulgs the night before. Little was said during the meal, for Captain Darby bade them to eat while the food was hot. But when at last they pushed away from the table and resumed their places near the fire, filling clay pipes with some of Tuck's Downdell leaf, the talk turned again to the Vulgs.

"Ye've done the right thing, raising the alarm through the countryside," said the Gammer. "Now the brutes'll meet prepared Warrows. And that ought to put a stop to the disappearances."

"On the morrow I'll dispatch heralds to all nearby Thornwalker companies," said Captain Darby, "and start the word spreading. It won't be long till the whole Bosky knows."

"Uh . . . Captain Darby," said Tuck, "would it be possible to send a patrol out to look for the ponies that survived? My grey seems to have gotten away, and one pack pony, with Patrel's lute strapped to it. Two others fled, also."

"My chestnut," said Danner.

"And my piebald," added Patrel.

Tarpy said nothing, for, full of good food and drawn up to a warm fire, exhausted by the all-night battle with the Vulgs, he had fallen asleep, his pipe slipping from his lax fingers to drop to the plank floor.

"You must be weary," said Captain Darby, his eyes soft upon the sleeping young buccan. "Patrel, take your comrades to the tents of your squad. Get some rest. Tomorrow we will begin search patrols into the countryside, looking not only for your steeds, but also for places where Vulgs may hole up during the day. Ah, but if we only had Dwarves as allies, then could we root out the underground haunts of these beasts. Tomorrow we also shall begin night patrols, Vulg hunts, and Thornwalks to keep more of the beasts out." Captain Darby stood and gestured for the four young buccen to seek out their tents and sleep.

They awakened Tarpy and donned their jackets and cloaks, gathering up their packs and bows. "Wait," said the Gammer, "I've something to say." The granther Warrow got to his feet. "When I organized the Wolf Patrols, I thought that it was only them raiding flocks that we had to deal with—and perhaps in the beginning that was true. And we've done a fair job at that: most Wolves in Northdell have come to fear the sight of Warrows. Oh, we know that it's only the strange winter that has driven them to kill livestock—they are only trying to survive—but it's been touch and go for many a Northdeller, and I expect more Wolves to push through the Barrier ere this winter ends, for it's bound to get worse. Before you know it, the other Dells will likely feel the bite of Wolf jaws; though that may not be, for the Wolves have made themselves scarce since the Patrols started and now seem to leave the livestock alone—in which case we'll leave them be, too.

"But, none of us thought that we'd be dealing with Vulgs. Oh, to be sure, there's been talk of Vulgs in the Bosky for two or three weeks, but it's just been tavern talk heretofore, rumors. Ah, but now you four have proven it to be more than just ale tales: it's fact, not fancy.

"Thanks to you, the Bosky will be warned, and the four Warrow kindred will ever be in your debt, for the preservation of the Warrow Folk is what the Thornwalkers are all about. Look around you. This very building symbolizes the four kindred. The logs represent the trees where dwell the Quiren Warrows, my folk, and I dare say ancestors to Tarpy and Patrel; the stone represents the field houses of the Paren Warrows, perhaps kith to Danner, here, by the look of him; the wicker comes from the fens of the Othen Warrows, like Captain Alver down in Reedyville; and the sod represents the burrows of the Siven Warrows, Captain Darby's folk, and it seems Tuck's, too. But whether Bosky folk live in tree flets, stone field houses, fen stilt houses, or burrows, none are safe where the Vulg walks, for Vulgs slink in secret through the night.

"But now, the secret is out. We know what we are dealing with, though we don't know why they've come to the Bosky. Be that as it may, I for one thank you for all the Warrow kindred." And the Gammer bowed to the four and clasped each one's hand.

When the Gammer took Tuck's hand, the young

buccan said, "Sir, please do not forget our slain comrade, Hob Banderel, for he was there, too."

"I haven't, and I won't," said the Gammer, solemnly.

"Thank you, eld buccan," said Tarpy, last to shake hands.

"Eld buccan?" laughed the Gammer. "Nay, bucco, it's been seventeen years since my eighty-fifth birthday. Next I know, you'll be shaving another twenty-five years off o' that, calling me buccan. Nay, the clock doesn't run in that direction, and it's seventeen years a granther am I. But I thank you just the same, Tarpy Wiggins, for you almost make me feel spry." Amid a round of quiet smiles, the Gammer herded the four out of the building.

As Patrel led the weary Warrows to the tents of his squad, they could hear Thornwalkers calling farewell to Gammer Alderbuc as the granther prepared to ride back to Northdell, to set out on his journey back to the town of Northdune along the Upland Way. They could also hear Captain Darby giving orders to summon the squad leaders to the headquarters building to tell them of the Vulgs in the Bosky and to lay plans.

Late in the night, Tuck woke up from deep slumber, still exhausted. Yet he stayed awake long enough to update his diary by the flickering yellow light of a lantern. Then he fell back into troubled, dream-filled sleep—but what he dreamt, he did not recall.

"Time for duty, slugabeds." Patrel shook Tuck awake. "It's midmorn. Stir your bones, break your fast, meet your squadmates." Danner and Tarpy sat up, rubbing sleep from their eyes. "I've got our orders. We stand the early nightwatch at the ford—sundown to mid of night."

With Danner grumbling and Tuck and Tarpy yawning great gaping yawns, Patrel led them to a common washtrough where they broke through the thin layer of ice to splash frigid water on their faces. "Brrr!" shivered Tarpy. "Surely there's a warmer way to get clean."

"Oh yes," answered Patrel, pointing to one of the tents, white wisps of steam leaking here and there from seams. "There is the laundry and bathing tent. Our squad gets to use it on Tuesdays."

"Tuesdays?" asked Danner. "Is that all? I mean, just once a week?"

"Yes," laughed Patrel. "But by the time you've chopped the wood for the heating fire, hauled water from the spring for the tubs, and done all the other work needed to get a bath and do your laundry, then once a week will seem often enough for that privilege."

"What other chores will we have?" asked Tuck, rubbing his face on the common towel and passing it on to Danner, who looked at it with some dismay before using it, too.

"Well, each squad is fairly self-sufficient," answered Patrel. "At times, on rotation, each of us will cook for the other members of our squad, and sometimes for Captain Darby, too, though we all pitch in every day to clean the pots and pans. And occasionally we'll help lay up supplies in the storehouse. Everyone cuts firewood, not only for the squad's needs, but for headquarters, too." Patrel continued to name the other chores they would per-

form, and it soon became clear that each Warrow
was expected to care for his own needs, in the main,
but that there were several jobs shared by all.

Patrel's squad consisted of twenty-two young
buccen, including Tuck, Danner, and Tarpy, who
were introduced at the breakfast campfire. The three
were accorded smiles and nods and a friendly wave
or two. Little was said as they ate, and Tuck's eyes
were drawn to the Great Spindlethorn Barrier
looming near. Dense it was; even birds found it
difficult to live deep within its embrace. Befanged
it was, atangle with great spiked thorns, long and
sharp and iron-hard, living stilettoes. High it was,
rearing up thirty, forty, and in some places fifty feet
above the river valleys from which it sprang. Wide
it was, reaching across broad river vales, no less
than a mile anywhere, and in places greater than
ten. And long it was, stretching completely around
the Boskydells, from the Northwood down the Spindle, and from the Updunes down the Wenden, until
the two rivers joined one another; but after their
joining, no farther south did the 'Thorn grow. It
was said that only the soil of the Bosky in these two
river valleys would nourish the Barrier. Yet the
Warrows had managed to cultivate a long stretch
of it, reaching from the Northwood to the Updunes,
completing the Thornring. And so, why it did not
grow across the rest of the Land and push all else
aside remained a mystery, though the grandams
said, *It's Adon's will*, while the granthers said, *It's
the soil*, and neither knew the which of it for certain.

Here at Spindle Ford, as well as at the one bridge
and at the other fords on the roads into the Boskydells, Warrows had worked long and hard to make

ways through the Barrier, ways large enough for commerce, for waggons and horses and ponies and travellers. Oh, not to say that the Barrier couldn't be penetrated without travelling one of these Warrow-made ways, for one could push through the wild Spindlethorn. It just took patience and determination and skill to make it through, for one had to be maze wise to find a way, usually taking days to wriggle and slip and crawl the random, fanged labyrinth from one side to the other. And never did one penetrate without taking a share of wounds. No, even though Warrows seemed skilled at it, and legend said that Dwarves were even better, still ways through the Barrier must needs be made for travel and commerce.

But the work was arduous, for the Spindlethorn itself was hard—so hard that at times tools were made of its wood, such as arrow points and poniards, fashioned directly from the thorns. And the wood burned only with great difficulty and would not sustain a blaze. Yet again and again, over many years, Warrows cut and sawed and chopped and dug, finally forming ways through the Barrier. And as if the Spindlethorn itself somehow could sense the commerce, the ways stayed open on the well-used routes; but on those where travel was infrequent, the 'Thorn grew slowly to refill the Warrow-made gap. Some had, in fact, been allowed to grow shut. But here at Spindle Ford, the way had remained open, looking to all like a dark, thorn-walled tunnel, for the Great Barrier was thickly interlaced overhead.

All these thoughts and more scampered through Tuck's mind as he took breakfast and gazed at the

Barrier looming at hand. But his reflections were broken as he took on a share of the after-breakfast cleanup chores. Then Patrel spoke to the others of the events at the Huggs' farm and the fatal attack of the Vulgs at the Rooks' Roost. And when Patrel came to the end of the account, Tuck noted that he and Danner, Tarpy, and Patrel, were being eyed with a high respect akin to awe.

Patrel assigned one of the squad members, Arbin Digg—a slightly rotund brown-haired blue-eyed young buccan from Downyville—to show Tuck, Danner, and Tarpy where things were around the camp, and especially to show them Spindle Ford.

"Ar, so you actually fought with Vulgs, and killed some, too," said Arbin as they strode toward the gaping, tunnel-like hole arching away into the Spindlethorn Barrier toward the Spindle River and the ford. "Good show. Gilly, over in the third squad, he thought he might've seen one about two or three weeks ago, but he wasn't certain. Here now, let me ask you, are they the great brutes we've all heard about?"

"Nearly as big as a pony," answered Tarpy, "though who'd want to ride one, I can't say."

"Asking a Vulg for a ride would be like begging a Dragon to warm your house in the winter," snorted Danner. "He'd warm it, all right—right down to the very ashes."

"Are you saying that the only way you'd get a ride from a Vulg is on the inside?" Arbin asked.

"Perhaps, Arbin, perhaps," responded Danner, "though I don't know what they ordinarily eat. The ones we met seemed to kill just for the joy of slaughter."

"Wull then, I don't believe I'll ask a Vulg for a ride," said Arbin, "or a Dragon to warm my house, either." He led them into the Barrier.

Although the day outside was bright, the light sifting through the entangled Spindlethorn to the roadway fell dim unto the eye, and the sounds of the Warrow encampment faded away and were lost. Only the muffled footsteps sounded within, and Tuck had visions of walking in a dagger-walled cave.

"They say in the summer when the leaves are asprout that torches are needed to light the way through, just as if it were night," said Arbin, looking at the tangled thorn-weave overhead. He had shown them the brands set in rows at the entrance—wooden stakes, with oil-soaked cloth layered over one end, to be used as torches for wayfarers to light their way through at night. "In autumn, when the leaves fall, they make a roof in places. Snow, too, can pile up and make solid ceilings overhead here and there. But sooner or later, leaves or snow, it works its way through, and the road must be cleared at times."

On they walked, through the wan light, a mile, then two. Ordinarily they would have ridden ponies to their posts, but first-timer Thornwalkers always were taken afoot, to get the "feel" of the passage. At one place, Arbin pointed out sections of a large movable barricade, now set to the side, made of Spindlethorn. "There's one of the barriers. I suppose we'll be putting it in place one of these days, and start warding it, now that there seems to be trouble Beyond, Outside. It's one of several Thornwalls that we can put up, though only two, one on each side of the ford, are actually in place now." Arbin pointed ahead. "Ah, look, the end is in sight."

Ahead they could see an archway of brightness, where the daylight shone at the end of the Spindlethorn tunnel. Shortly they came to the Beyonder Guard barrier, and with shouts of greetings all were welcomed by ten Warrows warding there. At roadside, a string of ponies stood, munching grain from nosebags. Arbin explained to the guards that they'd come to see the river and beckoned the three to follow him, slipping through the thorns of the barricade where it was slightly ajar. "This here is the aft-guard. Over there is the fore-guard, where there's another wall like this one, just on the other side of the river, just inside the tunnel," he said, as he led Tuck, Danner, and Tarpy out blinking and watery-eyed into the daylight.

All told, two and a half miles they had walked, and had come at last to the edge of the river, the shallows of Ford Spindle. Wide it was, and ice-covered, although here and there, both upstream and down, dark pools swirled as the river rushed and bubbled over and around upthrust rock, the churn keeping the water ice-free.

Across the ford they could see the mouth of the tunnel as it continued on through the 'Thorns growing on that side, where the Barrier reached another two miles before the Realm of Rian began.

Out onto the ice Arbin led them, to stand at river's center. They looked up and down the frozen length to where it curved away beyond seeing, a white ribbon wending between two looming, fifty-foot high, miles-wide walls of thorn. Overhead slashed a bright blue ribbon of sky, impaled upon the long spikes, tracing the course of the waterway.

"It's a wonder, ain't it?" asked Arbin, pointing

both ways at once, his arms flung wide. "Kind o' gives me the shivers." Tuck had to agree, for a more formidable defense he had yet to see. "Come on, buccoes," said Arbin, "I'll show you the fore-guard."

On they went, over the ford to just inside the tunnel, where they came to another barrier. Ten more of the squad stood at this post, the barricade shut, though a small crawlway twisted through, with a barrier set to drop and plug it. Ponies stood near.

"Who's up the road?" Arbin asked one of the warders.

"Willy," came the reply.

Arbin turned to the three. "The Beyonder Guard always has a point buccan, one with sharp eyes, good hearing, and a swift pony, out at the far edge of the Spindlethorns, out where the Bosky ends and Rian begins. If someone approaches, then he'll come pelting back here ahead of 'em to warn us. If it looks like trouble, and if there is time, then we'll open the wall and in he'll gallop and we'll slam shut the barricade behind him. But if they're right on his heels, then through the crawlway he'll scoot and we'll drop the thornplug to stopper it. O' course, the aft-guard will be signalled so that they can prepare, too.

"If it's a fight, then we climb up on these stands and shoot down at them, though we've never had to do that yet. Meanwhile, the aft-guard will send a fast rider back to warn the camp and to bring reinforcements. If by some chance the foe breaks through here, then there's the aft-barrier on the other side of the ford where we'll get to. Beyond that is another one, and finally the Deep Plug back at the campsite. And the Deep Plug will cork up this tunnel till Gyphon, Himself, comes back."

At the mention of Gyphon's name, Tuck felt a deep foreboding, and a cold shudder ran up his spine as if from an icy wind blowing. But Tuck said nothing of this dark portent, and soon they turned and walked back the way they had come.

That night, Tuck, Danner, and Tarpy were assigned with seven others to the barrier on the near side of the ford. A fire was built out beyond the open barricade, out where it would cast light upon anyone coming across the shallows, and the buccen alternately took turns standing guard and warming by the fire. On Tuck's turns to warm himself, he jotted notes in his diary by the firelight.

At mid of night, the watch was changed, and Patrel's squad rode back to the campsite, Tuck, Danner, Tarpy, and Patrel himself riding double with other Warrows of the squad.

The next morning, Tuck's grey pony and Danner's chestnut were found by a patrol from the fifth squad, but as of yet there was no sign of Patrel's piebald or the pack pony.

Tuck, Danner, and Tarpy had spent the morning studying, memorizing a section of a map; and at midday the squad Walked the Thorns in that area, going some five miles to the north by pony before returning, searching diligently but vainly for splits and cracks in the land where Vulgs might lie up during the time the Sun was on high. They kept their eyes out for Wolves, too, but saw none. And they inspected the Barrier for breaks, but of course there were none.

Again at night they stood Beyonder Guard at the ford, but nothing of note occurred.

For six more days the routine did not vary, except Tarpy was called upon to cook for the squad. As usual, the food was jovially vilified by all, except, since it was Tarpy's first go at cooking, the jokes were a bit more gentle than would be the case were he a cooking veteran.

Patrel's piebald pony came wandering alone into the camp on the following day, seeming no worse for the wear. As chance would have it, on this day the fourth squad, Patrel's, was to begin Wolf Patrol, roving wide across the countryside and looking for sign of Wolf, and now Vulg, too. The trio of Danner, Tuck, and Tarpy were pleased, for they had studied hard and the features of the maps were firmly implanted in their memories, hence they were to be permitted to join the wide-ranging search. But Tuck was to be disappointed, for he was to be left behind. He had forgotten that he was the cook for the day, and his duty was to prepare a hot meal for the squad's return at dusk.

All day Tuck jittered about nervously, fretting about Danner and Tarpy and Patrel and all of his other squadmates, wondering if they were safe and if they had seen any Wolves or Vulg sign or had found any Vulg lairs. And the day dragged by on leaden feet. At last it was dusk, and Tuck had the meal hot and waiting, but still they had not yet returned, though other squads had.

An hour passed, then another, and Tuck worried about the food and felt anger that they hadn't come to eat it when it was first ready. But then he thought how foolish it was to get upset over a meal when someone could be hurt or a fight with Vulgs could be raging. But most of all he fretted and paced and stirred and took the cauldron off the cooking irons only to put it back on when it had cooled a bit.

Finally they came, plodding wearily into camp. Tarpy was first. He slid off the back of his new white pony and tiredly removed the saddle, blanket, and harness and slapped the steed on the rump, sending it scudding into the rope pen to the awaiting hay. The others, too, came stringing in to do likewise.

"We found the pack pony," Tarpy said to Tuck as he dished up a hot, steaming, thick stew into Tarpy's mess kit. "Dead. Vulg slashed. Patrel's lute smashed beyond repair. We searched for hours but found no Vulg dens. Ah, me, but I'm tired."

Another ten days passed, and each day the young buccen saddled up and scoured the countryside, tracking down rumors of Vulg sightings or starting at farms where Vulgs had slaughtered livestock or had been seen, but to no avail. Neither Vulg nor Wolf was spotted. Someone suggested that perhaps the Vulgs were laired inside the Barrier, and special missions to examine the 'Thorn forayed out repeatedly, to return scratched or pinked by the spikes.

"Ah, it's no good," said Tarpy, dabbing at a puncture wound in his forearm as the squad sat at supper. "It's like trying to search out an endless maze. If they're in there, then it's one puzzle we won't solve in a lifetime."

"It's a puzzle all right," said Patrel, "for surely we should have sighted some by now. Oh, perhaps not Wolves, for they have gotten wily and now hunt their normal game in the woods. But our night patrols should have turned up a Vulg or two by now, and our day patrols, at least one den." Patrel fell into thoughtful silence.

"What's needed here," said Danner, "is for us to lay traps for them. Or to wait for them to come to us. We need some kind of bait, or an advantage of some kind."

"How about dogs?" asked Tuck. "I'll wager that dogs'd find the lairs."

"Ar, they tried dogs over at the Eastdell Second," said Patrel, "and they had no more luck than we. You know, it's as if the Vulgs came to the Bosky on some *mission* and, having accomplished it, are now gone. But what that mission may have been, I cannot say."

Neither, of course, could anyone else say, and again Tuck felt the icy fingers of an unknown doom walking up his spine.

The next day at sundown, they returned from patrol to find the camp all astir. A waggon train of refugees from Challerain Keep had passed through, following along the Upland Way; their goal was the Realm of Wellen to the west. Danner, who had cook duty, described the train.

"Long it was, perhaps a hundred or so waggons, loaded with food and household goods, and driven by *Men*, mostly oldsters, and *Women*, with their offspring, too. Big, those Folk are—nearly twice my size, and I'm no tiny dink like Tarpy, here.

"And the escort, soldiers on horseback, with helms and swords, and spears, too. Lor! Big horses, big Men." Danner paused in reflection, and it was the first time in Tuck's memory that he'd ever seen Danner impressed. "It took nearly two hours for the train to pass through," continued Danner, "and the Captain of the escort, well he was closeted with Captain Darby for most of that time. Then he just up and rode off as the last waggon trundled through. And then they were gone." Danner took a bite of bread and chewed unconsciously, his amber eyes lost in elsewhen thought.

A hubbub of questions and comments burst forth from the squad, washing over Danner, and Tuck was caught up in the fervor, his own supper forgotten, more than a little envious that he'd missed seeing the train. But before Danner could respond to the babble, Patrel came to the fireside and called for quiet.

"Captain Darby will speak to us tonight, in less than an hour, so eat up and finish the meal chores quickly. We are to assemble shortly at headquarters. Hop to it, now, for we've little time as it is."

Hurriedly, Tuck wolfed down his meal, cleaned his mess kit, and pitched in with the pots and pans. Soon the chores were done, and the squad collected with the others at the main building. Captain Darby was there, his face enshadowed by a lantern swinging from a pole by the door. He spoke to a few nearby, then sprang upon a bench and overlooked the company. The night was cold, and a light snow had begun to fall. Warrows stamped to keep their feet warm, and their breath rose up in a great white plume as if from some huge aggregate creature. Squad call was made, and each was there except the third squad, who had Beyonder Guard duty.

"Buccen," Captain Darby began, his voice raised

so that all could hear, "some of the rumors are true: There *is* trouble brewing up north, beyond the Keep. High King Aurion prepares for War: *War with Modru, the Enemy in Gron.*" A collective gasp of dismay welled up from the assembled Warrows, for this indeed was dire news, and many muttered grim words and spoke with their squadmates. Captain Darby let the talk run on for a bit, then held up his hand for silence. When it returned he continued.

"I had a long talk with Captain Horth, leader of the waggon train escort. He said that the call had gone forth for the allies of the High King to rally to his aid. Why the summons has not yet come to the Bosky, neither he nor I can say. But I believe that it will, and so we must begin to think upon going. Those who will it may take their leave and join the Allies at the Keep. Yet the Bosky must not be left unguarded and undefended should the foe come nigh, hence that, too, must be considered."

Again a babble rose up from the assembled young buccen. *Leave the Bosky? Fight a War way up north? High King's call?* Tuck, too, felt a wrenching at his heart, just as he had when Old Barlo had told him he would be leaving Woody Hollow, but this was even more unexpected. He had never dreamt that he might be asked to fight the foe in a strange land, especially when the Bosky itself was in danger from Vulgs. Yet how best to avenge Hob—face the enemy here, or in a far Land? For it now seemed certain that the High King's summons would come to the Boskydells, and Tuck would have to answer to his conscience no matter which way he chose. He was caught up in a dilemma: Could he leave the Bos- kydells to answer the High King's muster if Modru's

Horde marched this way? But on the other hand, could he refuse the High King's call to colors at the Keep? For if he and enough others answered the summons and went north, perhaps the Enemy in Gron could be defeated ere War came south. What to do? *Torn between love of home and duty to King,* Tuck realized, but knowing this did not help resolve the question.

"What about Modru? How do they know it's him?" someone called to Captain Darby, breaking Tuck's train of thought. Again a hubbub arose, but it quieted when the Captain raised his hands. "Captain Horth said that there's a great wall of darkness stalking down the Land from the north. Eerie it is, and frightening, too, like a great black shadow. And inside the darkness is bitter winter cold and the Sun shines not, though it rides the day sky. And there be fell creatures within that blackness, Rūcks and such, Modru's lackeys of old, a gathering of his Horde. And it is reported that some skirmishes with the Enemy's forces already have occurred."

Shouts broke out among the Warrows. *Black shadow? Rūcks and such? Modru's Horde? This is awful! Legends come to life!*

Again Captain Darby called for quiet, but it was a long time coming. At last, though, he said, "Hold on, for we know not whether these things be true, or are common events made dire in the telling. The black wall, for instance, could be but a cover of dark clouds. It does not have to be Modru's hand at work. But even if it is, till the High King calls we will concentrate on the defense of the Bosky, by Beyonder Guarding and Vulg Hunting. Yet when King Aurion's muster is sounded, then you must choose.

But for now, we Walk the Thorns." Calling his squad leaders to him, Captain Darby leapt down from the bench and strode inside.

Tuck, Danner, and Tarpy trudged back to their tent, each immersed deep in his own thoughts, and Tuck's entry into his diary that night took longer than usual.

The next day the squad was assigned Beyonder Guard, this time on the late night shift, mid of night till sunup. As was the case with this shift, on the day before beginning the duty the squad was given no daylight assignment so that they would be rested and alert when their late assignment began. Hence, they lazed the day away in small tasks and idle talk—talk that inevitably turned to Modru.

"Why now?" asked Tarpy. "I mean, well, after four thousand years, why does Modru threaten now?"

"What I'd like to know is, what kind of creatures are in his Horde?" queried Arbin, as he fletched another arrow, sighting down its length. "I know about Rūcks, Hlōks, and Ogrus, or at least what the tales tell. They're supposed to be all alike, just different sizes. The Rūck is the smallest, a bit larger than we—say, four foot tall; the Hlōk, big as a Man, I hear tell; and the Ogru, or Troll, as the Dwarves call him, twice Man-size."

Danner, who was the only one there who'd recently seen a Man, and who knew how *big* they were, snorted. "Hah! *Twice Man-size?* I think the old legends exaggerate. Why, that'd make the Ogru the greatest creature on the land."

"Except for Dragons," chipped in Tuck, "but none

of those have been seen for five hundred years or so—or so they say."

"You're forgetting one Dragon that's been seen recently," smiled Arbin.

"What do you mean?" spoke up Tarpy, puzzled. "What Dragon has been seen recently?" He appealed to the others with outstretched hands, palms up.

"The Dragon Star!" shouted Arbin in glee, having lured Tarpy into his word trap. Tarpy made a face, and the others smiled ruefully, shaking their heads.

"Now there's a thing folks will talk about for ages to come," said Delber, a fair-haired young buccan from Wigge, "the Dragon Star."

Delber was talking about the great flaming star with its long burning tail that had come blazing out of the heavens five years past, nearly to strike the world.

For weeks before, its light could be seen, appearing at sunset, and it burned through the night. Night after night it grew brighter and larger, plunging through the star-studded sky. And its fiery tail, called "Dragon's Breath" by some, and "Dragon's Flame" by others, grew longer and longer. An awful portent it was, for the hairy stars had presaged dire events since the world began. On it came, rising each night, inexorably sweeping closer. Now it was so bright that it could be seen even in the dawn light, as it set while the Sun rose.

But night was its true Realm, for then it silently clove the splangled sky, looming ever larger, ever brighter. And then folk noted that it seemed to be changing course, shifting, for slowly its tail swung behind till it no longer could be seen, *as if the Dragon Star had turned and was hurtling directly for Mithgar*.

Some folk prepared for the cataclysm: cellars were dug, and food was canned and stored away. The sale of charms against the Dragon Star became brisk, though even the sellers said they were not at all certain that the amulets would work. And it was commonly told that Mithgar was doomed. And onward it came, now an enormous blaze in the night.

And then the last night to live arrived, but in spite of the impending death of the world, most Bosky folks had worked their fields and livestock and trades as usual, though the taverns after the Sun set seemed more crowded than was ordinary.

That night the great Dragon Star rushed across the sky of Mithgar, so bright that books could be read by its light. As if in escort, myriads of blazing, burning points of light seared and streaked across the heavens, brighter than the brightest fireworks. Huge glowing fragments were seen to splinter from the Dragon Star and hurtle down through the sky toward the ground, and great, loud blasting booms shuddered over the Land, breaking windows and crockery. One great flaming piece, gouting fire and rucketing boom after boom, seemed destined to destroy the Bosky, but it seared a great blazing south-to-north path, hurtling to smash somewhere far beyond the Northwood, in Rian or perhaps even further.

People wept and cried out in fear, and some swooned while others drank in the taverns. Some fled to their burrows, and others took to their cellars. But most simply sat and watched and waited, with their arms around their buccarans or dammias, or about their sires and dams, or their buccoes and dammsels, or granthers and grandams, or uncles, aunts, cousins, or other relatives or friends, for they knew nought else to do.

Yet the mighty Dragon Star hurtled not into Mithgar, but instead rushed past. Still, its great glowing tail long washed over the world: it was said to the vast woe of Mithgar. For days upon days the bright glow of the Dragon Star could be seen in the sky, in the daytime now as it sped for the Sun. And the Sun at last seemed to swallow it, but later spat it out the other side. And the Dragon Star hurtled back into the heavens, now chasing its own tail, or Breath, or Flame, as the case may be, growing fainter every day, until at last it was gone.

For weeks afterward, a day did not pass that the Sun and sky did not show sullen red in the foredusk—blood red, some claimed. At night, great blowing curtains of shifting light glowed and shuddered in the sky—Mithgar's Shroud, some called it. A caul fell upon the face of the Moon and did not fade for weeks. And a raging fever plague swept the Land; many died. Milk soured, cows went dry, crops failed, hens stopped laying, dogs barked without reason, and once it rained without letup for eight days. It was said that two-headed calves and sheep without eyes were born, and some claimed to see snakes roll like hoops.

Wherever Warrows gathered, great arguments arose. Many believed that *all* of these strange things were the doings of the Dragon Star. Others said, "Rubbish! Most of these happenings are ordinary events; we've seen 'em before. And some o' these stories are just wild tales. Only a *few* things might be laid at the feet of the Dragon Star."

Slowly the Land returned to normal: the plague abated and finally died out, Mithgar's Shroud and the bloody sunsets gradually disappeared, cows came afresh, hens laid eggs, and the crops grew. But no one who had seen the Dragon Star would ever forget it; it would be an event talked about for generation upon generation, until it, too, joined the other epic tales and legends told 'round the hearth, as it was now being talked about around the Thornwalker campfire.

"Yar, I seen it," said Dilby Helk, peering at the other squad members, "but who didn't? I can 'member sitting on the hilltop near our farmstead with my elden grandam. And she said, 'No good'll come of this, Dilbs,'—she always called me Dilbs—'mark my words. It means the death of the High King, or something else just as bad, or worse.' And I said, 'What could be worse, Granny?' And her face went all ashy and her voice all hollow, and she said, 'The Doom of Mithgar.' Wull, I'll tell you, I was ascared!" Dilby's eyes were wide and lost in the memory, then he shivered and looked up at the others and gave a nervous laugh. "Ar, but the High King's alive and Mithgar's still here, so I reckon as she was wrong."

For a moment no one spoke. Then Tarpy said, "Maybe she was right, what with Modru stirring up north. Perhaps the Dragon Star came to forewarn us of that."

"What if it was a sending of Adon?" speculated Arbin. "He might have tried to tell us of this coming War, but we just couldn't read His message."

"Ar, sending!" burst out Danner, disgusted. "Why not say it was sent by Modru? Or even by bloody Gyphon, Himself? Hah! The Doom of Mithgar, indeed."

"Yes, Mr. Danner High-and-Mighty. Sendings!" cried Arbin, his face flushed with anger. "Don't look down your crusty beak at me! Everyone knows about sendings and omens. Plagues are sendings of Gyphon, the Great Evil. If not from Gyphon, then plagues come from His servant Modru, the Enemy in Gron. And as to omens, well just look the next time you see a flight of birds, for they tell of fortunes, sometimes good, sometimes bad. So you see, Mr. Wise Danner, the Dragon Star could well have been a sending of Adon."

Now Danner's ire, too, was up. "Ask yourself this, Arbin Oracle: If I shied a rock at a bird on a limb, and somewhere else you saw it flying in fright, what would it auger, what great omen of fortune would it tell you? Would it be a sending of Modru, or Gyphon, or one of High Adon? Answer me this, too: If Adon wanted to say something, why wouldn't He just come right out and say it plain? Why would He cast it in runes that nobody can read? Sendings! Omens! Faugh!"

Arbin leapt to his feet, his fists clenched, and so, too, did Danner. And it would have come to blows except Tuck stepped in between and gently pressed Arbin back, saying, "Hold on, now, and save your fighting for Modru." He turned to Danner and placed a hand on his forearm and said, "Squabble with Vulgs, not Warrows." Danner shook off Tuck's grip and, glowering at Arbin, sat back down. Talk ceased.

The tense silence was finally broken by Tarpy.

"Look, we can't have you two buccoes forever glaring at one another like circling dogs. Let's just leave it at this: Sometimes events seem like sendings and omens, sometimes not, and who's to say the which of it? Perhaps some things *are* portents while others are *not*, even the flights of birds—there may be times that they mean something and other times not. Yet I think none of us here will ever read a winged augery. But this I say: Until we know the truth about sendings, omens, whatever, there's got to be room for different beliefs and respect for the right to hold diverse opinions." Little Tarpy glared at Danner and Arbin, both of whom towered over him. "Have you got that? Then formally put your wrath behind you." Both Danner and Arbin stood, albeit somewhat reluctantly, and stiffly bowed to one another, to the smiles of the other squad members.

Tuck and Tarpy and eight others were assigned to the fore-barricade while Danner was among those that drew the aft-gate for their Beyonder Guard duty. Just prior to mid of night, they rode down the long black tunnel of thorns to their posts, greeting the squad there with *Halloos* and *Hai-rois* and *Ai-oi, where you been? Have you bitten any Vulgs lately? What's the news from Modru?* and other such banter. The relieved squad mounted their own ponies and rode back toward the encampment, leaving Patrel's squad to stoke the fires and prepare for the long watch. The fore-barrier was opened, and Dilby rode out to relieve the point-watch at the far side of the 'Thorn. After a while they could see the approaching torch of that young buccan, and as he rode up to the fore-barricade it was opened long enough for

him to pass through on his way back to camp. Tuck
watched as he rode across the frozen river and was
passed through the aft-barricade.

An hour dragged by, and then another, and few
words were spoken. In the main, the gurge of swift
water under ice and the pop of pine knots in the
fire were the dominant sounds of the night. All of
the ponies and half of the young buccen dozed while
the other half drank hot tea and kept a sharp watch
out. Another hour passed, and Tuck, on rest, was
just nodding off when Tarpy shook him awake.
"Tuck! Look sharp! Dilby comes, and he's riding
fast!"

Tuck scrambled up, and Warrows nocked arrows
and stood ready, their senses alert. Arbin scuttled
out the crawlway, kicked up the fire in front of the
barricade to better see by, and scurried back through,
making ready to drop the Spindlethorn plug into
the crawlway if necessary. The signal was given to
those across the ford to close the aft-barricade. They
could see Dilby's torch bobbing closer and now hear
the pony's hoofbeats as it raced toward the barrier.
Patrel came running across the river, arriving just
as Dilby pounded up.

"A rider comes!" Dilby cried. "At speed! Sounds
like a horse, not a pony. Let me in!" Quickly they
opened the barricade and shut it just as fast once
Dilby was through. He threw a leg over the pony
and leapt to the ground, giving his report to Patrel
as the others took up their posts on the ramparts
of the barrier. "I was at the point and thought I
could hear something coming up the road, far off.
I put my ear to the icy ground, nearly froze it, and
listened. The sound became plain—a horse, I think,

at speed, running along the road, headed for the ford."

"Oi! A light!" cried Delber, and all peered beyond the barricade to see a torch, its light growing swiftly. Now they could hear the pounding of hooves, this time horse rather than pony. On it came, growing louder, until a black foam-flecked steed, ridden by a haggard Man, burst into the firelight to thunder to a halt at the barrier.

"In the name of the High King, open up, for I am his herald, and War is afoot!" cried the Man, holding his torch aloft so that all could see that indeed he was garbed in a red-and-gold tabard, the colors of High King Aurion.

"Your mission?" called down Patrel.

"Ai! Modru gathers his Horde to fall upon Challerain Keep," cried the messenger, his horse curvetting, "and I am sent to muster this Land, for all must answer to the call if the Realm is to brave the coming storm."

"Open the barricade," ordered Patrel, and Tuck and Tarpy and two others leapt down to do so. "What news?" he called as the four set aside their bows to move the barrier.

"Darkness stalks the north. Prince Galen strikes within the Dimmendark. Young Prince Igon has slain Winternight Spawn. And Aurion Redeye fortifies the Keep," answered the herald.

The barrier at last was open, and the Kingsman rode through, but at the sight of the yawning black maw of the thorn tunnel on the far side of the ford, he paused and sighed. "Ah, Wee One," he called up to Patrel, "riding through this Great Thornwall is like passing through the very gaping Gates of Hèl."

"Would you have a hot cup of tea before going into those gaping Gates?" asked Tuck, looking up, marvelling at how huge both horse and Man seemed to be.

"Would that I could, but I must away," smiled the Man down at Tuck. "And shut that thorngate soon," he gestured at the barricade behind, "for I ken something follows me."

At a light touch of spurs to flank, the black steed trotted forward out of the mouth of the Thornwall and onto the frozen river, gingerly stepping toward the far bank, the strike of iron-shod hooves knelling through the ice. The Warrows watched his progress toward the far side and signalled the Beyonder Guard at the aft-gate to let the Man pass.

And thus it was that while all eyes were riveted upon the Man, a great snarling black shape hurtled through the open fore-barrier, racing to overhaul the herald. *"Vulg!"* cried Tarpy, snatching up his bow. Yet ere he could nock an arrow, the black beast was beyond range, but Tarpy sprang after.

"Close the barrier! More come!" shouted Patrel, and several leapt down to do so, while others spun to see three more hideous Vulgs speeding toward the barricade. *Thuun! Hsss! Thuun! Ssss!* Arrows were loosed at the creatures as the thorngate slammed to, walling them out.

Tuck, too, had snatched up his bow and raced after Tarpy, fumbling for an arrow as he ran. The Vulg was swift and closed upon the Kingsman with blinding speed.

" 'Ware!" shouted Tuck as he pounded onto the ice, five running strides behind Tarpy.

The herald turned in his saddle to see what was

amiss just as the great black Vulg sprang for his throat, and but for Tuck's warning he would have been slain then and there. He threw up an arm to ward the beast, and the Vulg hurtled into him, knocking him from the saddle, though his left foot was caught in the stirrup. The Vulg rolled on the ice, and his claws scratched and clicked as he scrambled to his feet, and his baleful yellow eyes flashed evil. The horse screamed in terror and reared up and back, dragging the Kingsman under. Tarpy had reached the steed and grabbed at the reins, and Tuck slid to a stop over the Man as the Vulg bunched and leapt at Tarpy, snarling jaws aslaver. *Thuun! Sssthwock!* Tuck's arrow buried itself in the Vulg's chest, and the beast was dead as it smashed into the horse, knocking its feet from under. Squealing, the steed crashed down onto the ice. Rending cracks rived the surface, and a great jagged slab tilted up and over. Tuck, Tarpy, and the Man—each desperately clawing at the canting ice—the screaming, kicking horse, and the dead Vulg all slid down to be swept under by the swift current. *And the slab slammed shut behind them like a great trapdoor.*

The icy shock of the frigid water nearly caused Tuck to swoon, so cold it was that it *burned.* But ere he could faint, the racing current rammed him into a great rock, and the jolt brought him to. Up he frantically swam, to collide with the underside of the ice, and he all but screamed in terror. His fingers clawed at the hard undersurface in panic as the merciless torrent swept him along. He needed to breathe but couldn't, for the bitterly cold water was everywhere, though breath raced by only inches away. Numb he grew, and he knew he was dead, but he held on until he could last no more. Yet, *lo!* his face came into a narrow pocket of air trapped between hard ice and gushing water, and he gasped rapidly, his cheek pressed against the ice, his panting breath harsh in his ears. He clutched helplessly at the smooth frozen undersurface, trying to stay where he was, but there was nought to grasp and his fingers no longer did his bidding.

He was swept under again, dragged down away from the ice, his saturated clothes weighing him under. Again the frigid current whelmed him into a great rock, and he was slammed sideways into a crevice, jammed there by the surge at the riverbed, far below the surface. He reached down and numbly felt a river rock and forced his fingers to close, to grasp it up from the bottom, and he clawed his way up the crevice. He would try to hammer through the ice, though he had little hope of succeeding.

Up he inched, buffeted by the whelming surge, pressed into the cleft of the great rock, nearly pinned by the force. Up he struggled, straining every nerve, every sinew, his lungs screaming for air. Up, and his grip failed him and the rock plummeted, whirling away from his benumbed fingers, but the furious battle upward went on. Up he clawed, and against his will his lungs heaved, trying to breathe, to find air and draw it past clamped lips. He knew he could hold out no longer. *No!* his mind shouted in anger, and with all his might, all his energy, he gave one last desperate surge upward. He came into the sweet night air, and his lungs pumped like bellows, for he had come up in one of the dark gurging pools where ice had not yet formed.

With enormous effort he crawled up onto the great stone thrusting above the water and lay against the icy rock, gasping for air. He could no longer feel his hands, and uncontrollable shudders racked through his body. He was cold . . . so cold . . . so bitterly cold, and he knew that he was dying. Yet from the depths of his being he willed himself to get up, to stand, but he only managed to roll over onto his side. He lay there panting, with his cheek pressed against the cold, hard stone, and only his eyes moved at his will.

Down between the great walls of thorn looming darkly upward he could see a ring of torchlight, perhaps one hundred yards away, at the ford. But one torch was much nearer, darting from place to place. Closer it came, held high. It was Danner! He came searching the pools! Tuck tried to speak, to call out, and his voice was but a feeble croak, lost in the churn. Again Tuck called, this time louder, though still faint. Danner jerked about and held up his torch to see the Warrow crumpled on the rock, and he darted to the pool, stopping at the edge of the ice.

"Tuck!" he cried, "I've found you! You're alive!" His voice sounded as if he were weeping. "Har! Yar!" he shouted at the others, his cry loud between the thorn walls. "This way! Hoy! Bring rope!" He turned back to Tuck. "We'll throw you a line and pull you out of there."

"I can't use my hands," Tuck managed to say. "They don't work anymore. I can't even sit up." And Tuck found that he was sobbing.

"Don't worry, bucco," Danner said, "I'll come and get you." Danner began stripping his clothes, muttering angrily to himself: "Witless fools! Trying to flip that slab back over." Other young buccen came pelting up, wondering in their eyes at the sight of Tuck. "I told you!" spat Danner. "Search the pools! Some now stay with me! The rest search for Tarpy . . . and the Man! Who has the rope?" They stood agape a moment until Patrel barked out orders, and four stayed with Patrel and Danner while the others began the search.

Danner tied the line to himself, and Patrel and the other four took a grip on it. Then the young buccan plunged into the water, crying out with the shock and pain of the cold, but swiftly he reached the rock, the current carrying him. Up onto the stone he clambered, shivering uncontrollably, his teeth achatter. Pulling in some slack, he sat Tuck up and looped the line over him, using a great slip-knot. "All right, bucco," his voice diddered with the cold, "in we go now. The current will carry us out of here."

Tuck was of no help, but Danner managed to get the two of them into the bitter rush, and Tuck lost consciousness. With Patrel and two others anchoring the line, paying it out, Danner kept Tuck afloat while the swift current carried them onward to the downstream rim of the frigid pool, where waited Argo and Delber, who pulled first Tuck and then Danner up onto the ice. Hurriedly, his feet trailing behind, they half carried, half dragged Tuck back to the fire, where they stripped his clothes from him and warmed him and wrapped him in two blankets taken from the bedrolls behind the ponies' saddles. Danner, too, moaning with the cold, came to the fire, limping, with Arbin helping him. He, also, was first warmed, then wrapped in blankets by the fire. Tuck came partly awake, and hot tea was given to both, Patrel holding the cup to Tuck's mouth, urging the buccan to sip.

A time passed, and Tuck was now sitting. His hands were beginning to tingle needle-sharp when at last the other buccen returned from the search. Tuck looked up as Dilby came to the fire. "Tarpy?" Tuck asked, and he burst into tears when Dilby shook his head, no.

When Captain Darby and the healers came, sent for by Patrel, both Tuck and Danner were taken by pony-cart back to the Thornwalker campsite. Neither said much on the trip, and in the tent Tuck was given a sleeping draught for his painfully throbbing hands and fell into a deep, dreamless state. Yet Danner awoke after but a few hours of restless sleep to see Tuck awkwardly gripping a pencil and determinedly writing in his diary. *He's putting it all down in his diary, you know, to get it out of his mind,* muttered Danner to himself, and he fell once again into troubled slumber.

Tuck awoke to Danner shaking his arm. "Up, bucco. They've gone off without us, as if we were sick or something," said Danner. "Well, we've got to show 'em we're tougher than they think. How are your hands? It was my feet that nearly gave out on me."

Tuck flexed his fingers. "They feel just a bit strange, somewhat like they're swollen. But that's all." He looked up at Danner and their eyes met, and Tuck began to weep.

"Come on, bucco," said Danner, his own voice choking, "don't go into that now."

"I'm sorry, Danner, but I just can't help it." Tuck's voice was filled with misery, and his tear-laden eyes stared unseeing into a private horror. "I can't wrench my mind away from it—the Man, the horse, Tarpy, all trapped beneath the ice, struggling for air, beating at the frozen surface. Oh, Lor! Tarpy, Tarpy. I close my eyes and see his face under the ice, his hands clawing, but he cannot get out." Sobs racked Tuck's frame, and Danner, weeping too, threw an arm over Tuck's shoulders. "If only I hadn't shot the Vulg just then," Tuck sobbed, "it wouldn't have struck the horse and the ice wouldn't have broken and . . . and . . ." Tuck could not go on.

"Hold it!" exclaimed Danner, leaping up and facing Tuck, his sorrow turning to anger. "That's stupid! If you hadn't feathered that brute when you did, then it would have bitten Tarpy's head off! Don't blame your fool self for an accident of misfortune. You did the right thing, and I mean *exactly* the right thing. It could have been you drowned under the ice instead of Tarpy—or the Man. Any one or all three could have come up in a pool like you did. No, Tuck, chance alone slew our comrade, and chance alone saved you, so if you want to blame someone or something, blame chance!"

Tuck, shocked from his grief and guilt and self-pity by Danner's angry words, looked up at the other buccan. A moment passed, and the only sound was Danner's harsh breathing. And then Tuck spoke, his voice grim. "No, Danner, not chance. I'll not blame chance. Chance did not send that Vulg after the Kingsman. 'Twas Modru."

Captain Darby called the Thornwalker Fourth together at the Spindle Ford, and a service was said for Tarpy, and for the unnamed herald. And through it all, Tuck's eyes remained dry, although many others wept.

And then Captain Darby spoke to all the company: "Buccen, though we have lost a comrade, life goes on. The High King has called a muster at Challerain Keep, and some from the Bosky are duty-bound to answer. I will send couriers to start the word spreading, and others then will respond to the call. Yet some must go forth now and be foremost to answer. It has fallen our lot to be the first to choose, and these are the choices: to remain and ward the Bosky, or to answer the King's summons. I call upon each now to consider well and carefully and then give your answer. What will it be? Will you Walk the Thorns of the Seven Dells, or will you instead walk the ramparts of Challerain Keep?"

Silence descended upon the Thornwalkers as each considered his answer—silence, that is, except for one who had already made up his mind. Tuck stepped forward five paces until he stood alone on the ice. "Captain Darby," he called, and all heard him, "I will go to the High King, for Evil Modru has a great wrong to answer for. Nay! two wrongs: one lies atop the Rooks' Roost, the other sleeps 'neath this frozen river."

Danner strode forward to stand beside Tuck, and so, too, did Patrel. Arbin, Dilby, Delber, and Argo joined them, and so did all of Patrel's squad. Then came others, until a second squad had formed. More began to step forward, but Captain Darby cried, "Hold! No more now! We cannot leave the ford unguarded. Yet, heed this: when others come to join our company, then again will I give you the same choice. Until that time, though, these two squads will be first, and the High King could not ask for better.

"Hearken unto me, for this shall be the way of it. Patrel Rushlock, you are named Captain of this Company of the King, and your squad leaders are to be Danner Bramblethorn of the first squad and Tuckerby Underbank of the second. Captain Patrel, as more squads are formed, they shall be dispatched to your command. And this is the last order I shall give you: Lead well. And to the Company of the King, I say this: Walk in honor."

The next morning, forty-three grim-faced Boskydell Warrows rode forth from the Great Spindlethorn Barrier and into the Land of Rian. They came out along the road across the Spindle Ford, each armed with bow and arrows and cloaked in Thornwalker grey. Their destination was Challerain Keep, for they had been summoned.

CHAPTER 4

CHALLERAIN KEEP

North, then east rode the young buccen, the Warrow Company of the King, along the Upland Way, the road into Rian. They were striking for the Post Road, some twenty-five miles hence, the main pike north to Challerain Keep. Tuck spent much of the time riding among the members of his new squad, getting acquainted. Some he knew from days past, others he did not. Quickly he found that they had come from all parts of Eastdell—from the villages of Bryn and Eastpoint, Downyville, Midwood, Raffin, Wigge, Greenfields, Leeks, and the like, or from farms nearby. Other than Tuck, no one else in his squad was from Woody Hollow or even from its nearby neighbor, Budgens, though one young buccan was from Brackenboro. Yet soon the Warrows were engaged in friendly chatter and no longer seemed to be strangers. Why, Finley Wick from Eastpoint even knew Tuck's cousins, the Bendels of Eastpoint Hall.

They rode through a snow-covered region that slowly rose up out of Spindle Valley to become a flat prairie with but few features. Behind, they could see the massive Barrier clutched unto the land, looming sapless and iron-hard in winter sleep, waiting for the caress of spring to send the life juices coursing through the great tangle, to set forth unto the Sun a green canopy of light-catching leaves, to send the great blind roots inexorably questing through the dark earth again. Immense it was, anchored from horizon to horizon and beyond, a great thorny wall. Yet as the Warrows rode, distance diminished it until it took on the aspect of a vast, remote hill, stretched past seeing. At last it sank below the horizon, and although Tuck rode in the company of friends, still he felt as if he had been abandoned. Yet whether it was because the loss of the Thornwall meant that he'd truly left the Bosky behind, or whether he felt exposed and vulnerable because he now rode upon an open plain, he could not say.

Ahead, here and there, lone barren trees or winter-stripped thickets occasionally appeared, but they, too, were slowly left behind on the snow-swept prairie. A thin, chill wind sprang up, gnawing at their backs, and soon all cloak hoods were up and talk dwindled to infrequent phrases and grunts. On they went, stopping once to feed the ponies some grain and to take a sparse meal. At times they walked, leading the steeds, giving the animals some respite.

On one of these "strolls in the snow," as Finley called them, Tuck found himself trudging between Patrel and Danner. "I hope this blasted cold wind whistling up my cloak is gone by the time we make camp," said Danner. "I don't fancy sleeping in the open in the wind."

"I don't think we'll be in the open, Danner," said

Patrel, "if we reach the point where the Upland Way meets the Post Road, as planned, for that's at the western edge of the Battle Downs. We should be able to find the lee of a hillside there, out of the wind, and make the best of things."

Tuck nodded. "I hope so, but if we don't and if the wind doesn't die down, it doesn't give us much to make the best of, does it now?"

Patrel shook his head, and Danner looked at the sky. The wind mouthed at the edges of their hoods, and the ponies patiently plodded beside them. "Say," asked Danner, "how long will it take us to reach the Keep?"

"Well," answered Patrel, "let me see. One day to the Battle Downs, and then six more along the Post Road north to Challerain Keep. If the weather holds— by that I mean, if it doesn't snow—we'll be seven days on the journey. But, with snow, it could be . . . longer."

"Seven days," mused Tuck. "Perhaps that'll give me enough time to get skilled with my new bow— if I practice every morning before we set out and every evening before bedding down." Tuck's bow had been swept away, lost under the ice of the Spindle River when the Kingsman's horse had crashed through and Tuck had been dragged down by the whelming current. Another bow had been drawn from stores, one that most nearly matched Tuck's old one in length and pull. Yet Tuck would need practice to get the feel of it and regain his pinpoint accuracy.

"Look, Tuck," said Patrel, "I've been meaning to tell you something, but I just haven't been able to muster my courage to the point where I could. But it's just this. I'm dreadfully sorry about Tarpy's death, and I know how close he was to you. He was a bright spirit in this time of gloom, a spirit we will sorely miss in the dark days to come. But I just want you to know that I'll try with all my being to make up for the horrible mistake I made, the mistake that got Tarpy slain."

"What?" cried Tuck, dumbfounded. "What are you saying? If any is to blame, it is I. I shot the Vulg. The horse would not have fallen but for that. Had I only acted quicker, the Vulg would have been slain ere he sprang."

"Ah, but you forget," answered Patrel, "had I but ordered the gate shut immediately after the Kingsman rode through, then that Vulg would have been slain outside the barricade as were the three beasts that raced but Vulg strides behind."

"Nay!" protested Tuck, " 'Twas not your fault. If I had—"

"Ar!" interrupted Danner, scowling, his voice harsh. "If this and if that, and who's to blame. If I'd only ordered the gate shut; if I'd only listened to the Man's warning; if I'd only watched the road instead of the Man; if I'd only seen the Vulgs sooner; if I'd only shot sooner. If! If! If! Those are just a few of the ifs I've heard, and without a glimmering doubt there's many a more where those came from. Tuck, you had the right of it yesterday, though you seem to have lost it already, so I'll remind you: the only one to blame is Modru! Remember that, the both of you! It is Modru's hand that slew Tarpy, none other, just as he slew Hob." With that, Danner leapt upon his pony's back and spurred forward to the head of the column, shouting, "Mount up! We've a ways to go and little time to do it in!" And so went all the Company, eastward along the Upland Way.

The Sun had lipped the horizon when the Warrows came into the margins of the hill country called the Battle Downs, a name from the time of the Great War. They made camp on the lee of a hill in a pine grove and supped on a meal of dried venison and crue, a tasteless but nourishing waybread, and they took their meal with hearty hot tea. After supper, Tuck cut some pine boughs and lashed them together in a large target bundle, and long into the evening, by flickering firelight, the pop of the fire and the sigh of the wind were punctuated by the sounds of bow and arrow.

The next dawn, many were awakened by the *Shock! Shwok!* of Tuck's practice, and they wondered at his dedication, for they could see that his arrows struck true. "Cor," breathed Sandy Pender of Midwood, helping to retrieve the bolts, "but you're a fine shot. Perhaps even as good as Captain Patrel."

"Danner's the one you ought to see shoot," said Tuck. "He'd put us all to shame." Back went Tuck and continued his drill, standing far and near, uphill and down. He stopped to eat breakfast while his pony took some grain, and then he resumed. But at last it was time to get under way, and the Warrows mounted up, urging the ponies out of the grove to take up again the journey, now travelling north along the Post Road.

Midmorn it began to snow, though there was no wind, and the horizon was hidden behind a thick wall of falling flakes. The Warrow column pressed doggedly on, the hill margins of the Battle Downs off to their right, and the long flat slope of land toward the far Spindle River on their left. Dim grey silence fluttered all about them as they rode.

Still the flakes fell as the blear day trudged into the afternoon. Tuck was riding at the head of the column when he looked up to see horses and a waggon loom up through the snow. It was the fore of a refugee train, and the young buccen rode off to one side heading northward while the horses plodded and the wains groaned southward. Both Men and Warrows eyed each other as they passed, and Patrel spoke briefly with the Captain of the escort. The waggon train was nearly two miles long, and it took almost an hour for them to pass one another, for the last wain to disappear south in the snow as the last Warrow vanished north.

"They're headed for Trellinath," said Patrel. "Old Men, Women, and children. Across the Bosky, then south through Wellen and Kael Gap. Ah, me, what an arduous journey for them." Tuck said nought, and north they rode.

Four days later they camped for the evening in the last northern margins of the Battle Downs. They had ridden north for two days, swung east for two more, and now the road had begun to swing north again. They had settled up in a stand of cedar, perhaps a furlong from the road. The Sun had set, and a full Moon rode the night sky. Tuck had finished his archery practice and was sitting by the campfire writing in his diary.

"Two more days, perhaps three, and we'll be there, eh, Patrel?" he asked, pausing in his writing. At

Patrel's nod, Tuck jotted a note in his journal and snapped it shut, putting it into his jacket pocket.

Shortly, all except the sentinels had bedded down. But it seemed to Tuck that he had no more than closed his eyes when he was awakened to a darkened camp by Delber. *"Shhh,"* cautioned the Warrow, "it's mid of night and something comes along the road."

Tuck silently moved through the campsite and awakened others, and bows were made ready. Now could all hear the jingle of armor and clatter of weaponry amid the thud of many hooves. Below, a cavalcade of mounted soldiers cantered north through the bright moonlight. The Warrow company watched them pass, and made no signal. When they were gone, a new fire was kindled, and the young buccen went back to sleep.

All the next day they rode, and there was much speculation about the night riders. "Nar, I don't think they were forces of Modru, even though they did ride at night," said Danner. "Men they were, riding to the Keep."

"Yar, answering to the King's call, like us," said Finley. "Besides, were it Modru's forces, I think as we would'er sensed it. They say as the Ghûls casts fear."

"Oh, it's not the Ghûls that cast fear," chimed up Sandy, contradicting Finley, "it's Gargons. Turn you to stone, too, they say." At the mention of Gargons, Tuck's blood ran chill for they were dire creatures of legend.

"Wull, if it's Gargons as cast fear, what is it that

the Ghûls do?" asked Finley. "I've heard they're most terrible."

"Savage, horse-borne reavers they are," answered Sandy, "virtually unkillable, for it is said that the Ghûls are in league with Death."

"Ar, that's right," said Finley, "now I remember. But I seem to recall that they ride beasts like horses but not horses. And don't the Ghûls just about have to be chopped to shreds before they die?"

"Wood through the heart or a pure silver blade," murmured Tuck, remembering fables.

On they rode, all through the day, stopping but briefly for rests. The Sun swung through the high blue sky, but the land below was cold. The snow scrutched under the ponies' hooves, and the Warrows put up their hoods and looked upon the bright white 'scape through squinted eyes and saw only unrelieved flatness.

Slowly the Sun sank, and when night came they camped in a small ravine on an otherwise featureless plain of Rian.

The next day the land slowly changed into rolling prairie as the Warrow column went on. Occasionally they passed a lonely farmstead, but only one— a mile or so east of the road—had smoke rising from the chimney, and they did not ride to it.

That night they camped in the southern lee of a low hill where stood a copse of hickory, the thickset small trees harsh and grasping in the winter eve. The young buccen had settled in but an hour or two when drumming hoofbeats ran toward the north and a lone rider hurtled past on the nearby road. Again they did not hail. Yet, Finley was dispatched

up the hill to the crest to watch the rider in the
bright moonlight, to see him on his way.

"Ai-oi!" cried Finley from the hilltop. "This way,
buccoes. We've arrived!"

All the company scrambled up to Finley, and he
was pointing to the north. "There she be." And a
hush of awe befell them.

The land fell away before them, beneath the light
of the Moon. Along the road sped the rider, now but
a fleeting dark speck on a shadowy blanket of sil-
vered white. Yet off to the north all eyes were drawn,
for glimmering there, perhaps ten miles away, like
a spangle of stars mounting up a snow-covered tor
springing forth from the argent plains, winked the
myriad lights of their goal—Challerain Keep.

"Lor, but it's big. Look at all those lights,"
breathed Dilby in the silence as they stood and gazed
in wonder at the first city any of them had ever
seen. "Why, there must be hundreds, no, thousands
of them."

"Mayhap we look upon the campfires of an army
as well as the homelamps of a city," said Patrel.

"More like several armies, if you ask me," said
Danner. "See, to the right are what look to be three
main centers, and to the left, two more. I make it
to be five armies plus a city."

"Well, we will find out tomorrow when we ride
in," said Patrel. "But if we are going to be bright
for the King, then it's to bed we must go."

Tuck reluctantly turned and went with the others
down to the hickory thicket, to the Warrow encampment. His being was filled with the excitement of watching distant fires and speculating upon
the Folk gathered about them. His mind was awhirl

with thought, and he paused to scribe in his diary. Yet when he set it aside and took to his bedroll, sleep was a long time coming.

All the young buccen were eager to set out the next day, to gaze upon Challerain Keep, and to move through its streets. "Coo, a real *city*," said Argo as they broke camp and mounted up and rode over the crest of the hill to see from afar the terraced buildings mounting up toward the central Keep. "What will a village bumpkin like me, straight from the one street of Wigge, do in a great place as that is like to be? No matter where you turn, there'll be streets running every which way. And shops and buildings and everything. What with this, that, and the other, it'll be as confusing as the inside of the Barrier, and like as not we'll be lost before it's over."

Tuck felt as if Argo had voiced the silent thoughts of each and every Warrow. "You're right, Argo, it will be confusing to us all, but exciting, too. Hoy! Let's kick up this pace a bit!" They clapped heels into pony flanks, and, shouting with laughter and anticipation, the young buccen raced galloping down the white slopes, powdery snow billowing and pluming up from the ponies as they plunged through the deep drifts onto the great long flats leading toward the distant city. The pace slowed once they regained the Post Road, and steadily they went north. Slowly, ever so slowly, the distance diminished, but their excitement grew.

Long ago, in very ancient times, there had been no city of Challerain; it was merely the name given to a craggy mount standing tall amid a close ring of low foothills upon the rolling grassland prairies of Rian. Then there came the stirrings of War, and a watch was set upon Mont Challerain. Various kinds of beacon fires would be lit as signals, to warn off approaching armies, or to signal muster call, or to celebrate victory, or to send messages to distant Realms. These tidings were sent via the chain of signal fires that ran down the ancient range of tall hills called the Signal Mountains and south from there over the Dellin Downs into Harth and the Lands beyond. War did come, and many of those signal towers were destroyed, but not the one atop Mont Challerain.

After the War, this far northern outpost became a fortress—Challerain Keep. And with the establishment of a fort, a village sprang up at the foot of Mont Challerain. Yet it would have remained but a small hamlet, except the High King himself came north to the fortress to train at arms; and he established his summer court there, where he could overlook the approaches to the Rigga Mountains, and beyond, to Gron.

Year after year the King returned, and at last a great castle was raised, incorporating the fort within its grounds. It was then that the village grew into a town, and the town into a city. The city prospered, and it, too, was called Challerain Keep. This it had been for thousands of years.

As the Warrow column gradually drew closer, they began to discern some details of the city. The mount shouldered up broadly out of low rolling foothills upon the prairie and rose eight or nine hundred feet above the plain. At its peak stood a castle: rugged it looked, even from afar, not at all like an airy castle of fable, but rather like one of strength: crenellated granite battlements loomed starkly 'round blocky towers. The grey castle stood within grounds consisting of gentle slopes that terminated in craggy drops stepping far down the tor sides until at last they fetched up against another massive rampart rearing up to circle the entire mount. On these Kingsgrounds there were many groves, and pines growing in the crags, and several lone giants standing in the meadows, many trees bereft in winter dress. There, too, were several buildings, perhaps stables or warehouses—the Warrows could not tell—and, of course, the citadel itself.

Below the Kingsgrounds began the city proper. There stood tier upon tier of red, blue, green, white, yellow, square, round, large, small, stone, brick, wooden, and every other color, shape, size, and type of building imaginable, all ajumble in terraced rings descending down the slopes. Running among the homes, shops, storehouses, stables, and other structures were three more massive defense walls, stepped evenly down the side of Mont Challerain, the lowest one nearly at the level of the plain. Only a few permanent structures lay outside the first wall.

Out on the crests of hills to the east and west sprawled the encampments of massed armies, yet there seemed to be less activity than could be expected from the extent of the bivouac—fewer Men and horses, as it were, for the number of tents.

All this and more the Warrows saw as slowly they came toward the hills and unto the city. Finally, in late morning, the company rode up among the sparse buildings flanking the Post Road to come at last to the open city gates, laid back against the first wall with a portcullis raised high. Fur- and fleece-clad, iron-helmed soldiers from the nearby camps streamed to and fro. Atop the barbican stood several Men in red and gold—the gate guard—and one leaned on his hands on the parapet and looked down upon the Warrows with wonder in his eyes. And he called to his companions, and all looked in surprise at the small ones below.

"Ho!" called up Patrel. "Which way to the castle?" he asked, then felt very stupid, for, of course, the castle was at the very top of the mount. Yet the guardsman merely smiled and called back that all they had to do was stay upon the Post Road and it would bear them there.

In through the twisting cobblestone passage under the wall they rode, looking up at the machicolations through which hot oil or missiles could be rained down upon an enemy. At the other end of the barway another portcullis stood raised, and beyond that the Warrows rode into the lower levels of the city proper, and the smells and sounds and sights of the city assaulted them, and their senses were overwhelmed, for they had ridden into an enormous bazaar, the great open market of Rian at Challerain Keep.

The square was teeming with people, buyers and sellers. Farmers from nearby steads were selling hams, beef, sausages, bacon, geese, duck, and fowl of other sorts. They offered carrots, turnips, potatoes, grain, and other commodities. And many customers crowded around the stalls, purchasing staples. Hawkers moved through the crowds selling baskets, gloves, warm hats, brooms, pottery, and such. A fruit seller peddled dried apples and peaches and a strange orange fruit said to come from far south, from Sarain or Thyra or beyond. The odor of fresh-baked bread wafted o'er all and mingled with that of hot pies and other pastries. Jongleurs strolled, playing flutes and harps, lute and fifes, and timbrels, and some juggled marvelously. Here and there soldiers and townsfolk warmed themselves over fires of charcoal set in open braziers and talked among themselves, some laughing, others looking stern, some nodding quietly, others gesticulating.

Through the ebb and flow of the crowd rode forty-three Warrows on ponyback, hooves clattering on the cobbles. The eyes of the young buccen were filled with the glory and marvel of it—why, this was perhaps even more exciting than the Boskydell Fair—and they looked in wonder this way and that, trying to see *everything*. They were so over-whelmed that they did not note that townsfolk and soldiers were staring back at the Warrows in amazement, too, for here come among them were the Wee Folk of legend with their jewel-like eyes.

At last the column rode out of the market square. Now they moved between the shops of crafters—a cobbler's shop, a goldsmithery, mills, lumberyards and carpentries, inns and hostelries, blacksmith-eries and ironworks and armories, kilns, stone-works, and the like. And above many of the shops and businesses were the dwellings of the owners and workers. And the cobbled Post Road wended through this industry, spiraling up and around the mount, climbing toward the crest. Narrow alleyways shot off between hued buildings, and steep streets slashed across the Road. But for the signs at each corner, the Warrows easily could have been lost in the maze of the city. Following the well-marked Post Road, they clattered through the streets of shops and warehouses and workyards, yet as they rode they noted that many of these businesses stood abandoned.

Again they came to a massive wall and followed the road as it curved alongside the bulwark. At last they came to a gate, and it, too, was guarded but open. Through it and up they rode, now among colorful row houses with unexpected corners and stairs mounting up, and balconies and turrets, too, their roofs now covered with snow, bright tiles peeking out here and there. Yet here also, buildings stood empty. But where there were people, they stopped in the streets or leaned out of windows to watch the Wee Folk ride by.

Here there were but a few hawkers: a knife sharpener; a charcoal vendor; a horse-drawn waggon hauling water from the prairie wells up to households on the mount to augment the fluctuating supply provided by frequent but highly variable summer rains and winter snowmelts, caught by the tile roofs and channelled into catchments.

Once more they passed through a barway under a great rampart—the third wall—and again they wended among houses, now larger and more stately than those below, yet still close-set. Again there was an aura of abandonment, for people were sparse and homes unattended.

"Hey," said Argo to Tuck, "have you seen all these empty houses?" At Tuck's nod, Argo went on. "Well now I ask you, how can the market down at the first gate be doing such a brisk trade in an almost deserted city?" Tuck, of course, had no answer, and on they rode.

At last they arrived at the fourth wall, the one encircling the Kingsgrounds. When they came to the gate, the portcullis was down, although the massive iron gates themselves were laid back against the great wall. Up to the portal they rode and stopped, the clatter of pony hooves on cobbles ceased, and in the airy silence Patrel hailed the guard atop the barbican: "Hoy there! Guardsman!"

"State your business," called down one of the Men.

"We are the Company of the King," cried Patrel, and all the Warrows sat proud, "and we've come from the Boskydells in answer to his summons."

Impressed though he was by the very fact that he looked upon Wee Folk, still the Man atop the wall smiled to himself that such a small ragtag group would give themselves the auspicious title "Company of the King." Yet from legend he knew that another small group of these Wee Folk, these Waerlinga, had played a key part in the Great War; thus he was not at all prone to scoff at them. "One moment," he called. "I'll get my Captain."

The Man disappeared behind the merlons, and the Warrows sat calmly waiting. Shortly, another Man appeared, calling down, "Are you warriors come to serve the King in this hour of need?"

"Yes," called Patrel back up to the tower, but in a low voice he said to Tuck and Danner, "though *warrior* is perhaps too strong a term." Then again he called up, "We are the Company of the King,

Thornwalkers of the Boskydells, Land of the Barrier. We answer to the King's call, though the herald who bore us that message is dead, Vulg slain."

"Dead? Vulg slain?" cried the tower commander. "Enter. I shall meet you." He turned to the guard squad and ordered, "Open the waybar," and disappeared from view as Men rushed to winches. With a clatter of gears, slowly the portcullis was raised until at last it was up.

The column rode into the passage under the wall and waited until the second portcullis was raised, too, and at last rode out into the Kingsgrounds, where waited the guard Captain. "I will take you to Hrosmarshal Vidron, Kingsgeneral, Fieldmarshal. He must be told of the death of the herald. It is he you want to see, in any case, for he commands the Allies if the King himself cannot take to the field. Now, follow me, we go to the Old Fort." The Man leapt upon the back of a dun-colored horse, and along the cobbles of the Post Road they clattered, at times mounting up along craggy bluffs, drawing ever closer to the Keep.

Now the fortress in all of its massive strength could be seen. Grey it was and ponderous, with great, blocky granite buildings with high windows and square towers. Crenels and merlons crowned the battlements; massive groins supported great bastions outjutting from the walls. Stone curtains protected hidden banquettes, where would stand defenders in the face of attack. In awe rode the Warrows, never having seen such might, and Tuck wondered what his stone-cutting sire would say were he here.

At last they came to the fifth and final wall, the

last rampart ere the castle itself, and the massive main gate was shut. They did not go to this portal, however, but instead rode northward alongside the bulwark, striking for the north wall, for there was the Old Fortress, now incorporated into the barrier itself.

As the company slowly rounded a bastion upon the northwest corner, thin wind sprang up, and the young buccen raised their hoods. Yet they heard the drum of hoofbeats and across the slope below saw a spear-wielding youth bestride a galloping charger bearing down upon a pivoting Man-shaped target, wooden shield on one side, extended arm and chain mace upon the other. *Chunk!* The spear-lance was driven into the shield by the full weight of the running War-horse, and the target whirled under the impact, violently whipping the wooden mace ball at the passing warrior's head. But the young Man ducked under and was borne away by his courser, leaving the target spinning behind, the ball cleaving nought but empty air. Finally the target gyred to a stop, the pivot coming to a rest in a shallow groove so that the silhouette was square to the list. Again the youth and steed charged upon thundering hooves. *Thunk!* The spear crashed into the shield, and the mace spun and slashed in vain.

To one side and just upslope stood a pavilion, and several Men were gathered about a table, occasionally looking to the north and gesticulating, pointing, and arguing. *Thunk!* The horse and warrior raced cross-slope. As the Warrow column drew near, they came under the winter limbs of an ancient oak tree. Their guide said, "Stop and dismount here.

Which among you is Captain? Good! Come with me."

Patrel dismounted and signed Tuck and Danner to accompany him. Following the Man, the three bow-carrying Warrows strode off toward the pavilion, leaving the two squads behind looking at the huge battlements of the massive north wall and speaking in hushed tones. *Chunk!* sounded the spear on target.

Striding down to the tent, Tuck could now see that the Men were gathered about a table strewn with maps and scrolls; some lay flat with the corners held down by improvised paperweights—a helm, a dagger, a small silver horn, a cup. Again some Men pointed at the maps while others stared northward, and they seemed to be arguing a point. Tuck glanced north, too. Here, high on the mount, he could see miles upon miles of unrelieved snow stretching forth upon the plains below; a low, dark cloud-bank clung to the far horizon. *Thunk!*

The young buccen came unnoticed to the edge of the group and stopped where the guardsman indicated. The guide then made his way to the warrior at the head of the table, a large, robust Man, black hair shot through with silver, with a close-cropped silver beard. The Captain of the tower guard said a word or two, and Marshal Vidron's eyes flicked over the hooded three and briefly up to the forty under the oak. *Thunk!* The target spun wildly under the impact, mace lashing air.

"Faugh!" growled Vidron, glancing back at the small trio. "Saddle me not with infants!"

"*Infants? Infants?*" cried Patrel, wrath rising in

his voice. "Danner! Tuck! Arrows!" and swiftly the three nocked arrows to their bows.

"Hold!" cried one of the Men, grasping the hilt of his sword and drawing it, stepping between Vidron and the young buccen.

But Patrel looked angrily about and cried, "The whirling mace!" and turning, let fly at the spinning target. *Thock!* His arrow struck home, *intercepting the hurtling wooden ball in flight!* Now it gyrated wildly, yet *Thunk! Thock!* Tuck's and Danner's shots followed, and *two more arrows struck the flying ball!* Stunned, the Men were speechless as the Warrows turned back to face them in ire.

"Ai-oi!" shouted Vidron in wonder, "these *infants* have fangs!" Then he burst out laughing loud and long, and in spite of themselves the Warrows smiled at his pleasure. "Hai!" cried the Valanreach Field-marshal, "I, Hrosmarshal Vidron of Valon, name you Captain of the Infant Brigade!" He swept up the small silver horn from among the maps and scrolls and strode forward, presenting it to Patrel as a token of his newly bestowed rank. The Warrows and all the Men laughed in great humor as Vidron hung the horn from Patrel's shoulder by the green-and-white baldric. "Someday I shall tell you the history of that trumpet, lad," said Vidron. "It is a noble one, for it was won from the hoard of Sleeth the Orm by my ancestor Elgo, Sleeth's Doom."

"Aye, we know that legend, Sire, for it is famous and told as a hearthtale," answered Patrel. "Elgo tricked Sleeth into the sunlight, and the Cold-drake was done for."

Patrel excitedly examined the bugle. He saw it had riders on horseback engraved upon it, running round the flange of the horn bell among the mystic runes of power. Patrel then set the horn to his lips and blew a clarion call that rang bell-like upslope and down, and spirits were stirred and hearts leapt with hope. And the Warrow company under the oak sprang up and would have come running, but Danner waved them back. Patrel looked upon the trump in wonderment. "Ya hoy! A fine badge of office is this!" he cried, beaming up at Marshal Vidron.

Patrel saw before him a Man in his middle years, with eyes of black and a sharp penetrating gaze. He was clothed in dark leathern breeks, while soft brown boots shod his feet. A fleece vest covered his mail-clad torso, and his silver and black hair was cropped at the shoulders and held back by a leather band upon his broad brow. White teeth smiled through his silver beard. A russet cloak hung to the ground, and a black-oxen horn depended at his side by a leather strap over one shoulder and across his chest.

"From where do you hail, lads?" asked Vidron, not expecting the answer he got.

"From the Boskydells, Sire," answered Patrel, throwing back his hood.

"Waldfolc!" cried Vidron in amazement, and now he looked sharply at all three and at the company upon the slope, at last seeing the color and tilt of gemlike eyes and the shape of sharp-pointed ears, finally recognizing the Wee Folk for what they were.

"Ai, but I knew the Land of the Waldana was nigh, yet little did I think to see you Folk here. Ho, but I thought you mere lads from an outlying village, and not Waldana from the Boskydells, or even from the Weiunwood near. But today, it seems, legends bestride this mount. Our liege will want to see you, as will his younger son, whose target you just bested. Yet wait! He bears your arrows now."

Toward them galloped the horseman of the spear, and he carried the three arrows plucked from the wooden ball of the target mace. Up he thundered, checking his great roan horse at the last moment with the cry "Ho, Rust!" And the red steed skidded to a halt, while in one and the same motion the young Man of fifteen summers sprang down. "Who winged these arrows?" he asked, then his eyes alighted upon the three bow-carrying young buccen. *"Waerlinga!"* his voice rose in surprise. "Was it you who loosed these quarrels?" He raised the arrows in a clenched fist. "Hai! What splendid marksmanship! Would that I could shoot as well. Ai, but what are Waerlinga doing here?"

"My Lord," spoke up the Captain of the gate guard, "they hail from the Boskydells and bear dire news. I know not their names."

"Captian Patrel Rushlock of the Company of the King at your service, Lord," said Patrel, bowing most formally. "And these are my companions and Lieutenants, Tuckerby Underbank and Danner Bramblethorn, Vulg slayers, Modru foes. My company of Thornwalkers are there, upslope, awaiting the orders of the King."

"Oi! Warriors of the Thornwall, Vulg slayers, hail and well met." The youth's spear was raised in salute, and his eyes touched them all in admiration. "Here, take back your bolts of doom. Spend them on the night-spawn instead of riddling my hapless wooden foe. And you've come to the very storm front itself if you stand against Modru, for his Horde swirls and gathers as a winter blizzard about to strike. But ho, my manners: I am Igon, younger son of King Aurion."

Prince Igon! Tuck's stunned thoughts were set awhirl as he bowed to the young Man before him. Prince Igon stood tall and straight and gazed at them out of clear grey eyes. His hair was dark brown and fell to his shoulders. He was slender as is wont for one of his tender years, but he seemed to conceal a strength beyond his form. A scarlet cloak fell from his shoulders, and light mail gleamed on his breast. His breeks and boots were rust red, and in his hand he held the lancing spear. Upon his head was a leather and steel helm, embellished with black-iron studs. His face was handsome.

Tuck's thoughts were broken by Vidron's bold voice: "Captain Patrel, what is this dire news you bear?"

"Marshal Vidron, the herald sent to the Bosky was pursued by Vulgs and slain at the very gates into the Seven Dells. His message came, but barely," answered Patrel.

"When was this?" asked Prince Igon, casting a look of significance at Vidron.

"Why, let me see." Patrel paused. "I make it ten days past." He turned to Tuck and Danner, who nodded in confirmation.

"And this was the first summons to your Land?" asked Vidron, a frown upon his features.

"Why, yes," answered Patrel, puzzled at the direction these questions were leading. "None else came ere him."

"Rach! Then it is so!" gritted Prince Igon, smiting a fist against the table, setting the scrolls ajumble. "Modru sends his Spawn to intercept and slay our

heralds. Captain Patrel, he was the second messenger to be dispatched to your Land. I fear our Kingsmen to other Realms have been intercepted, too, for few have answered the call, and the camps below stand half empty."

"But wait," interjected Danner, "last night we saw the campfires of five armies. Surely that is enough soldiery to withstand a thrust by Modru."

"Ah, you saw but a ruse in the dark to deceive the night spies of the Enemy," rumbled Vidron. "At night we have the look of five armies, yet the Men of less than three. And even five armies are not enough to withstand *that*." Vidron pointed at the far horizon.

Tuck looked, this time closely, and saw that what he had thought was but a low dark bank of distant clouds to the north in fact were not clouds at all. Instead it seemed to be . . . it looked like . . . an immobile solid black wall, rearing up a mile or more to swallow the sky, the darkness fading at the towering limit of its ebon reach.

"Wha—what is that?" asked Tuck, his mind recoiling from the unnatural sight, fearful of the answer.

"Ah, that we do not know," answered Prince Igon, "though some call it the Dimmendark. A sending of Modru, it is, and the land beyond lies in eternal night—cold, cold night—Winternight. In the day when the Sun is on high, I have ridden my horse into the Dimmendark, and it is like passing from bright day through twilight and into Winternight. There in that spectral dark the land about can be seen, as if in strange werelight; yet the Sun above is but a wan paleness, dim, so dim, only faintly can the orb's disk be descried. And at night, the stars glimmer not, and the Moon cannot be seen, yet the werelight shines. And in these glowing lands of winternight gather Modru's Spawn, and they roam freely—Rukha, Lōkha, Orgus, Ghola, Vulgs, and perhaps other things as yet unknown, for there Adon's Ban strikes not."

"Ar, wait a moment," interrupted Danner. "That can't be so, for Adon's Ban shall rule for as long as night follows day and day follow night: that is His Covenant."

"My trusty Waldan," said Vidron, "you forget: in the Dimmendark eternal Shadowlight rules. Hence, there day does not follow night, nor does night follow day. *There, the Covenant has been broken.*"

Broken? The Eternal Ban broken? Tuck felt as if his heart had flopped over, for now Modru defied even High Adon. How could a meager number of Men and a handful of Warrows hope to withstand a might such as that?

"Ah, but for now, cast aside the thoughts of Winternight and the Dimmendark, and of Modru's Horde, too," said Prince Igon, "for there is nought we can do to change a jot of it at the moment. Instead, come, bring your company of Waerlinga. You must be hungry. I'll take you to the Old Fortress for a meal while Marshal Vidron ponders your assignment. And I'll take you to my sire, for the High King would meet with Waerlinga, and he would hear your tale of the Vulg slaying of the herald."

Nodding to Kingsgeneral Vidron and his staff, Prince Igon walked with Tuck, Danner, and Patrel, and the Captain of the gate guard, back to the oak where the Prince was proclaimed to all the young

buccen to their delight. A rousing cheer burst forth
when it was announced that they were going for a
hot meal, and amid happy chatter they mounted
up to follow Igon. Waving goodbye to the guard
Captain as he departed for the gate, the Warrow
company trailed the Prince on his steed, Rust, as
he rode for a point midway along the north wall.
Through a postern he led them and across the cobbled courtyard of the Old Fortress, at last coming
to some stables.

After seeing to the needs of their mounts, the young
buccen were led by Igon to empty barracks, where
they stowed their gear from the pack ponies. The
Prince then took them to a mess hall for the prom-
ised meal and broke bread with them. Igon was
astonished by their gusto, for they were such a small
Folk—their feet dangling and swinging as they sat
on the Man-sized benches, their eyes more or less
just above the level of the tabletop—yet they packed
away food like hungry birds, and in fact chattered
like magpies at a feast. All about them Men paused
to stare and smile. But the Warrows paid heed only
to the meal, for to them it was indeed like a feast,
the first hot food they'd had in eight days, and they
happily made the most of it.

"This is where you'll take all your meals while
you are at the Keep," announced Igon, and the company heartily approved. The Prince turned to
Patrel. "Now, Captain Patrel, you and your Lieutenants and I shall go and seek out my sire, for he
will want to hear your full tale, as I do. As to your
company, I can arrange for a guide to show them
about, or they can rest in the barracks."

"Cor!" proclaimed Argo, "what with my belly full,

it's me for a nap on that soft cot back there in the barracks, and a welcome relief it'll be from the hard ground or cold snow, for a change."

"Har! Me too," spoke up Arvin. "I've been looking forward to resting my bones ever since I laid my eyes on that beautiful mattress." There was a general murmur of agreement. "But first, in the back room I spotted a tub or three, and it's me for a hot bath."

Bath! cried several voices at once, and it was a mad scramble as Warrows rushed helter-skelter from the mess hall to be first in the tubs, and Tuck found himself wishing he could go along, too.

Laughing, Prince Igon stood to lead Patrel, Tuck, and Danner in search of the King.

Through labyrinthine corridors of hewn granite blocks the young Prince took the three Warrows. The long passages were dimly lighted by slotted openings to the outside day. Under massive archways and past great pillars they strode, the young buccen's mouths agape as they peered up at huge shadowy cornices with carven gargoyles staring stonily down. Up long flights of stairs they went, and then back down. Tuck was bewilderingly lost and wondered at the route they had taken, deciding he should have spent more time seeing to the way and less time peering into dark corners at stone carvings. At last they rounded a corner to come to a short passage leading to massive, iron-bound, studded oaken doors. The hall was flanked by pike-bearing Kingsguards in scarlet and gold, who struck clenched right fists to hearts when Prince Igon hove into view. Returning the salute, the Prince strode past with the young buccen in tow, stepping to the oaken portals. Igon grasped a door ring in each hand and pulled; the great doors divided in twain, and though massive, each panel easily and noiselessly swung outward, coming to rest against the stone of the passage. Through this entry he led the wondering Warrows.

They saw before them a great long chamber beringed by pillars spaced along the walls. There, too, were huge hearths, most without fire. Along the tapestried walls, staffs jutted out, from which depended the flags of many different Kingdoms. Overhead, great wooden beams spanned from wall to wall dangling chain-hung braces of night lamps, the chandeliers now dark, for daylight streamed in through high windows. Three broad steps down began the great stone center-floor, smoothly polished stone, ringed around by raised flooring for banquet tables. The amphitheater swept forward till it fetched up against four steps leading to a throne dais. Upon the top step sat a flaxen-haired lass listening to the deep converse between a golden-haired stranger and High King Aurion himself.

As young Prince Igon waited to be noted and summoned, he murmured to the Warrows. "On the throne sits my sire, but whom he converses with, I know him not. The Lady is Princess Laurelin of Riamon, betrothed of my brother, Prince Galen. The other maidens are her Ladies-in-waiting." Tuck then saw three young Women sitting on a bench, partially hidden by a pillar.

The High King, though he was seated, looked from afar to be a Man of middling height. One of his eyes was covered by a scarlet patch, the result of a blinding wound taken in his youth during an expedition against the Rovers of Kistan. Because of the patch, many villagers called him Aurion Redeye; and he was much loved, for though his spirit was bold, his hand was gentle. Although silver locks fell from his head, it was said that his grip was stronger than that of most Men. He was dressed in scarlet, much the same as Igon, but trimmed in gold. When Tuck looked at him he thought of iron.

On the other hand, Princess Laurelin looked to be but a slip of a girl. Dressed in blue, she sat upon the step, her arms clasped about her knees, her face turned toward the King such that Tuck could not see her features. But her wheaten hair was beautiful to behold, for it fell to her hips.

Lastly, the stranger: Something there was about him, for as the day shone through a high portal down upon the throne dais, it seemed that he was wreathed in a nimbus of light, his golden hair gathering sunbeams. Grey-green was his cloak, as if it were woven of an elusive blend of leaf, limb, and stone—and his boots, breeks, and jerkin were of the same hue.

The King looked up, and his face broke into a smile. "Igon, my son!" he called, and beckoned the youth to him.

The Prince said, "Come," and he led the Warrows down the steps and across the center floor to the foot of the throne dais, where he stopped and bowed. "Sire," he said, "I present Captain Patrel Rushlock and his Lieutenants, Danner Bramblethorn and Tuckerby Underbank, Waerlinga three from the Land of the Thorns."

"Waerlinga!" breathed King Aurion, rising to his feet as the Warrows deeply bowed. "Welcome, though

I would that times were better." His voice was firm, and his one eye glittered blue and clear.

Igon turned to the Princess as she gracefully rose to her feet. Slender she was, and small. "My Lady Laurelin," he said, inclining his head. Decorously she curtsied as the Warrows bowed to her. Tuck looked up and gasped in wonderment, for she was most beautiful—high cheekbones, wide-set grey eyes, delicate lips—and her dove-grey eyes caught his and she smiled. Tuck blushed, flustered, and looked down at his feet.

King Aurion presented the golden-haired stranger. "Lord Gildor, once of Darda Galion, the Larken-wald beyond the Grimwall, now a Lian Guardian who brings us news from Arden Vale and from the Weiunwood, though grim it is."

Tuck again gasped, this time in astonishment, for the bright Lord Gildor was an *Elf*, with green eyes atilt and pointed ears 'neath his yellow locks. In the shape of these two features, eyes and ears, Elves are much the same as Waerlinga. Yet, unlike the Wee Folk, Elves are tall, being but a hand shorter than Man. In this case, the slim, straight Gildor stood at the same height as the young Prince Igon.

King Aurion stepped down to the Warrows. "But come, let us sit and talk. You must be wearied by your travels," he said, and led them all to a small throne-side alcove, where they each took a comfortable seat.

"Grim news?" asked Prince Igon, turning to the Elf. "It seems to be a day of ill tidings, for the Waer-linga's news is dire, too. What sinister word do you bear, Lord Gildor?"

At a nod from King Aurion, Gildor spoke: "The

Dimmendark marches down the Grimwall Mountains, the abode of ancient enemies, freeing them from High Adon's Ban. Even now Arden Vale lies deep in Winternight, and the 'Dark stalks south, into Lianion called Rell, and, on the far side of the Grimwall, it sweeps along the margins of Riamon. I fear Modru has in mind to strike at Darda Galion, for this he must do ere plunging into Valon, and beyond to Pellar. But though my heart calls me to rush to aid Darda Galion, here I have come instead, for here I can best serve Mithgar, at Aurion's side."

Gildor fell silent and for a moment nought was said, and Tuck saw that others, too, had had to choose between love of home and duty to the Realm.

"You know that you have my leave to go," said Aurion, but Gildor gave a faint shake of his head.

"Your pardon, Lord Gildor," said Patrel, "but it was said that you bear news from the Weiunwood, home of our distant kin." Weiunwood lay to the east of the Battle Downs, some thirty leagues south of Challerain Keep.

"Ah yes," answered Gildor. "Your Folk of the Weiunwood have allied with the Men of Stonehill and a small band of Lian Guardians from Arden. Even now, hidden holts are being prepared and plans laid for battle should Modru's Horde come."

"Who leads the Warrows?" asked Danner.

"Arbagon Fenner," smiled Gildor, "and a feisty Waerling is he." But the young buccen shook their heads, for none knew him. "The Men are led by Bockleman Brewster, owner of the White Unicorn Inn of Stonehill. Young Inarion leads the Elves."

King Aurion spoke to the Prince. "And your ill tidings, Igon: what grim news do you bear?"

At Igon's indication, Patrel spoke to the King. "Ten nights past your herald arrived at the Boskydells, bearing word of the muster here at Challerain Keep. Unbeknownst to us, pursuers followed, and while crossing Ford Spindle he was Vulg attacked. Though the foul beast was slain by Tuck, here, still your Man's horse fell to the ice and broke through, and herald, horse, dead Vulg, Tuck, and one of our comrades named Tarpy were all swept under the ice by the swift river current. Only Tuck survived, thanks to Danner's clear thinking in that time of crisis." Patrel paused, and Tuck could feel the Lady Laurelin's soft gaze upon him, sympathy in her eyes. "Though your herald is dead, still the word goes forth across the Bosky," Patrel continued, "borne by the Thornwalkers; hence, in this, Modru has failed to stop the call from spreading through the Seven Dells. Four Vulgs did he send to haul down your messenger; we slew them all. Yet I am told by Prince Igon that this was the second herald sent to the Boskydells, and that Modru's hand must have stopped the first. That explains why the word came late, for Warrows in the Bosky had wondered why no call had come, though rumors of War nested in every tavern. I wonder if other messengers to other Lands have failed to reach their goals, but instead have been intercepted and slain by the foul beasts of Modru, like the Vulgs we slew."

"Aye," said King Aurion, and though his mood was somber, still he looked with admiration upon these casual Vulg-slaying Waerlinga in Thornwalker grey. "Many a herald did we send, but few nations received our first summons, though here and there now the muster begins. We are reduced to playing a sham at night to make our forces appear larger than they are, though whether or not the Enemy is deceived I cannot say. We will know that we have succeeded if we are given enough time for our armies to come ere the storm strikes.

"Yet it is not only armies we await at the Keep. Waggons have been summoned to bear our loved ones to safe haven, whether or not they desire to go." Aurion cocked his shaggy white brow at Laurelin, but she did not look at him, keeping her eyes instead upon her folded hands.

"My Liege," her voice was soft but unyielding, "I cannot flee whilst my Lord Galen yet roams the Dimmendark. He is my betrothed, but even more so, he is my beloved, and I must be here when he returns."

"But you must go, Lady Laurelin," said Prince Igon, "for 'tis your duty to see to the needs of the people above all else, and your presence will buoy up their hearts and spirits in a time of great distress and darkness."

"You speak as if Duty o'errules all else, my Lord Igon," said Laurelin, "even Love."

"Aye," answered Igon, "even Love; Duty must go before all."

"Nay, Prince Igon," interjected Gildor. "I would not gainsay thee, yet I think that Honor must go above all, though each of the three—Love, Duty, Honor—must be tempered by the other two in the crucible of Life."

"Naytheless," said King Aurion, touching his brow above the eye-patch, "when the waggons arrive, refugee trains will be formed to take the old, the halt and lame, the children, and the Women hence from

here, including you, my daughter-to-be." Laurelin
would have protested but the King held up his hand.
"It is my royal edict that this thing be done, for I
cannot wage a War where the helpless and innocent
are caught in the midst of raging combat. I cannot
have my warriors battling with one eye on the foe
and the other upon their loved ones, for that is a
road to death.

"Yet this I will do, though it goes 'gainst my better judgement: You may delay your departure till
the very last caravan, but then you must leave with
it, for I would not have you fall into the Enemy's
clutch." The thought of Laurelin in the grasp of
Modru made Tuck shudder, and he futilely strove
to banish the image.

"But now, my friends," said King Aurion to Lord
Gildor and the Waerlinga, "you must excuse my
son and Princess Laurelin and me, for, you see, this
is the final market day, the last before all are evac-
uated from the city—if the dratted waggons will
ever get here, that is. We three must needs make
an appearance at the bazaar, for, as Prince Igon has
so succinctly put it, 'tis our duty. The folk expect
to see their good King Aurion Redeye, and the handsome Prince, and their Lady-to-be."

"So that's the answer!" burst out Tuck, striking
the table. "Oh . . . er . . ." He was embarrassed. "I
mean, well, we were wondering at the large crowd
in the market square, what with the city being half
deserted, as it were. Now you have answered our
question: it is the *last* market day, for some time to
come, I ween . . . sort of a 'Fair' one might say,
though a dark event it is you celebrate."

"With darker days yet to come, I fear," sighed

the King, standing, and so they all rose. He turned to Lord Gildor and the three Waerlinga. "I thank you all for your news, though ill tidings it is. We shall speak again in the days ahead. My Lady." He held out his arm, and Princess Laurelin took it. He led her from the hall, and they were followed by the Princess's Ladies-in-waiting.

"I'll meet you at the gates," called Igon after them and turned to the Warrows. "But first I must lead you back to your barracks. Lord Gildor, are you quartered?"

"Yes, the King has given over the green rooms to me," answered the Elf. "Here, I'll walk with you as you go, for it is on the way."

The next morning at breakfast, again the Warrow company chattered like magpies as they ate, for they had much to talk about. Tuck, Danner, and Patrel had spoken to all at length the previous day upon returning from the King, and the news they bore fired the furnaces of speculation. But though the ore they smelted was high-grade, much dross was produced for every pure ingot. The gathering War dominated all thought, and the conversations turned ever to it, as iron pulled by lodestone.

Patrel's meal was interrupted by a page, summoning him to attend Hrosmarshal Vidron. As before, Patrel took Tuck and Danner with him. Again they were led through a maze of passages in the labyrinthine Keep, yet this time Tuck paid more attention to their route, recognizing parts of it. They were brought up the steps of one of the towers and left on a bench at the door outside the Kingsgeneral's quarters. They could hear angry voices behind the door, muffled, but the words were distinct.

"I say, Nay!" cried a voice. "I remind you, I and my Men are not in your command. Instead I take my instructions directly from the King and none else. And we are sworn to but one duty, and that is to protect the person of the High King. I will not remove any from that charge and place them at your behest, Fieldmarshal."

"And I tell you, Captain Jarriel, it is already decided!" thundered the voice of Marshal Vidron. "You will reassign forty Men from the duty of guarding Challerain Keep to field duty under my command."

"And what? Replace the forty with those pipsqueaks? With those runts?" Captain Jarriel shot back. "You lief as well just hand the King over to Modru himself, for all the good those mites will do under an attack."

"Hey, he's talking about us!" exclaimed Danner angrily, leaping to his feet; he would have stormed through the door except he was restrained by Tuck and Patrel.

"May I remind you, sir," boomed Vidron, "that these Folk are renowned for their extraordinary service to the Crown. Or have you forgotten their role in the history of the Ban War, the Great War itself, when last we faced the Enemy in Gron, the very same Enemy, I might add?"

"Faugh! Hearthtales and legends! I don't care what fables you might believe about these Folk, for I intend to take this matter up with the King, himself. Then we shall see!" The door was flung open, and a warrior in the red-and-gold tabard of the Kingsmen strode angrily out and past the Warrows to disappear down the tower steps.

Just as angrily, Danner strode through the open doorway and into the Fieldmarshal's quarters with Patrel and Tuck behind. Vidron was sitting on the edge of his bed, pulling on a boot while an orderly hovered nearby.

"Pip-squeaks and runts we are?" Danner demanded. "Just who was that buffoon?"

The Kingsgeneral looked at the spectacle of a fuming Warrow: feet planted wide apart, clenched fists on hips, jaw thrust out, all three feet seven inches aquiver with rage. And then Vidron burst out laughing, falling backward on his bed, his foot halfway into the boot. Great gales of laughter gusted forth, and every time he tried to master his guffaws they would burst out again. Tuck and then Patrel and finally Danner could not help themselves, and they laughed, too. At last Marshal Vidron struggled upright. "By the very bones of Sleeth, each time I meet you three, humor drives ire from my heart. It is not every day that I am brought to task by an angry Waldan, bearded in my very den, as it were. Ah, but you are good for my spirit."

"And you, sir, are good for ours," replied Patrel. "Yet Danner's questions remain, and I'll add my own: Why have you summoned us?"

Grunting, Vidron pulled the boot the rest of the way on and stood. The orderly held the Fieldmarshal's jacket as Vidron slipped his arms in. "Well, Wee Ones, for your information, that 'buffoon' is Captain Jarriel. His company wards the Keep, the castle itself, that is, and guards the person of the King. A loyal Man, he is, and one I would gladly have in my command, but he stubbornly sees only one way to perform his charge of office. Because of his duty, he disagrees with the assignment I have for your company of Thornwalkers, yet had he but listened, I would have told him that High King Aurion himself suggested your assignment."

"And what, prithee, is it that we 'pip-squeaks' and 'runts' are to do?" asked Patrel, smiling.

"Why, patrol the Keep. Guard the King. Keep watch from the ramparts of the castle," answered Vidron.

"Just a moment, now," objected Danner. "We are here to tackle Modru, not to hide away behind the walls of some remote castle."

"Ah, as much as we all would like to brace that foe, each and every one of us cannot," said Vidron. "Heed me, Danner: think not that there is but one way to perform a duty, for to do so would make you the same kind of 'buffoon' as is Jarriel. Hearken unto this, too: by your company of *Waldfolc* warding the castle, forty Men can be freed to take the field against the Enemy, and forty Men on horseback can range farther faster than forty Waldana on ponies, whereas forty Waldana on Castle-ward, clear of eye and skilled in archery, are as good as, nay, better than forty Men in the same assignment. It is as simple as that."

Danner seemed unwilling to accept the argument until Patrel spoke. "Well said, Marshal Vidron. And if I have understood you aright, the King has so ordered, correct?" At Vidron's nod, Patrel said, "Then it is settled. To whom shall we report for duty, and when?"

"Why, to Captain Jarriel, of course, and this

morning at that," answered Vidron, pulling a bell cord. "Now, now, before you object, Jarriel is a fair Man, just stubborn. Give it a try. Should it become unbearable, try harder—then see me. After all, by then I'll need a laugh or two. Ah, here is your page now."

With misgivings, the Warrows left Hrosmarshal Vidron's quarters, following the page to Captain Jarriel's command post, located centrally within the castle at the junction of two main corridors. They had to wait a short while, for Captain Jarriel was not there.

"Perhaps he is seeing King Aurion," suggested Tuck, but there was no way of knowing. At last the Captain arrived, and the Warrows were summoned. Tuck expected Danner and the Man to exchange angry words, but, true to Vidron's appraisal, Captain Jarriel spoke only of duty to the King when he met with the Warrows, dealing with them as if the dispute had never occurred.

A page was assigned to show all the members of the Waerling company the ins and outs of the castle. They were to become familiar with its layout, at least the major corridors and rooms, as well as the ramparts and battlements. Then they would take on duties alongside the Men of the Castleward.

All that day and the next, every moment was spent learning the environs of the Keep. Also on the second day, they visited the King's armorers to be measured for corselets made of overlapping boiled leather plates affixed to padded jerkins, these to wear as armor while guarding the walls of the Keep. On the third day, the day watch on the north wall was assigned to Tuck's squad, while Danner's took on the south rampart.

"Har!" barked Argo as they overtopped the ramp alongside the bastion gorge and came upon the banquette behind the crenellated battlement. "I said it before and I'll say it again: these walls were not meant to be patrolled by Warrows. Cor, I can't see over the merlons at all, and only by walking along the weapon shelf can I look out through the crenels."

"Ar, but what would you see?" asked Finley, who then answered his own question: "Nothing but that black wall out there, and who wants ter see that? Nar, we're here to feather the Horde, if and when they try to climb these walls." Finley walked over to a set of machicolations, sighting through the holes where they would rain arrows down along the ramparts should the enemy attempt to scale them.

Tuck spaced the young buccen along the stone curtain, relieving the Men warding the north wall. True to Argo's word, they walked along the weapon shelf to see out upon the land. And far to the north, darkness loomed.

Even though the Sun marched across the sky, still time seemed suspended, for nothing moved upon the snowy plains beyond the foothills. It seemed as if the Land held its breath, waiting . . . waiting. And Tuck's eyes were ever drawn toward the far Dimmendark.

In midwatch, Patrel came to take the noon meal with Tuck. And as they sat eating, Tuck said, "I keep thinking about Captain Darby's words back at Spindle Ford, when he asked for volunteers to answer the King's call. 'Will you Walk the Thorns, or will you walk instead the ramparts of Challerain

Keep?' That's what he asked us. At the time I didn't consider his words prophetic, yet here I am, upon the very walls he spoke of."

"Perhaps there's a bit of a seer in each of us," answered Patrel, taking a bite of bread. He chewed thoughtfully. "The trick is to know which words foretell and which don't."

They ate in silence and gazed upon the land. At last Patrel said, "Ah, it looks so dangerous, that black wall out there. And who knows what lurks in the darkness beyond? But this we must do: tonight, and every moment off duty that can be spared, have your buccen fletching arrows, for there may come a time when we will need all the bolts we can get." Tuck nodded without speaking as he and Patrel watched the brooding land.

The Sun continued its slow swing across the sky, and in late afternoon Princess Laurelin and one of her Ladies came to the north battlement. The Princess stood gazing far over the winter snow, her eyes searching along the edges of the foreboding black wall, the distant Dimmendark. She was wrapped in a dark blue cloak, its hood up, concealing her face so fair, though a stray lock of her flaxen hair curled out. She seemed to shiver, and Tuck wondered if the cold stone chilled her, or was it instead the far dark loom.

"My Lady," he said approaching her, "there is a warm charcoal fire along the wall a bit, yet the view to the north is the same." He led her and her Lady-in-waiting to the brazier where the hot coals burned.

Laurelin warmed herself and then stepped to a nearby crenel. Long she looked, and Tuck stood on the shelf at her side gazing northward, too. At last she spoke: "There was a time, a happier time, when on clear days a low range of hills could be seen to the north. The Argent Hills, my Lord Galen called them. Often we stood upon this very wall and spoke of living alone in a cottage by a stream in the pines there. Daydreaming. Now the Argent Hills can be seen no longer, for they have been swallowed by that terrible blackness. Yet I know that they are still there, behind the dark wall, just as is my beloved." Laurelin turned, and she and her Lady went back to the narrow span leading into the castle. Tuck said nought as he sadly watched her go. And behind to the north, the Land waited in airy silence.

The next evening, Laurelin again came for her sunset vigil along the north wall, searching the plains and horizon just before the dusk, while Tuck stood quietly by.

Long moments fled, and the plains were empty of returning warriors. At last Laurelin spoke: "Ah, but I do not like looking for my Lord out over the barrows of dead heroes. He stands in harm's way, and gazing past graves would seem to portend no good."

"Graves, my Lady?" Tuck's voice was filled with puzzlement.

"Aye, Sir Tuck, graves." Laurelin pointed down into the foothills near the north wall. "Do you see that tumbled ring of stone jutting up through the snow? It stands in the center of the barrows of nobles and warriors felled in Wars past."

Tuck looked, and in the deepening shadows he saw snow-covered rounded mounds of elden turved barrows. But his eye was drawn to the center of all mounds, where an ancient ruin of fallen stone lay ajumble—a ruin that once was a ring of tall standing stones. And in the midst of the ring . . . "My Lady, what is that in the stone ring's center?"

"A crypt, Sir Tuck, a crypt, hidden in summer by a tangle of vines and in winter by a blanket of snow." Laurelin's eyes grew reflective. "Lord Galen took me once to see it—the ancient tomb of Othran the Seer, according to legend, Othran who came from the sea, they say, a survivor of Atala, lost forever. But that is only legend, and none knows for certain. Yet the worn carvings in the stone are arcane runes of an elden time, and only the Lian Guardians are said to have read them, for the Lian are skilled at tongues and writings."

"Runes?" Tuck blurted, drawn by the mystery of a lost language.

"Aye." Laurelin thought a bit. "My Lord Galen says that there is an eld inscription:

> *Loose not the Red Quarrel*
> *Ere appointed dark time.*
> *Blade shall brave vile Warder*
> *From the deep, black slime.*

Those are the words the Elves are said to have ciphered from yon stone."

"What do they mean?" asked Tuck. *"Red quarrel, vile Warder, appointed dark time."*

"I cannot say," laughed Laurelin, "for it is a riddle beyond my knowing. Sir Tuck, you ask me to answer an enigma that has stumped the sages ever since Elf first came upon the crypt in elden times, since Man first settled these lands and chose to place his barrows around an ancient tomb, even then a ruin, in the hope that the wraith of the mystic seer of Atala would give guide to the shades of Man's own fallen heroes."

Tuck looked down upon the tower in wonder as Laurelin spun forth the eld tale. Slowly the shadows mustered unto the low foothills, and when the Princess fell silent, darkness covered the land. Finally Laurelin bade Tuck goodeve and disappeared into the castle. Tuck watched her go, and then his vision was drawn again toward the darkness where stood the jumbled ring of stone. And he pondered the riddle of the carven runes, etched words of a long-lost tongue.

On the third evening Laurelin, looking down at Tuck, asked the small Warrow, "Do you have a beloved? Oh, I think you must. Do I see a sweetheart's favor around your neck?"

Tuck fumbled at Merrilee's silver locket, lifting the chain over his head. "Yes, my Lady," he answered, "only, in the Boskydells a sweetheart is called 'dammia,' er, I mean, I would call her 'dammia' while she would call me 'buccaran.' That is what we Warrows name each other, uh, Warrow sweethearts, that is. And yes, this is my dammia's favor, given to me on the day I left my home village of Woody Hollow." Tuck handed her the locket and chain.

"Why, this is beautiful, Tuck. An ancient work. Perhaps from Xian, itself." Laurelin pressed a hidden catch and the locket sprang open. Tuck was dumbfounded, for although he had touched the locket often, he had not known that it actually opened.

"My, she is very pretty," said Laurelin, looking closely. "What is her name?"

"Merrilee," said Tuck, his hands atremble, yearning to take the locket back to see what face it held.

"A lovely name, that." Laurelin glanced to the brooding north. "My Lord Galen wears mine own golden locket at his heart, but no portrait has it, just a snippet of my hair. It must ever be so, that warriors in all times and all Lands have carried the lockets of their loved ones upon their breasts. If not lockets, then other tokens do soldiers bear into danger, to remind them of a love, hearth, home, or something or someone else dear to their hearts." Laurelin clicked shut Tuck's silver locket and handed it into his trembling hands, and turned once more to look beyond the abutment and across the winter plains.

Tuck eagerly fumbled at the locket, discovering at last that it opened by pressing down upon the stem where attached the chain. *Click!* The leaves of the locket fell open in his hand—mirrored silver on the left, and a miniature portrait of . . . it *was* Merrilee! *Oh, my black-haired dammia, you are so beautiful.* As he stood upon the cold granite rampart, all of his loneliness, his longing for quiet evenings before the fire at The Root, and his love for Merrilee welled up through his very being, and his vision blurred with tears.

"Ah, Sir Tuck, you must miss her very much," said the Princess.

Blinking back his tears, Tuck looked up to see Laurelin's sad grey eyes upon his blue ones. "Yes, I do. And, you know, I didn't realize just how much until I saw her portrait just now." Tuck shuffled his feet, embarrassed. "You see, until you opened the locket, I didn't know she was there, all the time secretly next to my heart."

Laurelin's laughter had the ring of silver bells chiming in the wind, and Tuck smiled. "Ah, but Sir Tuck, did you not know?" asked the Princess. "We Women and dammen do practice our secret arts to remain in the hearts of our Men and buccen." And they laughed together.

Yet in the waning light of day and by candleflame throughout the night, again and again Tuck gazed at Merrilee's likeness, for now it seemed she was closer to him, and he could not seem to get his fill of her image. The young buccen of his squad smiled to see him peering at the locket, but Danner merely snorted, "Faugh! Moonstruck calf!"

The next afternoon when Laurelin came to the north wall, there was a deep look of sadness about her, and desperately she scanned the sullen horizon.

"My Lady, you seem . . . disturbed." Tuck looked out over the remote snowy plains.

"Have you not heard, Sir Tuck?" Laurelin turned her gaze to him, her grey eyes pale. "The waggons arrived yestereve. Even now a first caravan presses south, and a second one forms. A train will leave each day, bearing Women and children, oldsters and the infirm, until we are all gone. And my beloved ranges far north, and I fear I will not get to see him ere I must board the last wain of the final caravan."

"And when might that be, Princess?" Tuck turned to Laurelin, and her face was shadowed within her hood.

"The first day of Yule," said Laurelin, forlornly. "That day, too, I become nineteen."

"Ai!" exclaimed Tuck. "The last of Yule is my dammia's birthday, and for her it is an age-name birthday, too. It's when Merrilee turns twenty, no longer a maiden but a young damman she becomes. Oh my, but neither she nor you have been given much cause to be merry."

"High King Aurion has granted me but one more day of vigil after this eve. But on my birthday, the shortest day of the year—First Yule, just two days hence—the last waggon train departs, bearing south to Pellar. And I go with it, to Caer Pendwyr." The Princess looked crestfallen.

"Ai-oi! But it *is* your birthday," said Tuck, attempting to brighten her spirit. "At least we have that to celebrate, though I have no gift for you, nought but a smile, that is."

Tentatively the Princess smiled back, brushing aside a stray flaxen lock. "Your presence alone is gift enough, Sir Tuck. Yes, your presence gladdens me. Please do come to my birthday feast tomorrow night on Yule Eve. High King Aurion holds the celebration in the Feast Hall, and all the Captains are to attend. Ah, but they are such stern warriors, all cheerless but for Marshal Vidron, Igon, and, of course, the King himself."

"But, my Lady," protested Tuck, "I am no Captain. I and Danner are but Lieutenants. It is Captain Patrel you would invite."

"Nonsense!" Laurelin tossed her head. "I'll invite whom I please. After all, it is *my* birthday we celebrate. Yet, would it make you happier, I invite all three—Captain Patrel, Sir Danner, and yourself, Sir Tuck."

"But we have nought to wear except our rude clothes, not fine jerkins nor shiny helms nor—" Tuck's protests were interrupted by a stamp of Laurelin's foot.

"But me no buts, Sirrah!" she exclaimed, her sad mood now replaced by one of amused determination. A smile played at the corner of her mouth, her eyes twinkled, and her mode of speaking now dropped into that of formal court parlance: "I shall see to the petty details of thy raiment. Tomorrow eve, gather thy two friends unto thee at the change of watch. I will meet thee here at the wall, as is my wont, and then we will get thee hence to be fitted, for I have secret knowledge of the whereabouts of clothes just thy size but fit for a Prince. Then thou shall be dressed for my party, be it one of farewell or of a birthday anniversary or simply a celebration of the coming Yule."

Tuck threw up his hands in surrender, resigned to the inevitable, and the Princess laughed at the look upon the face of her diminutive, newfound confidant. Then, while Laurelin spoke of Lord Galen and Tuck listened, the Warrow and Princess gazed over the waiting snow until it became too dark to see.

During the early part of the next day-watch, one of Laurelin's Ladies-in-waiting came first to Tuck, then to Danner, and lastly to Patrel and took their measurements with a tailor's tape. Yet when queried by the curious Warrows as to what was to be done with the figures, the Lady merely smiled and answered not their questions.

That day all three were the targets of the jests and japes of their fellow Warrows: "Ar, keeps yer thumbs out o' the soups if you please, me buccoes," said Dilby. "Mind your p's and q's, and stay off the Ladies' toes when you dance," laughed Delber. "Watch out for lettin' your little fingers droops as you takes your tea," cautioned Argo. "Mind you now, eats with your knifes and forks, and don't go tearing into it with just yer little teeths like a common hanimal," added Sandy. Throughout the day the good-natured remarks assaulted Tuck's, Danner's, and Patrel's ears, accompanied by raucous guffaws.

An hour before sunset, Laurelin came alone to stand at the wall and search for sign of the return of her betrothed. Long she sought, but again the vigil bore no fruit, for the expectant plains lay empty as great flat shadows mustered upon the distant prairie. The darkening land seemed poised upon the brink of doom, yet nought stirred in the deepening gloom. As the last of the Sun dipped below the horizon, the ward-relief appeared, and so, too, did Tuck and Danner and Patrel. Sadly, Laurelin turned away from her watch, for this was her last night. Tomorrow would see her depart south, and who, then, would look for her beloved? She sank to a ledge and put her face between her hands and wept silently.

Laurelin cried as Tuck, Danner, and Patrel stood helpessly by, not knowing aught else to do. At last Tuck took her hands in his own and said, "Fear not, my Lady, for as long as I can I will come hence to be your eyes, to watch in your stead. And when Lord Galen comes at last, I will tell him of your lasting love." And Laurelin clasped Tuck to her and wept even more so. And he held her and soothed her while a tear ran down Patrel's cheek, and Danner, in dull rage, looked out over the empty stillness toward Modru's black wall.

After long moments, Laurelin's tears began to subside, and she looked at the three Warrows and then quickly away, as if afraid to catch their eyes with her own. "I am shamed by my outburst, for often I have been told that a Princess should not be seen to weep, yet I could not help myself. Oh my, I seem to be lacking a kerchief."

Patrel stepped forth and gave her his own. "A gift my Lady, for it is your birthday eve."

"I have acted more as if it were a funeral, keening my lamentation," said Laurelin, wiping her tears away, gently blowing her nose.

"Then, Princess, I suggest we give over this whole night to the singing of dirges," smiled Patrel, and Laurelin laughed at the absurdity. "If not dirges, then, let us instead celebrate, for I know where they're holding a party tonight, though we have nought but rags to wear."

Again Laurelin laughed, and she rose up and clasped one of Patrel's hands and twirled him about. "Ah yes, such lowly beggar's garb you wear," Laurelin crowed, "yet I know where we can remedy that, and then perhaps all four of us can slip into that party of yours and not be cast back out the door. Come." And smiling secretively unto herself, the Princess led the three Warrows into the castle, to the old living quarters of the royal family, to a long-abandoned room. Inside was a waiting valet, there to attend the three young buccen, much to their surprise.

"I shall return in a trice," said Laurelin, mischievously. They heard the sound of a distant gong. "Hasten, for the guests now gather and we would not be late to the feast." She slipped out the door and left them with the valet.

In an adjoining room three hot baths had been prepared in great copper tubs, and the Warrows wallowed and sloshed in the soapy suds. But they were soon herded out by the servant, who bade them to hurry and dry themselves for betimes the Princess would return. They found awaiting them soft silken garments, both under and over—stockings and shoes and beribboned trews, blue for Tuck, scarlet for Danner, and pale green for Patrel, with jerkins to match—and they fit as if sewn for them by the royal tailors. As fine as these clothes were, the three young buccen had a greater surprise in store, and they were astounded.

The valet presented them with three corselets of light chain mail. Silveron was Tuck's, amber gems inset among the links, with a bejeweled belt, beryl and jade, to be clasped about the waist. Danner's ring-linked armor was black, plain but for the silver-and-jet girt at his middle. And Patrel was given golden mail with a gilded belt: gold on gold. Helms they wore, simple iron and leather for Tuck and Patrel, a studded black one for Danner. And at the last they were given cloaks, Elven-made, the same elusive grey-green color as was worn by Lord Gildor.

They gaped at each other in astonishment. "Why,"

said Danner, "we look like three warrior Princelings!"

"Just so," came a tinkling laugh. Laurelin had returned, now dressed in a simple yet elegant gown of light blue that fell straight to the floor from a white bodice. Blue slippered feet peeked under the hem. Her hair was garlanded with intertwining ribbons, matching those crisscrossing the bodice. A small silver tiara crowned her head.

"You *do* look like Princelings," she said, "but that is befitting mine escorts, warriors three."

"But how . . . where?" stammered Tuck, holding out his arms and pirouetting, indicating the raiments and armor upon Danner and Patrel and himself. "Tell me the answer to this mystery before I burst!"

"Oh, *la!*" laughed Laurelin, "we can't have you bursting on my birthday eve. As to the mystery, it is simple. Once apast, my Lord Galen showed me where first he and then Igon quartered as children. Here I knew were closets of clothing worn by the seed of Aurion. And I thought surely some would fit you three, and I was not wrong. But happiest of all, here, too, was the armor of the warrior Princelings of the Royal House of Aurion. The silver you wear, Sir Tuck, is from Aurion's own childhood, handed down to him from his forefathers. Silveron it is, and precious, said to be Drimmen-deeve work of old. And, too, Sir Tuck, I chose the silver armor for you because you wear your dammia's silver locket." Laurelin smiled as Tuck blushed before the other young buccen.

The Princess then turned to Danner. "The black, Sir Danner, comes from Prince Igon's childhood, made just for him by the Dwarves of Mineholt North, who dwell under the Rimmen Mountains in my Land, Riamon. It is told that the jet comes from a mountain of fire in the great ocean to the west."

Laurelin spoke to Patrel. "Your golden armor, Captain Patrel, is Dwarf-made, too, and came from the Red Caves in Valon. It was my beloved, Prince Galen, who wore it as a youth, and I hold it to be special because of that."

Princess Laurelin turned again to Tuck. "There, you see, the riddle is now solved, though simple it was, and hence you must not burst after all. You are, indeed, wearing clothing and armor fit for Princelings, yet they never graced a more fitting trio." The Princess smiled, her white teeth showing, and the young buccen beamed in response.

Again they heard the tolling of a distant gong. "Ah, let us begone," said Laurelin, "for the time is upon us. Captain Patrel, your hand please." And thus they went forth from the abandoned quarters and through the corridors and down the steps to the great Feast Hall: Captain Patrel, in golden armor, with the hand of the beautiful Lady Laurelin, gowned in blue; black-armored Danner to Patrel's right; and silver-armored Tuck to Laurelin's left. Each of the Elven-becloaked Warrows strode with a helm under one arm, and a silver horn of Valon on green-and-white baldric hung at Patrel's side. And when they came through the main doors and into the long Feast Hall, all the guests rose and murmured in wonderment, some at the great beauty of the Princess, others at the Waerling warriors by her side.

Across the wide floor they strode, unto the steps

of the throne dais, and thereupon sat Aurion Red-eye; scarlet-and-gold raiments were upon him, and he looked every inch the High King. To his right stood youthful Prince Igon, in red, and Lord Gildor, in grey. To Aurion's left stood Hrosmarshal Vidron, dressed in the green-and-white colors of Valon. The Warrows bowed low, and Laurelin made a graceful curtsy. Aurion acknowledged their courtesy by in-clining his head, and then he rose and walked down to the Princess and took her hands in his and smiled.

Then Aurion turned to the guests. His voice was firm and all heard his words: "This is the eve of the twelve days of Yule, a time of celebration, for it marks the ending of an old year and the beginning of the new. Tomorrow, First Yule brings with it the shortest day and longest night as the old year lays dying, and some may take that as a bleak omen in these dark times. Yet I say unto ye all, First Yule is also a time of new beginnings. Hearken unto me, though Twelfth Yule is reckoned as the first day of a new year, I ween that First Yule marks its true beginning; for it is thereafter that the days grow longer as the land begins the slow march toward the shining days of summer, and that is a bright omen of hope.

"But First Yule also has brought us great grace and beauty—the Princess Laurelin. If there be omen seekers amongst ye, look upon this Lady in blue, and ye can do nought but see good fortune in your rede."

King Aurion led the Princess to a throne to one side, where she was seated and flanked by the ar-mored Waerlinga. The King turned to his guests and proclaimed, "Let the celebration begin." And there rose up a great cheering in the Hall that made the very rafters ring.

Spectacle and entertainment filled the Hall as the grand party got under way, with jugglers and wrestlers, dancers and buffoons, prestidigitators and a Man who spewed fire from his mouth, and others, all strutting in file through the doors and around the floor to be seen before they were to perform.

Next, servants bearing platters laden with food paraded into the Hall. There were roast pig and lamb, beef and fowl, and vegetables such as carrots, parsnips, beans, red cabbage, and peas, and great pitchers of frothed ale and dark mead, and apples and pears, and even the strange new fruit from Thyra, orange and tangy and full of juice.

The tables were set and groaned beneath the weight of the feast. The Warrows' eyes grew big at the heaped mounds of food, for trenchers were they all, but never had they seen such a spread of banquet.

The King stood and escorted Princess Laurelin to the royal table, and Prince Igon, Lord Gildor, Marshal Vidron, and Tuck, Danner, and Patrel accompanied them. The Princess was seated, and King Aurion raised a horn of honey-sweet mead; so did they all. "Yule and Lady Laurelin!" he cried, and a great shout went up: *Yule and Lady Laurelin!* And the Princess's eyes were bright with tears as she signed for the feast to begin. And so it did.

Food and drink and entertainment occupied Tuck's senses as the party pulsed into the night . . . and good conversation, too:

"We celebrate this same festival in my Land of Valon," said Marshal Vidron to Tuck as they watched a juggler. "Only there we call it Jöl rather than Yule. But that is because the old language, Valur, still names many things in the Valanreach, though the Common Tongue, Pellarion, makes up our everyday speech. Ah Valur, a language rich in meaning, once spoken by many, but now known only to my countrymen. Yet Valur will live forever, for it is our War-speech, the battle-tongue of the Harlingar, the Vanadurin, Warriors of the Reach!" Vidron raised his cup in salute and took a great gulp of mead.

"Yule has had many names in many tongues," said Lord Gildor, his Elven eyes aglitter, "yet it always has been the same twelve days of winter festival throughout the years. And though days, months, and years mean little to my Folk, memories are important to us. And many a happy memory centers about Yule, or Jöl, Yöl, Üle, or whatever it may be called. Yes, I can remember a time such as this when it was still called Gēol, and we celebrated even though Modru threatened the Land in that Era, too."

"You can *remember*?" exclaimed Danner, hushed awe in his voice. "But that was . . . that was back before the Ban, four thousand years . . ." Danner's words trailed off in wonder.

"Yes," smiled Gildor, his voice soft, "I can remember."

A roar went up from the guests, and nothing more was said as they watched wrestlers grapple on the central floor. At last, one of the young soldiers hefted the other and spun him about and flung him to the mat, pinning him. Great shouts of praise rose up from the assembly.

"Ah, if I am not mistaken," said Aurion to the Princess, "that young Man, the victor, is from Dael in your Land, for I have seen him wrestle before. He has great strength and agility, as many in Riamon do."

Laurelin smiled brightly, but behind her eyes loomed sadness. "What a grand party," she said to the King, "yet many of this gay troupe will be on the waggons with me on the morrow."

"And I ride with the escort," said young Igon, glumly, "when I think it would be better that I return to the Dimmendark to stand beside Galen against the foe."

"My son," said Aurion, "I need you in Pellar. You but ride with the escort to Stonehill, beyond the range of Modru's Vulgs. Then you will leave the train behind, and with six fast companions you will go apace to Caer Pendwyr to rally the Kingdom to our aid."

"Sire, I will obey thy command," replied Igon, his speech now courtly, "though I think thee but try to place one of thy heirs temporarily beyond harm's way." King Aurion's face flushed, and he glanced at Vidron as if to a conspirator. Prince Igon spoke on. "I think others, Captain Jarriel for one, can do this deed thou hast given me as well as I if not better, whereas I have fought and slain foe in the bitter Winternight and that is what I am suited to do. Aye, 'twas perchance by accident that we stumbled across the enemy, still that does not alter the fact that Galen and I slew five between us. It is this task I would return to: to stand with Galen against the foe."

"Son, you spoke that others could do this deed I

have given you," responded Aurion, stonily, "and you name Captain Jarriel, for you know I send him south as your counsel. But this I say unto you: Captain Jarriel cannot command the jealous generals of rival factions to set aside their pettishness. Only one of the Royal Family can fire the will of the armies with the resolve and unity needed to meet and do battle with Modru's Horde. And that is the command I have thrust upon you: to muster the forces and return unto me with them."

"The commanding of that army, Sire, should be Galen's task, not mine, for he is elder, by ten years," answered Igon.

"But he is not here!" snapped the King, his voice rising, the flat of his hand slapping the table, setting cups atumble. Then his look softened, and his speech became as courtly as was Igon's. "Ah, mine son, in thy veins flows the same blood as mine own, yet thine is made hot by youth. I know thou wouldst sally forth to join thy brother and meet the foe, for that is a hard thing to resist. Yet set aside thy rashness at this time, and see that a royal hand is needed to bring mine Host northward apace. Thou knowest that the first heralds were Vulg slain, and perchance the second, and only slowly doth the word go forth unto the Land. Hence, the muster has not yet truly begun. This, then, is the eleventh hour of our need. Thou, or Galen, or I must go and return with that which will whelm the Enemy." King Aurion placed a hand upon Igon's. "Fate hath decreed that it is thou who must gather mine Host, for Galen is to the north, and I must remain here to take the field if Modru comes. This, then, is my charge unto thee: Bring unto me mine Host."

The youth bowed his head to the King and placed his free hand upon Aurion's. "Sire, I am at thy command," said Igon, acceding to Aurion's reasoning. And the King stood and raised up Igon and embraced him, and then they each drained a horn of mead.

Prince Igon turned and spoke to the Princess. "It seems, my Lady Laurelin, that we are to be travelling companions, at least for a while. Hear me now: I take upon myself a sword-oath to ward you to safety on our travel to Stonehill; let the Enemy in Gron beware."

Laurelin smiled radiantly up at him. "I am most pleased to have you as a protector, Lord Igon, though I would that neither of us had that journey to make."

The feast went on. A sleight-of-hand artist made doves appear from kerchiefs, and flowers from empty tubes, to the delight of all. Then one came who swallowed swords—making Tuck's stomach queasy—and threw knives with wondrous skill. Finally a harper played, but his song was of love lost and sad unto the heart. Patrel looked at Laurelin and saw that tears glistened upon her lashes, and he nudged Tuck and Danner, who saw her sadness, too.

The small gold-clad Warrow took a great draught of ale and called the harper to him. "Have you got a lute?" Patrel asked. "Good! May I borrow it?" In a trice the Wee One held a fine lute in his hands, and he turned to the Princess.

"My Lady, it is nearly mid of night, and in but a few moments you will be nineteen. We of the Boskydells have nought to give you as a present on this your birthday eve, yet there is a happy song, really nought but a ditty, that perchance will cheer you. It is called *The Merry Man in Boskledee*, and practically every Warrow in the Boskydells knows it and the dance that goes along. I propose that Tuck and Danner and I perform it as the Warrows' gift to you."

Tuck and Danner were both thunderstruck. Had Patrel actually proposed that *they* sing a simple Warrow song before all of these *Warriors?*

"Patrel!" hissed Danner, "you can't be serious. This hardly seems the time or place for a nonsense tune."

"Nonsense!" roared Vidron, his mood jovial. " 'Twere no better time than now for a happy jig."

"Oh yes, please do," begged the Princess, turning to Tuck and Danner, "for I need the cheer."

Tuck looked into the pleading eyes of the Lady and could not refuse, and neither it seemed could Danner. And so, after a good stiff glog of mead, they most reluctantly stepped down upon the central floor and walked to the fore center.

King Aurion himself called for quiet, and a hush fell over the guests. Patrel plunked the strings, tuning the lute, and said under his breath to to the other two, "Give it your best go." At their nods his fingers began dancing over the strings. And such a bright and lively tune sprang forth that it immediately set toes to tapping and fingers to rapping, and lustily the Warrows began to sing:

Oh—Fiddle-dee hi, fiddle-dee ho,
  Fiddle-dee hay ha hee.

Wiggle-dee die, wiggle-dee doe,
  Wiggle-dee pig die dee.

Once there was a very merry Man
  Who came to Boskledee.
His coat was red and his horse was tan,
  And mittens, well he had three.

He was so tall but his horse so small,
  His feet dragged on the ground.
He didn't dismount when the steed was tired,
  He simply walked around.

A great roar of laughter rose up from the assembly, and here Tuck and Danner, silver- and black-armor clad, danced a simple but rigorous to-and-fro jig to the beat of the tune, occasionally linking arms to wildly circle oppositely.

Oh—Ho ho ho, ha ha ha,
  Higgle-dee hay hi hee.
Har har har, ya ya ya,
  Giggle-dee snig snag snee.

He tumbled hand springs, wore seven rings,
  Shot fireworks in the air.
His pants were orange and his shoes bright green,
  He cried, "Let's have a fair!"

He strummed upon a six string-ed lute
  And sang so merrily.
His voice, it broke with a great loud croak,
  And he laughed in happy glee.

Again the warrior Captains howled in mirth and banged the tables with their mead cups. Laurelin and Igon ran down hand in hand, and they joined Danner and Tuck in dancing the jig. To and fro, back and forth they danced, bright smiles upon their faces. Blue, red, silver, and black, all whirled and stepped to the notes played by gold. And the assembly roared its vast approval.

> *Oh—Har har har, fa la la,*
>   *Cackle-dee ha ho hee.*
> *Ho ho ho, tra la la,*
>   *Giggle-dee tum ta tee.*

> *He disappeared with a flash and a bang*
>   *And maybe a puff of smoke.*
> *He left behind his clothes and his lute,*
>   *His steed, and a couple of jokes.*

> *And now there is in old Boskledee*
>   *Fireworks at the annual fair,*
> *Where we wear bright clothes and ride ponies*
>   *With gay songs filling the air.*

> *Oh—Tiddle tee tum, ho ho ho,*
>   *Tra-la-la lay la lee.*
> *Fiddle-dee fum, lo lo lo,*
>   *Ha-ha-ha ho ha hee.*

> *Oh—Fiddle-dee fum, lo lo lo,*
>   *Ha-ha-ha ho ha hee.*
> *Tiddle tee tum, ho ho ho,*
>   *Tra-la-la lay la lee—Hey!*

And with final *Hey!* Patrel twanged the lute and the fling stopped, the four dancers embracing and laughing in joy and panting with exertion. A great, wild cheering broke out, with whistling and cup banging and stomping and clapping. Marshal Vidron roared in laughter, while King Aurion banged his cup and Lord Gildor clapped. Laurelin and Igon, Danner and Tuck, and Patrel all bowed to one another and to the crowd, and Laurelin's eyes fairly danced with happiness.

But then:

Boom! Doom! The great doors of the Feast Hall boomed open, echoing through the chamber like the knelling of doom, and a begrimed warrior trod into the Hall, his left arm gashed and bleeding. Smiling countenances turned toward him, but gaiety fled before his unyielding pace. Silence clanged down like the stroke of an axe blade upon stone, and the only sound to be heard was the hard stride of the Man down the long floor. And as the soldier passed the Warrows and Laurelin and Igon, and strode toward the King, Tuck was whelmed by a dreadful foreboding, and it seemed as if he were rooted to the floor. All eyes were locked upon the warrior as he came unto the throne dais. He struck a clenched fist to his heart and knelt upon one knee before the King, and blood dripped upon the stone. And in the hanging quiet, all heard his words:

"Sire, on this dark Yule Eve, I bear thee tidings from my Lord Galen, though ill word it is: The Dimmendark now stalks this way, the Black Wall moves toward Challerain Keep. And in the Winternight that follows, the Horde of ravers marches. The War with Modru has begun."

CHAPTER 5

THE DARK TIDE

A great uproar filled the Hall, and hands grasped futilely at weaponless girts, for all had come to the feast unarmed. Shouts of anger boiled up, and clenched fists struck tables in rage, and some tore at their hair. Tuck's heart thudded in his chest, and a cold chill raced through his veins, and from his confused wits one thought rose up above all: *It comes!*

At a sign from Aurion, a steward struck a great staff to the floor three times, and the knell of the gavel cut through the din. At last quiet returned to the Hall, and the King bade the warrior to speak on.

"Sire, I did but come from the Dimmendark five hours past," he continued. "Two of us were entrusted by my Lord Galen to bring this word. Three horses each had we, and all were ridden unto foundering. Yet I and my last steed were all that won through, for my comrade was Vulg slain along the way, and I am Vulg wounded."

"Modru's curs!" spat Aurion, his fists clenched in fury, and the scarlet patch upon his left eye seemed to flash anger. Shouting wrath filled the Hall.

"Oh my, your arm!" Distress was in Laurelin's voice, and she moved at last, rushing to the soldier's side. She gently took his arm and called out through the roar for a healer, sending a nearby page darting from the chamber after one.

Tuck's own paralysis was broken, and he joined Laurelin. Together they used the warrior's dagger to cut away his tattered sleeve, revealing a long, ugly gash. "This scratch was made at the very gates of the first wall," grunted the soldier, gratefully accepting a horn of mead from Patrel and quaffing it in one gulp. Danner refilled the cup from a pitcher. "Why, you are Waerlinga!" he exclaimed, seeing for the first time that he was attended by Wee Folk.

Again the gavelling of the steward's staff cut through the clamor, and slowly quiet was restored. "Your name, warrior," called Aurion, as Igon moved to stand beside his father.

"Haddon, Sire," answered the Man.

"Well done, Haddon! You have brought vital news, though dire it is. Say you this: How much time have we ere the Black Wall sweeps unto Challerain Keep?"

"Perhaps two days, three at most," answered Haddon, and a grim murmur ran throughout the assembly.

"Then we must make final our plans," Aurion called out to the gathering, and all fell silent. "It is now mid of night. First Yule steps into the Realm, and Princess Laurelin paces forward into her nineteenth year. Good times lay behind us, and better time yet lay ahead, but in betwixt will fall drear days. Modru's Horde now strikes south. Here at these walls they must be held. Go now unto your beds and rest, for we must be in the fullness of our strength to meet this foe." Aurion swept up a goblet from a nearby table and raised it on high. *"Hál!"* he cried in the ancient tongue of the North. *"Hēah Adoni cnāwen ūre weg!"* (Hail! High Adon knows our way!)

And the assembled raised their own horns and cups. *Hál! Aurion ūre Cyning!* (Hail! Aurion our King!) And all drained their goblets to the bottom as through the doors returned the page with a sleepy healer in tow, nightcap still aperch his head. But all sleep fled from his eyes as he examined the wound.

"Vulg bite?" The healer's voice was startled. "Foul news. We must get this warrior to a cot. The fever has begun, and we need blankets, hot water, a poultice of gwynthyme, and . . ." His voice sank into mumbles as he rummaged through his healer's satchel. Laurelin sent pages scurrying to fetch the healer's needs.

With the healer and young buccen following, the Princess led the warrior through a postern behind the drapes in back of the throne. The door led to an alcove where there was a divan and fireplace and several chairs. Haddon's cloak and armor, jerkin and padding were removed, and he was made to lie down, though he protested that he was too grimy for the couch. A page bore hot water in, and the healer laved the wound as Laurelin spoke with Haddon.

"My Lord Galen, is he well?" she asked.

"Aye, my Lady," answered Haddon, pride in his voice. "He has the strength of two and the spirit of ten. And cunning he is, clever as a fox, for many a trap of his has the foe sprung to their woe."

"Does he say when he might return here to the

Keep?" Laurelin filled a basin with water, exchanging it for the one now tinged red with blood.

"Nay, Princess." Haddon's brow now beaded with sweat. "He harasses the Horde's flanks, trying to turn their energies aside. Yet there are so many, and he now has less than a hundred in his ranks. We were sent to spy, not to thwart an army, yet I do not think he will flee back to the Keep." Laurelin's pale eyes were bleak as she heard this news.

The door opened and in strode Aurion, followed by Igon, Gildor, and Vidron. As Gildor drew the healer aside and spoke quietly with him, Aurion sat by the side of the couch.

"How many does Modru send against us?" asked the King, peering into Haddon's face, now flushed with fever.

"Sire, they are without number," answered Haddon, his voice weak and falling toward a whisper. A shudder of chills racked the scout's frame, but his low voice spoke on: "Sire . . . the Ghola . . . Ghola ride in their ranks."

"Guula!" cried Vidron, and his countenance was grim.

"Do you mean Ghûls?" asked Patrel.

"Aye, Waldan," answered the Hrosmarshal. "This foe is dreadful: Man-height, with lifeless black eyes and the blanched skin of the dead. Dire in combat, virtually unkillable, they take dreadful wounds without bleeding or falling. Lore has it that in but a few ways can they be slain: a fatal wound by a pure silver blade, wood driven through the heart, fire, beheading or dismemberment, and the Sun. Skilled with weapons they are, and cruel beyond measure. They ride to battle mounted upon Hèlsteeds, horselike but with cloven hooves and hairless tails." Vidron fell silent, stroking his silver beard and thinking deeply.

The healer came with a goblet containing a sleeping draught. "Sire, he must rest, else he will die. And we must sear the wound, for he will fall into foam-flecked madness otherwise. A poultice to draw the poison is needed, lest it run wild through his veins, if it does not do so even now."

As Tuck heard the healer's voice, his mind went back to the fright-filled night atop Rooks' Roost, the night Hob died from Vulg bite, and he realized at last that they had not had with them the means necessary to stay the young buccan's death; yet knowing this did not take the sting from behind Tuck's eyes.

The King nodded to the healer, and Haddon was held up to drink the potion. The warrior's eyes slowly glazed over, yet he roused long enough to beckon the King unto him. Aurion leant down to hear Haddon's faint whisper, listening closely. Then Haddon's eyes closed, and he said no more.

As Gildor withdrew a glowing dagger from the fire, Igon asked, "Sire, what said he?"

Wearily the King turned to them all. "He said, 'Rukha, Lokha, Ogrus.' "

There came a cry and the sound and smell of searing flesh as Gildor set the ruddy dagger to the Vulg wound, while the healer prepared a gwynthyme poultice, and Laurelin wept for Haddon's pain.

"Rūcks, Hlōks, and Ogrus?" asked Delber, voicing the question for all the Warrow company.

"And Ghûls, too," said Argo. "Don't forget the Ghûls."

"I knew it! I just knew it!" exclaimed Sandy. "That Black Wall stood out there like Doom, lurking on the horizon. You could feel it in the air, like a storm about to break. And now Modru comes at last."

All the company murmured in agreeement, for each Warrow there had felt the menace crouched over the Land; and Tuck, Danner, and Patrel had come in the wee hours of the morning to tell them the dire news.

"Hold on, buccoes," said Patrel above the babble. When quiet returned, he spoke on. "Now I've told you about the Ghûls and their rattailed Hèlsteeds, just as Vidron described them to us, only he called 'em Guula while Gildor called 'em Ghûlka. But let me tell you what he and Gildor said about Rūcks, Hlōks, and Ogrus." Again a low murmur washed throughout the company until Patrel raised his hands for quiet.

"It seems that most of what we've been told in the past is correct," said Patrel in the hush. "The Rūck is a hand or three taller than we, and, unlike the corpse-white Ghûl, the Rūck is night dark. He's got bandy legs and skinny arms. His ears look like bat wings, and he's got the eye of a viper—yellow and slitty. Wide-mouthed he is, with gappy, pointed teeth. He's not got a lot of skill with weapons, but Gildor says he doesn't need much 'cause there's so many of 'em; they just swarm over you, conquering by their very numbers. Vidron calls 'em Rutcha and Goblins; Gildor calls 'em Rucha; but by any name, they're deadly."

Patrel paused and a hubbub rose up, and Dilby

called out above the babble: "What do they fight with, Danner? Did Gildor say?"

"Ar, cudgels and hammers, mostly. Smashing weapons, he said," answered Danner. "The Ghûls use spears and tulwars; the Rūcks, smashing weapons, though some use bows with black-shafted arrows; Hlōks usually wield scimitars and maces; and the Ogrus fight mostly with great Warbars. All of them use others weapons, of course—whips, knives, strangling cords, scythes, flails, you name it—but in the main they stick with those I named first."

"Gildor says that the weapons with an edge or a point may be poisoned," added Tuck. A low growl rumbled through the company.

"Yar, a minor nick from one of those can do you in days later if not treated quickly," said Danner.

"What about the Hlōks," asked Argo, "and the Ogrus? What do they look like?"

"The Hlōk is Man-sized," answered Patrel, "like the Ghûl. Their looks are different, though, the Hlōk being more Ruck-like in appearance, darkish, viper eyes, bat-wing ears. His legs are straight, and his arms strong. Unlike their small look-alikes, the Hlōk is skilled with weapons, and clever, too. And cruel. There's not as many Hlōks are there are Rūcks, but the Hlōks command the Rūck squads, and in turn are commanded by the Ghûls."

"Who tells the Ogrus what to do?" asked Finley. "Ar, and what be they like?"

"As to who commands the Ogrus, Gildor didn't say," answered Patrel. "Whether it be Ghûls or Hlōks or someone else, he did not tell the which of it. But this he did say: Trolls—that's what Gildor calls Ogrus—Trolls are huge, a giant Rūck some say, ten or twelve feet tall. They've got a stonelike hide, but scaled and greenish. Ordinary weapons don't usually cut Ogrus, and the only sure way to kill them is to drop a big rock on 'em, throw them off a cliff, or stab them with 'special' swords—that's what Gildor called them, 'special.' But I think he must mean 'magical,' though when I asked him about it, he didn't seem to know what I meant by the word 'magic.' "

"He did say that Ogrus sometimes could be slain by a stab in the eye, or groin, or mouth," added Tuck. "And, oh yes, fifty or more Dwarves have been known to band together in a Troll-squad and hew an Ogru down with axes, but at a frightful cost to the Dwarves."

"Hey," said Finley, "if ordinary weapons won't cut Ogrus, how come Dwarf axes work to slay them?"

"I don't know," answered Tuck. "Perhaps Dwarf axes are 'special' weapons."

"Nar," said Danner. "I think they just know where to chop."

"Anyhow, buccoes, that's all Gildor and Vidron told us," concluded Patrel. "All we have to do is wait and we'll see for ourselves, 'cause they're coming: Vulg, Rūck, Hlōk, Ogru, Ghûl: it's them we'll be fighting alongside the Men. Yet, that's a couple or more days in the future, and now we must gather some sleep, for our watch on the ramparts is but a few hours ahead, and our eyes need to be even sharper in the coming times."

And so they all took to their cots, but slumber was a long time coming to some, and others slept not at all. And they tossed and turned to no avail,

occasionally rising up to see Tuck in a far corner
scribing in his diary by candlelight.

The next morning a bleak grey dawn saw the
Warrows come to the ramparts. North they looked,
but the glowering skies were too sullen and the
early light too blear to see the wall of Dimmendark.
After the watch was set upon the bulwark, Delber
and Sandy were left in charge while Tuck, Danner,
and Patrel entered the castle to seek out the Princess. They went to bid her farewell, for this was the
day she would leave. They took with them the clothes
they had worn to her birthday feast, and also the
armor, to return it. They found her in her chambers,
taking one last look before departing.

"Oh pother!" she declared. "If ever you needed
armor, now is the time, for War comes afoot."

"But my Lady," protested Patrel, "these hauberks
are precious, heirlooms of the House of Aurion. We
could not take them. They must be returned."

"Nay!" came the voice of the King as he stepped
into Laurelin's parlor behind them. "The Princess
speaks true. Armor is needed for my Kingsguards.
Even now the leather-plate armor made for your
company these past days is ready in my armories
for your squads to don. But though I did not think
of the Dwarf-made armor of my youth or that of
my sons, Lady Laurelin remembered it. Now, too,
she is right, yet not only because armor is needed,
but also because you are the Captain and Lieutenants of the Wee Folk company, and my Men will
find it easier to single out a Waerling in gold, silver,
or black to relay my orders to. And so you will keep
the mail corselets." He raised his hands to forestall

their contentions. "If you take issue with the gift, surely you cannot oppose me if we call it a loan. Keep the Dwarf-made armor, and, aye, the clothes, too, until I personally recall them. And if I never do so, then they are to remain in your hands, or in the possession of those you would trust. Gainsay me not in this, for it is my command." The Warrows bowed to the will of the King.

Laurelin smiled and her eyes were bright. "Oh, please do dress again as you were last night, for that was a happy time, and I would have you bid me farewell accoutered so."

Hence it was that in the grey morn the three Warrows were arrayed once more in armor and Elven cloaks, in steel helms and bright trews and soft jerkins—silveron and blue, gold and pale green, black and scarlet. 'Neath overcast skies they stood in the courtyard at the great west gate as wounded Haddon was gently placed in the first of the two wains standing on the cobbles. Prince Igon stood by his horse, Rust, with stern Captain Jarriel at his side holding the reins of a dun-colored steed. King Aurion and silver-bearded Vidron were there, too, along with Gildor the Elf Lord. Princess Laurelin came last of all.

"Advise Igon well, as you would me," said Aurion to Jarriel, and the Captain struck a clenched fist to his heart.

King Aurion then embraced his son. "Gather mine Host to me, my son, yet forget not your sword-oath to the Lady Laurelin." And Igon drew his sword and kissed the hilt and raised the blade unto the Princess. Laurelin smiled and inclined her head, accepting Igon's oath to see her safely to Stonehill.

Then the Lady Laurelin made her farewells: King Aurion she embraced and kissed upon the cheek, bidding him to whelm Modru and keep her Lord Galen safe. Of Lord Gildor she asked only that he serve the High King until the War was ended, and Gildor nodded, smiling. To Marshal Vidron she said nought but hugged him extra tight, for he had been like a father to her in this Land so far away from Riamon her home, and Tuck was amazed to see a glittering tear slide down the gruff warrior's cheek and into his silver beard. Captain Patrel she named minstrel of her court, and to Danner she smiled and called him her dancer. Last of all she turned to Tuck and kissed him, too, and whispered to him: "Someday I hope to meet your Merrilee of the silver locket, just as someday I would that you and my beloved Lord Galen could know one another, for I deem you would be boon companions. Keep safe, my Wee One."

And then Laurelin was escorted by Prince Igon to the last waggon, and she mounted up into it. At a sign from Aurion, the portcullises were raised and the great west gates opened. With a flip of reins and a call to the teams, the drivers slowly moved the wains forward and through the portal, the iron-rimmed wheels clattering upon the flagstones and cobbles, horses' hooves ringing, too. Igon followed behind upon Rust, who pranced and curvetted, eager to be under way, and Captain Jarriel upon the dun steed came after. Outside the gate they were joined by the escort, and slowly the waggons trundled down Mont Challerain, heading for the final caravan waiting below.

Behind stood Warrows, Men, and Elf, waving goodbye. Tuck's last sight of Laurelin was one of sorrow, for although he could see her returning the farewell, he also saw that she was weeping. And then with a clatter of gears and a grinding of metal, the portcullises lowered and the iron gates swung to, and Tuck stood staring at the dark iron long after the barrier clanged shut.

At last the three young buccen climbed up to the ramparts and stood long upon the south wall in the company of Danner's squad. They watched as the waggon train wended southward out through the first wall and into the foothills, driving toward the plains beyond. And they all had heavy hearts, for it seemed as if a brightness had gone from their lives, leaving behind cold bleak stone and grey iron and empty barren plains under drab leaden skies.

They were standing thus when Finley came. "Oh, hullo, there you are," he said. "I've found you at last. You'd better come, Cap'n Patrel, Tuck, Danner, come to the north rampart and look at Modru's Black Wall. It's growing."

"Growing?" barked Patrel. "This we must see."

Swiftly they strode along the castellated bulwark, coming soon to the north wall. Climbing upon the weapon shelf they looked through crenels northward. Tuck felt his heart lurch and the blood pound in his temples, for Modru's forbidding wall of Dimmendark now seemed half again as high as when last he had seen it.

"Summon Marshal Vidron," said Patrel, not taking his eyes from the growing darkness.

"It's been done, Cap'n," said Finley. "He's at the mid-wall gorge."

"Come then," Patrel bade Tuck and Danner, stepping down from the shelf and marching toward the mid of the bulwark. As they went to Vidron, King Aurion also came with Gildor, striding up the nearby bastion ramp. They came to the gorge, and again the young buccen mounted the shelf and looked at the far Black Wall.

At last Tuck asked, "Why is it growing?"

"It's not *growing*, Tuck," answered Danner, "it's coming *closer*."

Of course! Tuck thought, surprised that he hadn't seen it for himself. *How stupid can I be? No wonder it looms larger: it's moving toward us. Haddon said it was coming, and it is!* His thoughts were interrupted by the King.

"Like a great dark tide, it comes, drowning all before it," said Aurion. "How much time do you deem we have, Marshal Vidron?"

"Two days, perhaps, but no more," answered the Man from Valon, his hand stroking his silver beard. "Modru comes apace."

"Nay," said Gildor. "Not Modru: just his minions come, his Horde, but not him."

"What?" burst out Patrel. "Do you mean that he's not with them, that he doesn't lead his armies?"

"Oh, no, Wee One, he leads them aright, but by a hideous power, and he remains in his tower in Gron to do so," answered Gildor, his voice low.

Tuck shuddered, though he knew not from what. But Danner spat toward the north: "Modru, you cowardly toad, though you hide away now, someday you will yet face one of us, and in that battle you will lose!" Danner turned his back to the Dimmendark, leapt down from the weapon shelf, and marched angrily away to rejoin his squad along the south rampart.

Lord Gildor watched him go. "Ai, that one, he vents his fear in anger, though tell him not I said so. He will be a good one to stand beside in times of strife—if he can control his passion. Rare warriors like him I have seen in the past, though not of the Waerlinga: the more difficult the task, the greater is their grit to win through."

Tuck thought, *Gildor is right about Danner: the tougher a task, the more he strives. Grit, Gildor names it, though my dam called Danner "pugnacious," and my sire said he was "quarrelsome."*

"Aye," said Vidron, "I, too, have seen warriors who turn dread into rage, but at times the berserker comes upon them, and then they are awful to behold, for then they do nought but slay. Yet were this to happen unto one of the *Waldfolc*, he would not survive, for they are so small."

"Nay, Marshal Vidron," said King Aurion. "Were a Waerling to have the battle rage come upon him, to become a Slayer, I, too, think he would not survive—but not because he is so small: instead because he is what he is—a Waerling—and were he to become a Slayer, even in battle, he simply would not live beyond that time." A feeling of dire foreboding came over Tuck at these words, and he looked in the direction that Danner had gone.

All that morning, Captains and warriors came to the north rampart to watch the advance of the Dimmendark, and faces blenched to see the dreadful blackness stretching from horizon to horizon and stalking toward them. To the rampart, too, one at a time, came the young buccen of Danner's squad, now accoutered in their new corselets of leather plate, as were the Warrows of Tuck's squad. They watched the dark looming wall draw closer. Some made comments, but most simply stood without speaking and looked long before turning and going back to their posts.

"Ar, it looks like a great black wave," said Dilby as he stood beside Tuck.

"King Aurion said something like that, too, Dilbs," answered Tuck. "He called it a dark tide, though I think he meant Modru's Horde as well as the Dimmendark."

"Aurion Redeye can call 'em a dark tide if he wishes, but me, well, I think the Elves have the right of it when they call 'em *Spaunen*, though I would call them Modru's Spawn," Dilby averred. After a short pause, he spoke on. "I don't mind telling you, Tuck, seeing that Black Wall acomin', well, it makes me feel all squirmy inside."

Tuck threw Dilby a glance and then looked back at the blackness. "Me, too, Dilbs. Me, too."

Dilby clapped a hand to Tuck's shoulder. "Ar, squirmy or not, I hope it don't spoil our aim none," he said, and looked a moment more then stepped down from the shelf. "Ah, well, it's me for the south wall so as someone else can come here and see this black calamity."

"I'll go with you," said Tuck, jumping down beside Dilby. "I've watched Modru's canker long enough. Perhaps the view to the south will be more pleasant: perhaps Lady Laurelin's caravan is still in sight, though I would that it were gone far south days apast, for the Wall comes swiftly and the waggon train but plods."

To the south rampart they strode, where Tuck found Danner at the wall gazing south. Up beside him Tuck stepped and looked southward, too. "Oh, my!" gasped Tuck. "Have they gone no farther?" Out on the plains, seemingly but a short distance beyond the foothills of Mont Challerain, the caravan clearly could be seen, pulling up a long rise.

"They've been creeping like that all day," gritted Danner, grinding his teeth in frustration. "I keep telling myself that they're making good time, but deep inside I don't believe it. Look, you see that rise they go up now? Well that's the same one we galloped down on our last day toward the Keep. It took us a morning to arrive. It's taken the train about the same time to get from here to there. But, Tuck, I swear, their journey crawls slowly while ours trotted swiftly."

They stood and watched as the waggon train toiled up the slope. Tuck threw an arm over Danner's shoulders. "Were the waggons filled with strangers, mayhap the pace would seem right. Or if the Dimmendark came not this way, we would believe the caravan swift. Yet I think we see it move at a snail's pace because someone we care for rides in the last wain."

"Of course you're right," said Danner, "but knowing it does not help." The taller young buccan watched long moments more and then struck his fist to the cold grey stone. "Move faster, you slowcoaches, move faster!" he hissed through clenched teeth. Then, shrugging Tuck's arm from him, he turned and slumped down on the shelf and sat, letting his feet dangle from the ledge, his back to the cold stone merlon, refusing to look at the caravan.

Another half hour passed, then nearly an hour, and Patrel joined them. At last Tuck said, "There she goes, the last wain, over the hill." Danner scrambled to his feet, and the three of them watched as Laurelin's waggon slowly disappeared beyond the distant crest. And the white prairie lay empty before them.

Late in the day, Tuck and Patrel stood again at the north rampart as the Dimmendark inexorably drew closer. Often their eyes had intently scanned the edges of the Black Wall, but nought of note did they see as the 'Dark stalked south across the plain toward them. Tuck secretly hoped to see Lord Galen's troop ride forth upon the snow and come unto Challerain Keep, for he longed to meet this Prince who had won the heart of the Lady Laurelin. But no one came, and he, like Laurelin, began to fear that something had gone amiss. Yet Tuck told himself that Haddon the messenger had seen Lord Galen alive and well less than a day past. *Has it been such a short time?* he wondered. *Less than a day since we were having a grand birthday party? Ar, but it seems as if that happy time were years agone, and as if the dread of the coming Black Wall has been forever, instead of but a single dismal day.*

"Ai-oi!" Patrel's exclamation of puzzlement broke into Tuck's thoughts. "Look, Tuck, at the base of the 'Dark! What is it?"

Long did Tuck look, yet the distance and the failing light of the setting Sun through the overcast did not let him see clearly. "It looks like . . . like the snow is *boiling* all along the base of the Black Wall."

"Yar," agreed Patrel. "Boiling or swirling, I cannot say which."

"Swirling, I think, now that you've said it, Captain Patrel," confirmed Tuck. "But what would cause that? A wind, do you think?"

Patrel merely grunted, and the day faded into night, and they saw no more. At last the Warrows trooped wearily to their quarters as the Castle-ward changed.

The next morning the great Black Wall was less than ten miles distant and drawing closer. Each time Tuck looked at the looming darkness, his heart would thud anew, and he wondered at his courage: *Will I be strong enough when it o'ertops these ramparts, or will I run screaming?*

Now they could see that a wind blew wildly all along the Dimmendark front, as if the air were being violently shoved, plowed before the moving Black Wall. Like a tempest-driven ocean breaking upon an enormous black jetty, great boiling clouds of swirling snow were lofted high into the air. As to the 'Dark itself, the blackness rose from the plains, darkest near the ground, fading as it went up; yet high into the sky it reached before it could no longer be seen, perhaps a mile or more. And though the day was bright and the Sun shone golden, its light seemed *consumed* as it struck the Black Wall, as if swallowed by some dark monster.

Aurion, Gildor, Vidron, and the War-staff came often to the rampart, yet neither did their sight penetrate the churning snow or looming black, nor did aught emerge from the ebon wall.

The Sun stood at the zenith when at last the Dimmendark came upon Mont Challerain. Tuck stood braced upon the rampart and watched with dread as the Black Wall rushed forward. Before it the howling wind raced, and with it came the hurling snow. The Castle-ward was buffeted and battered by the shrieking gale on the rim of the Dimmendark. Tuck pulled the Elven cloak about his shoulders and the hood over his head, but still the swirling snow was driven into his squinting wind-watered eyes. The Sun began to grow dim as the dark tide swept on, as if a black night were swiftly falling, though it was yet high noon. Rapidly the sunlight failed as the Dimmendark engulfed the Keep: through dusk into darkness the day sped in but a trice, and night fell even though the Sun stood on high.

The shriek of the howling wind faded to but a distant murmur as the Black Wall swept on, and then even the murmur stilled. The lofted snow quietly drifted back down upon the ramparts and the ground. Tuck looked about in wide-eyed wonder. The Keep now lay in dark Winternight, and a bone-numbing chill stole upon the land. Above, the disk of the Sun could but faintly be seen, and then only by knowing exactly where to look. Yet a spectral light, a Shadowlight, shone out of the dark, as if from a bright Moon; but the source of the light seemed to be the very air itself, and not the Sun, the Moon, or the stars. Ebon shadows clotted around the feet of rock outjuts and seeped among the trees and hills, and vision was hard-pressed to peer into these pools of blackness. And even out where the land was more open, sight became lost in the Shadowlight, snubbed short by the spectral dark.

Tuck walked up and down the rampart, saying, "Steady, buccoes, steady." But whether he was trying to buck up his squad or was talking to himself, he did not know. Once more Tuck took up his position at the central bastion, and he stared out across the foothills. His eyes felt strange as he peered through the Dimmendark, as if the Shadowlight somehow contained a new color, perhaps a hue of deep violet, or beyond. Toward the open snowy plains he looked; he could see but a few miles through the ghostly 'Dark, yet still nought of any movement did he espy. And neither did Patrel, who joined Tuck in his vigil.

The awful cold crept into the very marrow of the bones, and Tuck sent his squad five at a time to their quarters to don their quilted down clothing. Patrel, who had gone, too, came bearing Tuck's togs, and Tuck quickly pulled the winter garb over his shivering frame.

"Trews and shiny armor are fine for birthday parties, but eiderdown is needed to withstand this cold Winternight," Tuck said as he slipped his jacket over the silveron mail and again affixed the Elven cloak 'round his shoulders, and cast the hood over his head. Slowly warmth returned to his body, and he and Patrel once more looked out upon the cold dark land.

At last the Warrows were relieved by the Men of the Castle-ward, though no one could tell when the Sun had set in the grim cold, for only near noon could the faint disk be seen, and it faded beyond sight as the orb fell toward the unseen horizon.

Time now was measured in candle marks and by the water clocks and sand, and though it was now reckoned to be nighttime, neither Moon nor stars shone through the Dimmendark from the skies above. Yet still the harsh land below could be seen in the spectral Shadowlight.

After a troubled sleep, the Warrows arose to, as Danner put it, "A dawnless 'day,' if time in the Dimmendark can be measured in 'days,' that is—though Lord Gildor says that the *days* have now fled, and the *'Darkdays* are come upon us."

Dread filled the mess hall, and voices were grim and hushed. And after breaking their fast, once more the young buccen took station upon the walls of the Keep and gazed out upon the darkling land, out into the Shadowlight. Time wearily passed, and the stone of the walls grew bitter, for the cruel grasp of Winternight clutched full upon the hills and plains, and hoarfrost crept upon Challerain Keep, and ice rimed the battlements and glittered coldly.

King Aurion with Lord Gildor came once more unto the north rampart, riding caparisoned steeds into the bastion gorge below. Now they were armed and armored, with the King bearing a great sword at his belt and a spear in his hand. Lord Gildor had a lighter sword at his own girt, with an Elven long-knife to one side. They were clad in chain mail and capped with helms of steel. The King wore red and gold, Lord Gildor, Elven grey. The King's grey horse, Wildwind, and the Elf's white-stockinged chestnut, Fleetfoot, pranced and sidled as they came into the gorge, but stood quietly as the riders dismounted.

Up the ramp strode the two to join Tuck and

Patrel, and Aurion stared out into the spectral dark, but little did he see in the ghostly werelight.

"How far see you, Lord Gildor?" asked the High King.

"To the fifth rise, no more," answered the Elf.

"Ai, that is a far sight in this icy shadow," said King Aurion. "Mine own one eye is accounted good among Men, yet I but see to the first, nay, the second rise. Perhaps a mile or two at most."

Aurion turned to Tuck and looked at the strange Warrow orbs, and even in the Shadowlight the young buccan's tilted eyes were bright and sapphire blue. "How far see you, Wee One?"

"Sire, I see north one hill further than Lord Gildor and even beyond a bit, out upon the plains, but after that I see nought but darkness," answered Tuck.

"Ai!" cried Gildor in wonderment. "Never before have the far-seeing Elven eyes been bested at sight. Yet here in this baffling shadow it happens. The vision of your strange eyes now proves to see beyond those of the First Folk in this Shadowlight. Yet, it is said among my kindred that the Waerlinga have talents not easily seen, and now I find it is true. Perhaps there is more to the tale of your Utruni eyes than I had thought true."

"Utruni eyes?" asked Tuck, puzzled. "Do you mean Giants?"

"Aye," answered Gildor. "It is believed among my Folk that the Wee Ones have in them something of each of the other Free Folk—of Elf, Dwarf, Man, and Utrun. In this case, even though the shape of Waerling eyes is the same as Elvenkind's, the hue is like that of the jewel-eyes of the Utruni."

"Jewel-eyes? The Giants had jewel-eyes?" blurted out Patrel.

"Yes," answered Gildor. "Great gems of eyes: ruby, emerald, opal, sapphire, amber, jade, and many other gemstones did their eyes resemble. Once I saw an Utrun with eyes of diamond."

"You *saw?* You *saw* an Utrun?" Tuck was astonished. "But I thought the Giants were no more."

"Nay, in that you are wrong." Gildor's own green eyes looked sad. "Though it has been many long seasons since I last saw Utruni, they exist still, but deep within the living stone of Mithgar, moving through the solid rock far below, toiling in their endless fashion to shape the Land. Aye, they live, but it is not likely that they will ever again help us surface dwellers in our petty struggles."

"Oi!" said Patrel, sharply. "I just remembered: there's an ancient Warrow legend that we are of the Giants."

"Ar, few would say they believe that hoary tale," said Tuck. "I mean, how could the smallest of Folk come forth from the largest?"

Gildor answered Tuck's question with a question of his own: "Who knows the way of Adon?" The Elf paused, then said: "Have I not said there seems to be in you something of each of the High Folk, even the Utruni? Mayhap that is why you see farther than Elves in this Shadow-light, for Utruni eyes are strange, too."

"And you say that we have eyes like theirs?" Patrel asked. "Gemstone eyes?"

"Nay, Captain Patrel, I say only that the hue of your eyes resembles theirs," answered Gildor. "The clear eyes of the Waerlinga are emerald green, or golden amber, or sapphire blue—three bright colors only, as you well know. Utruni eyes have many more hues, and seem to be the actual gemstones they resemble; moreover, they see by a different light than we, for it is told that they can peer a distance through solid stone, and that we are but insubstantial shadows to them. How they came to notice us in the Great War against Gyphon, only Adon knows, though fragments of lost legends have it that here, too, Waerlinga played some unknown but key role in gaining their aid."

"Are they as tall as I've heard?" asked Tuck.

"I know not what you have heard, but twelve to seventeen feet the grown ones reach in height," responded Gildor. "Yet wait, we could speak many days upon these strange Folk, and perhaps a time will come when we can talk at length about the Stone Giants, but now we must lay that aside and wrench our talk back to this War.

"King Aurion, I think we must turn the far-seeing eyes of the Wee Folk to our good. We know not how distant the eyes of the enemy forces can peer through this darkness sent by Modru, yet if the Waerlinga can see farther than the foe, then that will give us great vantage: advantage to set our forces beyond their vision and watch them come into our traps. Then we may strike swiftly and with deadly force, falling upon them out of the cover of their own dark myrk."

King Aurion struck a fist into his palm, and a fierce smile broke his frown. "Hail! At last a ray of hope. If you are right, Lord Gildor, if the Wee Folk can see farther than the eyes of the enemy, then they will prove to be the key to our tactics, for we shall place Waerling eyes throughout our forces and swoop down upon the Horde like hawks upon rabbits."

"*Hsst!*" Gildor suddenly held up a hand for silence, his head snapping up, and he listened intently. "A drum tolls." Swiftly Gildor drew sword from scabbard and held the weapon high, and *lo!* set within the blade was a rune-carved blood-red jewel, *and deep within the gem pulsed a ruby light!* "My sword Bale whispers that Evil comes," said the Elf, and he leapt to the wall and turned his head this way and that, trying to locate the drum sound. Tuck, too, as well as the others listened attentively, but they heard nought. "From the north it comes," said Gildor at last. Long moments fled, and all the while the faint glow grew within the scarlet jewel. Tuck knew that he looked upon one of the "special" Elven weapons forged long ago by the House of Aurinor. And the jewel-fire signalled that Evil came near, so they peered through the murk and listened, all eyes and ears.

"Hoy," breathed Patrel, "I hear it now."

So, too, did Aurion. And at last Tuck detected the faint pulse of a distant drum: *boom, boom, boom.* All about them on the walls, others, too, heard the regular throb: *boom, boom, boom.* Slowly, ever so slowly, the leaden pulse became louder. *Boom, boom, boom!* And Tuck's now-racing heart kept double time to the beat:*Boom! Boom! Boom!*

"So ho! Tuck!" A call from Finley sounded above the ominous pulse. "Look out beyond the hills!" *Boom! Boom!*

Tuck and Patrel peered intently to the north, and

Tuck's heart leapt to his throat, and his blood surged in his ears. *Boom! Boom! Doom!*

"What is it?" cried Aurion Redeye, his own sight unable to pierce the murk. "What see you?" Yet the Warrows did not immediately answer, waiting to be sure of their words ere speaking, and the beat of the drum came onward. *Boom! Doom! Doom!*

At last Patrel turned. "Modru's Horde," he said, his voice grim, a fell look in his viridian eyes. "Modru's Horde is come and their numbers are endless." *Doom! Boom! Doom!*

And out on the prairie vast arrays marched toward Challerain Keep, file after file emerging from the black Shadowlight, like a great flood of darkness pouring forth over the snowy plains, covering it with thousands upon thousands of Modru's ravers. Before them loped the evil black Vulgs, and within the ranks marched dark Rūcks and Hlōks. Upon Hèlsteeds amongst the Horde rode the corpse-white Ghûls. And they came to the pulse of a great War drum: *Doom! Doom! Doom!*

Into the foothills they came, flowing toward the Keep, and now Gildor's vision could see them, too, and his eyes glittered in the Shadowlight as he watched them pour forth, and now the ruby flame from Bale's blood-jewel flickered along the edge of the blade.

Doom! Doom! Doom!

King Aurion peered intently, and he struck the stone curtain in frustration. "Still I cannot see them. What are their numbers? The arrangement of their march? What kind of forces?"

Patrel spoke: "Thousands do I see. I cannot guess at their number, yet more come through the 'Dark behind. They are spread on a wide front, perhaps a mile or so. Most are what I take to be Rūcks, though among them stride the taller Hlōks, while one in a hundred are mounted Ghûls, and Vulgs range wide to fore and flank."

Aurion's face turned ashen to hear such dire figures, for his forces were meager compared to the Horde. "Is there aught else?"

"Nay, Sire," answered Patrel, "except that more march out from the 'Dark."

Doom! Boom! Doom! Boom!

The sound of drum was answered by a stirring call of Valonian horns, and Tuck looked down and saw the army of Challerain Keep march out to take up positions upon the hills below: pikemen to the fore with archers behind, foot soldiers with halberds and swords and axes came next, and mounted riders of Valon in back, with spears that would be couched for the charge through lanes when the enemy hove to.

"But Sire," protested Patrel, "they are too many and we too few to meet them in open battle. We have not one tenth their forces. It would be senseless sacrifice to set our handful 'gainst their Swarm."

"Pah!" grated Aurion. "Could I but see them, then would I know whether to strike hard or withdraw. Rather would I cleave into their ranks in fury than to fight like a cornered badger." He turned to Gildor.

"I think, Sire, that Captain Patrel is right," said the Elf as he sheathed burning Bale. But Aurion said nought in return, and Tuck's spirit wrenched in desperation as he watched the vast array inexorably march through the hills toward the King's forces. Yet Tuck, too, said nought, though his eyes brimmed with tears of distress.

Doom! Boom! Doom! Boom! Onward came the enemy. Vidron strode up the ramp and stood beside the King. At last the Horde hove into the range of Man-sight, and Aurion Redeye blenched to see the Swarm in all its numbers. With a groan, the High King signalled to Vidron, "Sound the withdrawal. They are too many to meet upon the field."

Vidron lifted his black-oxen horn to his lips, and an imperative call split the air: *Hahn, taa-roo! Hahn, taa-roo!* (Return! Return!) From the distant force below came a faint horn call. "Sire," rumbled Vidron, "Hagan questions the order."

Doom! Boom! Doom! Doom!

"Ah, Vidron, your Captains of Valon are brave, yet bravery alone is not enough to whelm that Horde. Only the numbers of mine own Host can even begin to challenge such a might, and they are yet far south." King Aurion looked weary. "We have no choice but to follow the War-council's plan to defend the walls."

Hahn, taa-roo! Hahn, taa-roo! demanded Vidron's black horn. Slowly the meager army of Challerain Keep withdrew, coming at last through the first wall, and the gates clanged shut behind.

Boom! Boom! Doom! Doom! Onward came the Horde, a dark flood. Now the sharp Warrow eyes could see that among the Hlōks were those who lashed at the Rūcks with whips of thongs, driving them forward if any lagged or strayed in the slightest.

Boom! Doom! Boom! Still the vast Horde poured forth out of the blackness, and among the ranks were carried standards bearing Modru's sigil—a burning ring, scarlet on black, the sign of the Sun-Death. And where the standards were, there, too, rode Ghûls upon Hèlsteeds, pacing the Swarm forth. And they came until they were just beyond bow shot from the first wall, nor could mangonels fling missiles to reach their ranks.

With a hideous, chilling howl, like that of a Vulg, a Ghûl in fore center flung up his hand, tulwar raised high, and so signalled all the Ghûls. A harsh blat of Rūcken horns sounded, discordant and grating, and the ranks of the Horde split, like a vast flood cleaving around a great rock, curving east and west and south again. Once more the chilling Ghûlen howl rent the air, and as if released from a duty, the Vulgs left the Rūcken Horde and raced away to the south. Swiftly they ran, as if following the wave of Dimmendark engulfing the Lands afar. At last their black shapes were lost to Warrow sight, and the beasts passed beyond seeing, leaving the Horde and Keep far behind. And still the Swarm curved 'round the mount, at last to come together on the far side, beringing the walls.

And then the great drum pulsed loudly: DOOM! DOOM! DOOM! and fell silent.

The Horde ground to a halt and stood facing Challerain Keep, and the only sound was that of a thin chill wind gnawing through the merlons on the ramparts of the besieged mountain city.

An hour passed, and then another, and still the Horde stood fast, facing the Keep. On the ramparts the King paced back and forth, like a caged lion, and he would stop for long moments to stare down at the silent foe and then resume his pacing. At last he called Vidron and Gildor unto him, and they spoke softly. After a moment he summoned Patrel.

Tuck, nearby, heard the King's words: "Captain Patrel, we must have sharp Waerling sight throughout the ranks of my forces, for only the strange jewel-eyes of your Folk have the vision to see afar through this myrk. And though it means a separation of kith from kith, friend from friend, and like from like, still I must ask that Waerlinga be at the right hand of as many of my Captains as are your numbers, save this: I would that you and your two Lieutenants remain with me and join my War-council, for I deem it will take all three of you to be our far-seeing eyes throughout the long days ahead."

Thus it was that the Warrow Company of the King was dispersed among the armies of Challerain Keep, and Tuck, Danner, and Patrel joined the War-council of the High King. Yet, as had been foreseen by the King himself, although the Wee Folk were honored by the special role given them by Aurion Redeye, still they were stricken by the sundering of their company. And Tuck was filled with the feeling that somehow he was abandoning the young buccen of his squad, or that he was being forsaken by them. Too, he felt guilty that he and Danner and Patrel would perhaps remain together while each of the other young buccen would be alone among strangers, the only consolation being that they were all still in Challerain Keep and would at times see one another.

Lord Gildor turned to Patrel. "Captain, if you will by my sharp-eyed comrade, then I'll teach you the harp while you show me the lute." Patrel's features split in a wide grin, and he inclined his head, accepting the Elf's offer.

King Aurion cocked his eye toward Marshal Vidron, who said, "Sire, it would please me if Sir Danner would peer through the blackness at my side." At the King's nod, Vidron strode off toward the south rampart to find Danner.

Thus it was that to Tuck fell the honor of being the far-seeing eyes of the High King. "Come, Wee One, walk with me while I take Wildwind back to the stables; you can lead Lord Gildor's Fleetfoot," said Aurion, and he and Tuck strode down to the horses while Patrel and Gildor remained behind upon the ramparts.

"Sire," a herald came breathless unto the King, "Lord Gildor sends word: something is afoot along the eastern flank."

"Sir Tuck!" called the King, and the young buccan popped out of the stall where his grey pony was stabled, a curry comb in his hand. "Swift, to the east wall we go," barked Aurion, and Tuck spun and set aside the comb while snatching up his cloak. Legs churning, the Warrow had to run to catch the King, as Aurion strode rapidly out and across the courtyard. Up a ramp they went and to the mid-gorge of the east bulwark. There stood Gildor and Patrel, while Danner and Vidron came from the south.

"There," said Gildor, pointing.

Tuck looked, and a large force of Ghûls, Hlôks, and Rûcks could be seen to the east, marching southward. Far they were, just within Gildor's seeing, and no sound came unto the ramparts from their distant tramp. Like a sinister gliding shadow, they flowed through the werelight and across the land. All this Tuck described to Aurion while Vidron listened, for the force was beyond Man-sight.

Patrel said, "Sandy spotted them about an hour ago. Out of the north they came, and south they go, but where they march, I cannot say."

"Perhaps they march upon Weiunwood," said Danner. His fists were clenched.

"Or Stonehill." Aurion's voice was grim.

"Mayhap they have discovered that Arden Vale is an Elven strongholt," said Gildor, gripping the pommel of his long-knife. "Perhaps they will strike east for Talarin's hidden valley. Yet I think they would assault that gorge from the Grimwall. Aye, it's Weiunwood or Stonehill they march upon."

Yet wood, village, or valley, none knew where the force was bound; and Man, Elf, and Warrow stood as the buccen watched the distant Horde silently pass once more into the ominous 'Dark. And when none of the Warrows could any longer see it, Aurion sent heralds to call his War-council together. But as the King turned to go down into the castle, *Doom!* the mighty drum of the Horde sounded. *Doom!* Again came the pulse, and from the walls Tuck could see a great stir among the Rücken ranks. His heart leapt to his mouth, and swiftly he nocked an arrow to his bow, his eyes never leaving the enemy. *Doom!*

"Pah! They break for camp," growled Vidron after a moment, "and not to charge the walls below." The Kingsgeneral sheathed his sword, and for the first time Tuck noted that he as well as Patrel, Danner, and Sandy had put arrow to string. But each one there upon the castle wall had readied a weapon of some sort at the boom of the great beat. Swords and poniards slid with metallic sounds back into sheaths, including Gildor's Bale. As Tuck returned arrow to quiver, he wondered if the others felt as foolish as he did, for even had the enemy charged, the fighting would not have been up here at the fifth wall, but instead down at the first wall, nearly a thousand feet below. *Doom!*

"Come," said Aurion, "let us to council." Down from the rampart they went, and into the Keep where pages went before, holding lanterns to show the way, for the pallid Shadowlight of the Dimmendark stole not into the castle. The King led them to a room where a great table stood in the center of the floor with massive chairs around, and maps and charts hung upon the walls. This was the Warcouncil chambers, deep within the castle—but even here the slow beat of the Rūcken drum sounded, muffled and distant. *Doom!*

Other Men came: Hagan of Valon, young and strong and flaxen-haired; Medwyn of Pellar, grizzled and gnarled but with bright, alert eyes; Overn of Jugo, fat he was, with a great black beard and bushy eyebrows; Young Brill of Wellen, tall and slender, an air of detached inwardness, some said he was a berserker; and Gann of Riamon, taciturn and reserved, perhaps the best tactician there. A mixed lot they were, yet warriors all, and with Vidron and Gildor they formed the High King's Warcouncil at Challerain Keep. Into this company came Tuck, Danner, and Patrel, and Tuck felt as out of place among these soldiers as would a child in a council of elders. *Doom!* All took seats 'round the table, including the young buccen, who found that they had to sit upon the chair arms to see and be seen over the flat expanse.

King Aurion spoke: "Warriors, we have fallen upon dire times." *Doom!* "The enemy numbers ten times our strength, and they surround our position: we are besieged. Too, others of Modru's forces move south, and we are helpless to stop them. Would that I knew where mine own Host stands, or when they will come. Even now the Legion may be marching north, yet we know not, for Modru's curs waylay the messengers, and perhaps the muster has not yet begun. But no word has come from the south, and with the Horde 'round our walls, none shall come lest it be borne by the Host itself.

"When last we met we chose two plans, each based upon the strength of the enemy: in the first we would take to the field and set our force 'gainst Modru's; in the second we would defend these walls, and hold until the Legion arrives. Well now the enemy is come, and his numbers would seem to leave us little choice but to defend the ramparts, for we are be-ringed by a mighty Horde, and, mark me, they will attack." *Doom!*

"I have called you unto me to ask if there be aught we can do but wait for the enemy to strike. Has any seen some weakness in the Swarm we can turn to our vantage? Have we any option but to ward the walls of Challerain Keep? Advise me now, I listen."

No one spoke for long moments, and, reluctantly, Tuck stood in his chair and was recognized. "I am sorry, Sire, for being so stupid, but I have a ques-tion: Why has not the enemy attacked? For what do they wait?"

The King looked to Lord Gildor, who said, "We

know not the mind of the Enemy in Gron, nor the full disposition of his strength. Yet the Horde without surely awaits something." *Doom!* "I know not what, but something evil, of that you can be certain." Lord Gildor fell silent, and Tuck felt a chill in the very marrow of his bones.

"How long can we last? Food and drink, I mean," asked Patrel.

"Perhaps six months, no more," responded fat Overn, "if we can repulse them from the bulwarks."

"Won't that be difficult?" interrupted Danner. "I mean, our warriors will be spread thinly along the walls. It looks as if they could break through anywhere."

"Yes, Sir Danner, you are right," answered Medwyn of Pellar. "It will be difficult, especially on the lower walls. In fact, those ramparts we expect to fall." *Doom!*

"*What?*" burst out Patrel. "You *expect* them to fall?"

"Indeed," answered Medwyn, "for the lower walls stretch around the base of the mount and our numbers are too few to defend their great length against such a vast Horde. But the higher up the mount we come, the shorter it is around, and the less length we have to defend. Thus, as we fall back to successive ramparts, our strength effectively multiplies, for the primeter of our defense grows smaller. Think of it this way: but a few sturdy warriors are needed to hold a narrow way—such as a bridge or a pass—for no matter how great is the enemy army, they can come at the defenders only a few at a time. Hence, a squad may defy a legion, just as we will defy the Horde—though we may have to fall back unto the last wall itself to do so." *Doom!*

Again Tuck's blood ran chill, and his mind was filled with visions of hordes of ravers swarming up and over the castle walls. *Doom!*

"But, Sire, I do not comprehend," said Patrel. "You expect to fight losing battles upon the lower walls, ever retreating higher until at last we defend only the castle, where perhaps our perimeter will be constricted enough to withstand this awful Horde. And for how long? Six months at most, for then our provisions expire. Sire, perhaps I do not understand the plan aright, for it seems to me that we but put our heads into a noose fashioned by the enemy, and he will draw it tight until we strangle." *Doom!*

"Nay, Captain Patrel," answered Aurion, "you understand the plan perfectly, for that is *exactly* our strategy, our road to victory."

"What?" burst out Danner. He leapt to his feet, his face livid, and shook off Tuck's hand, which reached out to restrain him. "A road to victory, you say? A path to destruction, I call it. I say let us cleave into their ranks and engage them in battle. If we are to die, let it be in full attack and not while trapped like cornered rats!"

Young Brill's eyes flashed hotly, and so, too, did Hagan's and Vidron's. These warriors seemed to agree with Danner, for this strategy suited their bold natures.

But Gann of Riamon quietly held the floor: "And what, Sir Danner, will such a move gain?"

"Why . . . why . . ." spluttered Danner, "we'll take many of the maggot-folk down with us. Die we will,

but a mighty swatch we shall cleave among them."
Doom!

"And then what?" Gann's voice was coldly measured.

"Then what, you ask? Then what?" Danner ground his teeth in fury. "Nothing! That's what! Nothing! We'll be dead, but so will many of the enemy. Yet we will have died a warrior's death, and not that of a trapped animal."

"Precisely," said Gann, now standing, "and therein lies the flaw in your 'plan.' You would have us sally forth and do glorious battle with the Horde. Yet you yourself recognize that such a course leads but to Death's domain. Perhaps, though, we will be mighty and slay two or even three of them for each of us who falls. Yet, heed me: when we have all died your 'warrior's death'—each of us having taken our quota of the enemy down into the darkness with us—*there will still be a vast Horde left standing, a Horde now free to ravage southward,*" Gann's fist smashed to the table, "*crushing those in its path.*"
Doom!

Gann's eyes swept 'round the table, and it became clear to Tuck that the Man spoke to Vidron and Hagan and Young Brill as well as to Danner. "Attack? Nay, I say, for that path leads to a roving Horde free to savage the Land. Defend Challerain Keep? Aye, I say, for then we pin the Horde unto this place. And when the Host comes, 'tis the Spawn who will be trapped, and not we." Gann sat back down, and Danner's smoldering amber eyes refused to look into Gann's cold grey ones, for the Warrow could see the clear logic of the Man's argument. But still Danner seemed unwilling to accept Gann's strategy, for it went against his grain.

"Ah, Wee One," rumbled Hagan, his voice deep, "we in the War-council thought the Horde might be large, though we did not expect the vast number that came. We have argued this plan and others many times. I know how you feel, for I sense we are much alike in this, you and I. It galls the spirit to be ever on the defensive, ever in retreat. Attack! That is our solution to life's ills. Attack!"

Tuck was amazed at Hagan's keen insight into Danner's nature, for Tuck knew the Man was *right*. Danner *did* attack when faced with life's ills, be it fear, trouble, a different viewpoint, or any other adversity: when Danner was crossed, he attacked. Even when it led toward undesired ends, Danner still attacked. Why Tuck had not seen this about Danner before, he did not know, for it now seemed so obvious. It had taken two complete strangers— Gildor earlier and now Hagan—to show Tuck this truth about Danner's nature, and Tuck did not think that either one of them would ever know just how clear his sight had been.

Tuck's thoughts were wrenched back to the problem at hand as Vidron spoke: "Aye. Gann's words ring true, and his strategy seems sound, for without moving we stop this Horde here in a place of great strength. We hold the high ground, and our defenses are mighty. But there are these problems with the plan: First, we may not be able to hold the walls 'gainst this might. Second, even if we do hold, our own Legion may not come soon enough or in enough strength to defeat this Horde. Third and last, Modru may have other Swarms raving across the Land that are the equal of or greater than that which we face: a smaller one passed to the east, as you well know. Three things I have named, and if one or more of these three are true, then this strategy is not best, though it may be too late to do aught else."

"Fie!" snorted Medwyn, starting to rise, but Aurion Redeye held up a hand, and reluctantly the Man from Pellar sank back.

"Let us not again stir up that particular hornet's nest of plans and counterplans," said the King, "for we have been stung too many times by the barbs of argument from both sides. The balm of logic here does little good to soothe away the passion, for there are too many unknowns, and the best way is not clear.

"Instead, this I ask, for ye have all seen the numbers of our enemy, and they are mighty: Is there aught else we can do, now that we know what we face? Does another plan come to mind we have not already discarded?" The King slowly looked 'round the table, his eye resting upon each one there: Gildor, Vidron, Gann, Overn, Medwyn, Young Brill, Hagan, Patrel, Danner, and finally Tuck. Each shook his head no, and Tuck felt as if he had somehow failed when it came his turn to answer. *Doom!*

"Then this War-council is done." Aurion stood, but before leaving he turned to the Warrows. "Sir Tuck, move your belongings into my quarters, for I want you at my side should I need eyes to see through the Dimmendark. Captain Patrel, you'll stay in Lord Gildor's rooms, and Sir Danner, with Marshal Vidron. I return to the walls."

The three young buccen entered the barracks to find that they were the last to remove their things to other quarters. The hall was empty and silent, abandoned, somehow forlorn. Tuck scooped up his bedroll and pack and took a long look around, and no happy Warrow chatter fell upon his ears, nor did smiling young-buccen eyes look into his own. A great lonely feeling welled up through his being, and his sapphirine eyes brimmed with unlooked-for tears. Without speaking, he turned and trudged toward the barracks doors, and Danner and Patrel walked with him. And as the trio crossed the courtyard, they did not look back.

Tuck went alone to the King's quarters, bearing a lantern to light the way. He placed his belongings by a couch in the anteroom, selecting it as his sleeping cot. When he returned to the wall, Tuck found the King on the west end of the north rampart. Vidron and Danner were there, too, as well as Argo, now assigned to the Castle-ward company on duty. As Tuck came up the ramp he saw that all eyes were straining northward, and there was a stir of excitement.

"What's all the fuss?" Tuck asked, joining the others.

"Out there, Tuck, look," said Argo, pointing far to the northwest. "Nearly beyond seeing. I can't quite make it out. What is it?" *Doom!*

Tuck looked and at first saw nothing. He scanned intently, but still could see only the distant dark.

Just as he was about to say he saw nought, a flicker caught his eyes, and at the very limit of his sight he saw . . . motion, but just of what he could not tell.

"Catch it out of the corner of your eye," said Danner, trying an old night-vision trick.

"I don't know," said Tuck after long moments, looking both sidelong and direct. "Perhaps . . . horses. A force upon horses, running swiftly."

"See!" crowed Argo. "I told you! That's what I think they are, too, Tuck, but Danner says no."

"Nar, I only said that it was too far to say," growled Danner. "Besides, it could just as well be Hèlsteeds as horses."

"Well, whatever it is, it's gone, lost in the Dimmendark."

King Aurion, again frustrated at not being able to penetrate the murk, cried, *"Rach!"* and struck the stone curtain with the edge of his fist. Then he mastered his ire and turned to Argo and said, "Pass the word among your Folk: search the very limits of the darkness for this and other sign. Mayhap some Waerling will see what we could not, and then we will know whether it is for good or evil." *Doom!*

When Tuck crawled wearily into his bed in the King's antechamber, the great Rūcken drum continued its leaden toll *(Doom!)*, sounding the pulse of the waiting Horde—but what they waited for, Tuck could not say. His mind was awhirl with the day's events, and though exhausted, he did not see how he could sleep with the Keep surrounded by the enemy and a great drum throbbing. Yet in moments he was in deep slumber and did not awaken when at last Aurion passed through on his own weary way to bed. And all of that night Tuck's dreams were filled with fleeting glimpses of swift dark riders sliding in and out of distant shadows—but whether they were Men on horses or Ghûls upon Hèlsteeds, he could not tell. And somewhere a great heavy bell tolled a dreadful dirge: *Doom! Doom! Doom!*

Twice more before Tuck returned to the ramparts, movement was seen upon the edge of darkness at the very limit of Warrow vision—yet none could say what made it. These as well as other matters were brought to the attention of the King as he took his breakfast with Vidron, Gildor, and others of the War-council. Rage crossed the King's features when a messenger came bearing the news that the Rukha now plundered the barrow mounds along the north wall. "If, for nought else, they shall pay for this," he said grimly, and Tuck shuddered at the thought of the maggot-folk digging in the barrows and looting the tombs of dead Heroes and Nobles and of Othran the Seer.

To take his mind from the grave robbers, Tuck turned to Danner. "I dreamt last night of riders in the dark, but whether they were Men or Ghûls, I could not say."

"Ar, dreams didn't disturb me. I slept the sleep of the dead," answered Danner.

"I kept waking in the night," put in Patrel, "and, you know, every time I looked up, Gildor was sitting at his window seat, softly strumming his harp. When I asked, he said not to worry, that the sleep of Elves is 'different'—but just how, he did not say."

I wonder what he meant, 'different'?" Danner pondered, but before they could say on, it was time to go.

They rose and donned their outer winter garb and then strode through the halls and out upon the cobbles. When they came into the frigid air, Tuck was grateful for his snug eiderdown clothing, even though it hid his splendid silveron armor, for he thought that only a fool would exchange warmth for vanity.

As they went toward the ramparts, Danner said to Tuck, "I've been thinking about the pickle we're in. What it all boils down to is that the Horde still waits . . . for who or what, no one can say; and our own forces stand ready to defend the walls, falling back until we are trapped in this . . . stone tomb. I don't like it, Tuck, I don't like it at all, this waiting to be trapped. Instead, give me the freedom of the fens and fields and forests of the Seven Dells, and the Horde will rot before they conquer me there."

"I agree with you, Danner," said Tuck. "This waiting is awful. All we seem to do is wait, peering out over the enemy into the darkness beyond, rushing from this wall to that to see something—who knows what—flickering through the shadows, and all the while just waiting, waiting for the blow to fall. I feel thwarted, too, Danner, and trapped, and it's only been *one 'Darkday!* Lor, what are we going to do if they stand out there for weeks, or months? Go crackers, that's what. But let me point out one thing: we are not *waiting* to be trapped, we're *already* trapped. Now we have no choice but to follow Gann's strategy and hope it works. By staying here, we pin the Horde, too. And when the Host comes, the tables will be turned, for then it will be the Swarm who will be trapped."

"Only if the Host comes in enough force, and only if we can hold Challerain Keep," said Patrel. "As the King said, even his Host will be hard pressed to defeat this Horde. "And as Vidron pointed out, should the Keep fall, the Horde will be free to strike southward." *Doom!*

On they went, and Tuck noted that ashes and cinders had been spread upon the paths and up the ramps and along the battlement ways, for the hoarfrost and ice made the footing treacherous. The cold was bitter, and hoods were pulled up and cloaks drawn tightly about to fend off the icy clutch.

At last they looked down upon the Horde, and it was vast and mighty *(Doom!)* and beringed the mount. Again Tuck felt a bodeful dread as he once more saw the great array. Yet the enemy had moved neither forward nor aback since he had last seen them; instead, they waited. *Doom! Doom!*

"Arg! That infernal drum!" cried Danner, his voice filled with ire. "If nought else comes of this, I'd like to stuff that Rūck drummer inside his own instrument and pound it to a fare-thee-well."

They all burst out laughing at Danner's words, especially Vidron, who found the thought of a Rutch trapped in a drum being whaled by a Waeran hilarious.

Their humor was interrupted by a cry from Patrel: "Ai-oi! What's that? A fire. Something burns."

Far to the north, visible as yet but to Warrow eyes, a blaze burned. Even as they watched, the flames mounted upward and grew brighter, winging light through the Dimmendark. Higher leapt the fire. *Doom!*

"Look!" cried Tuck. "Around the blaze, riders race." Silhouetted by the flames, the Warrows could see a mounted force raging to and fro in battle, but who fought with whom, they could not say.

"Ai! Now I, too, see the fire," said Lord Gildor, "but not the riders." Bitterly the King and Vidron and other Men on the wall stared with their Mansight to the north, as if willing their vision to pierce the murk. Yet they saw nought but shadow.

"What size the force?" barked Aurion. "Men or Ghola?"

"I cannot tell," replied Patrel, "for only fleeting silhouettes do we see."

Higher leapt the flames, and brighter. "It burns tall, like a tower," said Danner, "a tower where none stood before."

"Hola!" cried Vidron. "Now I, too, see the blaze— yet faintly, as a far-off candle in a dark fog."

"Or a dying coal from the hearth," breathed Aurion, who now at last could dimly see the fire.

"Hsst!" shushed Gildor. "Hearken below."

The blatting sound of Rücken horn was mingled with the harsh calls of Ghûls, and there was a great stir among the Horde. Tuck could see Ghûls springing upon the backs of Hèlsteeds and riding to the horn blares, gathering into a milling swarm. And then with a hideous cry, they raced away to the north, toward the swirling blaze.

"They ride as if to defend something, or to intercept a foe," said Vidron. "What of the other riders, the ones at the fire?"

"Gone," answered Patrel. "They're gone." *Doom!*

And Tuck realized that Patrel was right. For nought did he see but a far-off blaze threading upward in the distant shadow, and no longer did the fleeting silhouettes race past the flames. Tuck looked up at the King, who seemed lost in thought. And even as the Warrow watched, a flicker of understanding seemed to pass over Aurion Redeye's features, and he smacked a fist into the palm of his hand, and a gloating *"Hai!"* burst forth. Yet what his thoughts were, he did not say, but instead turned his gaze once more unto the dim red glow.

Below and racing north rode the Ghûls through the Winternight. Swift they were, passing through the foothills toward the prairie, and ere long they had ridden beyond Warrow vision into the Dimmendark, streaking toward a distant fire that shone like a solitary beacon through the blotting murk. Still the Warriors watched, and the flames grew dimmer, but at last the silhouettes of the Ghûls could be seen as they arrived at the waning blaze. *Doom*!

"I can no longer see it," growled Vidron, and the King, too, gnarled, for the fire now was too dim for Man-sight to detect. Yet the Warrows and Lord Gildor continued to watch the light fail. At last the Elf turned away, and not long after, the Warrows, for even their gem-hued eyes could see the fire no more.

"Well," asked Patrel, "what do you think it was?"

"Perhaps—" Gildor started to speak, but then: *"Hsst!* Something comes." Once more the Elf's hearing proved sharper than that of Man or Warrow, for they heard nought. Again Gildor leapt upon the wall and listened intently, turning his head this way and that. "I cannot say what it is, yet I sense that it evil." *Doom!*

"There!" cried Danner, pointing. "Something looms in the dark."

"What is it?" Vidron's voice was grim. "What comes upon us?"

"Look there, in front!" cried Tuck. "Ogrus! They must be Ogrus!"

And out upon the plains came giant plodding Ogrus, hauling upon massive ropes. Behind them, on great creaking wheels turning upon protesting iron axles, they towed a mighty ram, and catapults, and giant siege towers.

"Ai!" cried Gildor upon hearing the news, "now we know what it is that the Horde awaits—the siege engines needed to assault the Keep. What an evil day this is." *Doom!*

King Aurion stared through the 'Dark, and though he now could hear the grinding wheels and turning axles, still he could see nought. "Sir Tuck, what see you now?"

"Teams of Ogrus still pull the engines toward us," answered Tuck. "In the fore is a great ram, and then three catapults come next. But behind are four . . . no, five tall towers, each high enough to o'ertop the walls. 'Round them all rides an escort of Ghûls." *Doom!*

The King's face was pale in the Shadowlight, yet the look in his eyes was more resolute than ever.

"Hey!" cried Danner. "That's what we must've seen burning out on the plains." At Tuck's blank look, Danner explained, exasperated that Tuck did not see it for himself. "The towers, Tuck, the towers. One of them must have been what we saw burning."

Then a puzzled expression came over Danner's face. "But who would burn the tower? Surely not the Ogrus, for they would not torch their own engine of destruction."

"Lord Galen!" burst out Tuck, the pieces of the puzzle suddenly coming clear.

"Aye," said Aurion Redeye, a look of fierce pride upon his features. " 'Twas my son Galen and his company who did that deed, striking from the cover of the Enemy in Gron's own foul darkness, turning Modru's own vile cover 'gainst his lackeys, then melting away into the shadows ere the foe could strike back."

"Then it must have been Lord Galen and his Men we saw silhouetted by the flames of the burning tower," said Tuck. "And, too, now I think that the glimpses we've had of distant riders slipping in and out of shadow at the limit of our vision also were of Lord Galen's band."

"Just so." Gildor nodded, for he had sensed that the shapes seen afar only by the Warrows were not foe, yet he had said nought.

"I wonder how many towers they burned beyond our seeing?" asked Tuck.

"We know not, yet I would that it had been five more," answered Patrel, inclining his head toward the five great towers creaking toward the keep.

The King called heralds to him and said, "The machines of the Enemy have come, and now his minions will assault the walls of the Keep. Go forth unto all of the companies and have them make ready their final preparations, for the Horde will not long wait." And as the messengers sped away, Aurion Redeye turned to the Warrows. "I am told you are archers without peer. Have you enough arrows for the coming days?" *Doom!*

"Sire," Captain Patrel answered, "many a bolt have we fletched, for the arrows of Men are too lengthy to suit our small bows—though we could use them in a pinch. Little else have we done both on watch and off, yet the numbers of the Horde are such as to make me wish we had ten times the quarrels."

"We simply shall have to make every one count," said Tuck, "for as my instructor, Old Barlow, would say, 'The arrow as strays might well'er been throwed away.'"

"Hmm," mused Gildor, "your instructor had the right of it."

"Sire!" exclaimed Vidron. "Look! Now I see them come from the darkness."

At last the siege engines lumbered into the view of Man, and Marshal Vidron shook his head in rue, for they were mighty, and cunningly wrought to protect those using them. Forward they creaked, axles squealing—ram, towers, catapults.

"Ai! What a vile bane is that ram!" cried Gildor, pointing at the great batter. Now they could see that it had a mighty iron head, shaped like a clenched fist, mounted on the end of a massive wooden beam. "It is called Whelm, and dark was the day it rent through the very gates of Lost Duellin. I had thought it destroyed in the Great War, but now it seems that evil tokens have come upon us again." *Doom!*

Though Gildor seemed dismayed by the ram, it was the siege towers that frightened Tuck. Tall they were, and massive, clad with brass and iron. He did not see how Lord Galen's company could have set one afire. Yet inside was wood: platforms, a frame with stairs mounting up, ramps set to fall upon the besieged battlements—bridges for the foe to swarm across.

" 'Tis well that this castle is made of stone," said Vidron, "but I fear that the catapults will prove the undoing of the city below, for they are terrible machines and will fling fire. Much will burn to the ground." *Doom!*

Vidron's words made Tuck realize that they each had looked upon a different engine as being most dire: ram, tower, and trebuchet. Tuck wondered if Man, Elf, and Warrow—or other Folk for that matter—always viewed the selfsame scene through the eyes of their own People; or did each person instead see things through his own eyes? Tuck could not say, for he knew that individual Warrows saw a given event differently, yet he also suspected that each type of Folk shared a view common among their kind.

Slowly, the siege towers and catapults were drawn by the mighty Ogrus to places spaced 'round the mount, while the great ram, Whelm, was aimed at the north gate. The sound of the Rūcken drum pounded forth *(Doom! Boom! Doom!)* and the ranks of the Horde readied weapons: for the most part, cudgels and War-hammers and crescent scythes and great long dirks were brandished by the Rūcks. The Hlōks held flails and curved scimitars, wicked and sharp. The Ghûls, upon Hèlsteeds, couched barbed spears or bore fell tulwars. And great Troll Warbars were clutched in the massive hands of the Ogrus.

Yet the Horde did not attack. Instead, a blat of horns sounded, and a Ghûl and one other rode forth upon Hèlsteeds, while at their side loped a Rūck bearing the Sun-Death standard. Toward the north gate they paced.

"They come to parley," said Lord Gildor.

"Then I shall go forth to meet them," responded Aurion, turning to the ramp.

"But, Sire, I must protest!" cried Vidron. "There are two upon 'Steeds. It is a trap to lure you forth."

Aurion looked to Gildor, who in turn gazed long out upon the field with his sharp sight. "One is no Ghûlk," he said at last, "and he bears no weapon."

"Then he is Modru's messenger and speaks for the Evil One," said Aurion, "and the Ghol is his escort."

"Sire, let me go in thy stead." Vidron dropped to one knee and held the hilt of his sword forth to the King. "If not that, then at thy side."

"Nay, Hrosmarshal," answered Aurion Redeye. "Put thy sword away, until it is needed defending these walls. This I must do for myself, for I have been pent here too long—and I would have words with Modru's puppet."

"But, Sire, I beg thee, take one of us." Vidron's hand swept wide, gesturing to all the warriors upon the rampart.

Aurion turned. "I shall need sharp eyes at my side: Sir Tuck, you shall bear my colors." And as Vidron looked on in dismay, the King strode down from the wall with a wee Warrow running behind, legs churning to keep the pace.

And thus it was that Tuckerby Underbank was chosen to accompany the King; and he rushed to the stable and saddled his grey pony and rode down with Aurion, the young buccan bearing the High

King's colors: a golden griffin rampant upon a scarlet field.

Down the mount they rode, passing through the gateways of the upper walls. To the north gate of the first wall they came at last, and King Aurion bade the Warrow to give over his bow and quiver of arrows to the gate guard—for standard bearers at parleys are honor-bound to carry no weapons, else treachery would be suspected.

A small side-postern was opened, and the two rode forth: Aurion upon grey Wildwind, prancing and curvetting, the horse's proud neck arched, hooves stepping high; and Tuck upon a small grey pony, plodding stolidly at the War-steed's side. And scarlet and gold flew from the staff held by the buccan. As they approached Modru's emissaries, Tuck's blood ran chill at the sight.

In the Rūck, Tuck saw what Gildor had described: a foe who was swart, skinny-armed, bandy-legged, with needle-teeth in a wide-gapped mouth, batwinged ears, yellow viperous eyes—a hand or three taller than Warrows. Though repelled by the Rūck, Tuck felt no fear, yet the Sun-Death standard planted in the frozen snow gave the buccan pause.

But it was the Ghûl that set the Warrow's heart to pounding: Corpse-white he was, with flat deadlooking ebon eyes. Like a wound, a red mouth slashed across his pallid face, and his pale hands had long grasping fingers. Tall he was, Man-height, but no Man was this malignant being, clothed in black and astride a horselike creature.

As to the Hèlsteeds, Tuck was prepared for the cloven hooves, but when the great rat-tails lashed about, the buccan saw that they were *scaled*; and the eyes of the beasts bore *slitted* pupils. Yet neither Tuck nor his grey pony nor even Wildwind was prepared for the foetid maisma that the creatures exuded, a foulness that made Tuck gag and caused his pony and Aurion's horse to shy and skit. Only the firm hands of Warrow and King kept their mounts from bolting.

Last, Tuck's eye settled upon the third emissary: a Man, dark, as if from Hyree or Kistan. Yet he was strange, for spittle drooled from the corner of his mouth and his features were vapid, empty-eyed and slack-jawed, holding no spark of intelligence.

All this Tuck saw as they approached Modru's trio, standing midway between the Horde and the north gate. The Warrow and the King drew up facing the foul emissaries. The Ghûl looked from one to the other, his dead black eyes briefly locking upon Tuck's gemlike sapphire-blue ones, and dread coursed through Tuck's veins. The Ghûl escort then turned to Modru's messenger, and in a dreadful voice, *Like the dead would sound*, thought Tuck, the Ghûl spoke a word in the harsh, slobbering, foul Slûk speech: *"Gulgok!"*

The vacant features of the swart Man's face *writhed*, a malignant look of utter Evil *filled* his eyes, and his lips twisted into a cruel mocking snarl. With a cry, Tuck threw up his hand, and the King turned pale, for a great malevolence lashed out at them. And Tuck shuddered to hear the voice that followed, for it sounded like the hissing of pit adders.

"Aurion Redeye. I had not expected you," the voice gloated, and the evil eyes turned to Tuck and glittered. "This is even sweeter, for you draw mine other enemies into the trap with you." And Tuck felt the hackles on his neck rise, and his grip upon the staff showed white knuckles.

The vile stare turned back to the King. "Look around you fool. With your feeble one eye see the might that has come to throw you down, and think not to oppose it. This great boon I offer you: lay down your arms, surrender now, and you shall be permitted to exist in slavery, serving me for the rest of your days. Think upon this with the wisdom you are reputed to have, for no second chance will be offered. But you must choose now, for time slips swiftly through your grasp. What will you have, slavery or death?" The sibilant voice fell silent, and scornful eyes leered from mocking face.

"Pah!" spat Aurion. "Say this to your vile Lord Modru: Aurion Redeye chooses freedom!"

A bone-chilling shriek of rage burst forth from the swart emissary, and malignant hatred blasted down upon Tuck like a vile living force. "Then, Redeye, you choose death!" screamed the voice, and the cruel mouth screeched a harsh command at the Ghûl and Rūck—"*Gluktu!*"—using the foul Slûk speech.

The Ghûl flung up a tulwar and spurred his Hèl-steed forward, while at the same time the Rūck tugged at his cloak, drew a bow from concealment, and fumbled at a black-shafted arrow to aim at the King.

"*Treachery!*" cried Tuck, clapping heels to his pony and riding at the Rūck, and out of the corner of his eye he saw King Aurion draw gleaming sword from scabbard and spur Wildwind forward. But then only the Rūck commanded Tuck's view, for the swart maggot had set his black arrow to string and was drawing aim upon the King, the barb dripping a vile ichor. Raising the standard, Tuck brought it crashing down upon the Rūck's head as the pony raced by, and the force of the blow was so great that the pole snapped in twain, leaving Tuck gripping a jagged shaft. The black arrow hissed wide of the mark as the Rūck fell dead—skull crushed, neck broken.

Tuck wheeled the pony around, and he heard and saw the clang of sword upon tulwar. And the Ghûl was skilled, for his blade slashed through Aurion's guard and skittered across the King's chain mail. But again, Tuck did not see more, for he rode his pony to come between the battling pair and the other emissary, placing himself in harm's way to fend off a charge by the third foe. Yet the Hèlsteed moved not, and Tuck looked up into the visage of this enemy, *but the eyes were vacant and the mouth slack and the face now void of wit.*

Clang! Chank! Sword and tulwar clashed. *Thunk!* The King's blade bit deeply, cleaving a great gash in the Ghûl, yet the foe did not bleed and fought on as if unwounded. *Ching! Thock!* Now the tulwar slashed across the King's forearm, and blood welled forth. *Chunk!* Again Aurion's sword rived, once more the Ghûl's flesh gaped, yet it was as if nought had happened.

"His mount!" cried Tuck, and Aurion's sword slashed through the throat of the Hèlsteed. Black gore spewed forth as the creature fell, flinging the Ghûl off. Tuck heard the snap of breaking bones, yet the Ghûl rose to his feet as if unharmed and slashed his tulwar up at Aurion, but the blow was caught by the King's blade. Now the Ghûl emitted a chilling howl, and like cries answered from the Horde. Hèlsteeds bearing Ghûls raced forth from the ranks. Tuck saw them hurtle out, and in desperation he clapped heels to his pony and charged at the Ghûl, couching the splintered flagstaff like a spear, as he had seen Igon do at practice. Forward raced the pony. With a hideous *Thuck!* the jagged shaft caught the Ghûl full in the back and punched through, the splintered end emerging from his chest, and the jolting impact hurled Tuck backward over the cantle and to the frozen ground as the pony ran on. Dazed, the Warrow could hear the King calling his name. He floundered to his feet, only to be jerked up off the ground and flung on his stomach in front of Aurion Redeye across Wildwind's withers.

Tuck could not catch his breath as the King's grey horse thundered for the north gate, and the pounding gallop caused Tuck to retch and lose his breakfast. Toward the portal they sped, with Ghûls in pursuit. But Wildwind was not to be headed, and he raced under a canopy of arrows shot from the walls at the pursuers. With howls of rage, the Ghûls sheered off the chase as Wildwind came to the side-postern and through, closely followed by Tuck's free-running pony.

"Killed 'em! Killed 'em both, he did!" cried Hogarth, the Gate Captain, a fierce grin splitting his face as he pulled Tuck from Wildwind's back and to the ground. But Tuck could not stand and fell forward to his knees, his arms clutched across his stomach, face down as he gasped for air. He found he was weeping. Aurion leapt down beside him.

"He's got the wind knocked out of him," said

Aurion. "Stand back." And the King held the Warrow by the shoulders as the Wee One gasped and wept, while the Kingsmen upon the wall roared a mighty cheer.

At last Tuck got control of his breathing, and soon the weeping stopped, too. And the King said in a low voice that only the Waerling could hear, "Sir Tuck, you must mount up the wall so that all may see you. Heroes are needed in these dark times to rally the spirits of all of us."

"But, Sire, I am no hero," Tuck said.

The King looked at the Warrow in astonishment. "No hero, you say? Fie! Whether or not you feel like a hero, you are one, and we need you. So come, mount up to the parapet with me."

And so, up the ramp and to the battlements above the north gate went the King and Warrow, and all the Men shouted great praise. Tuck looked forth upon the field. Of the third emissary there was no sight, but out upon the snow, near the carcass of the Hèlsteed, lay a skull-crushed Rück and a shaft-pierced Ghûl, slain by Tuck's own hand. Yet Tuck did not feel the pride that the shouting Men took in him; instead, a sickening horror filled his being. For although it is one thing to kill a snarling Vulg with arrow as he had done at Spindle Ford, it is quite another thing to slay beings that walk about upon two legs and wear clothes and speak a language. Too, it had been so utterly violent—smashing, crushing, jarring, stabbing. The sight of his victims brought only a bitter nausea upon him.

But another sight there upon the field overrode his horror and filled him with dread: *Oh, please let it not be an omen*, he thought, as there on the field, where the Rūck had planted it, stood the Sun-Death sigil of Modru, and below it, lying crumpled in the snow, was the broken scarlet-and-gold standard of Aurion.

Tuckerby shook his head to dispel the foreboding thoughts and realized that he was being spoken to.

"Lor! What a close chase," said Corby Platt, returning Tuck's bow and quiver to the Warrow hero. Corby was a young buccan formerly of Tuck's squad but now assigned to the north gate. And he gestured at the slain enemy. "That's two for the Bosky, Tuck, and one o' them was a *Ghûl!*"

"Wood through the heart," said Hogarth, "that's what slew the Ghol—impalement. And it's a good thing, too, for King Aurion had not the time to dismember it, for the other Ghola were riding hard upon you. Hoy! but it was a fine bit of lancery, Sir Tuck."

"It wasn't as if I *thought* to do it—to spear the Ghûl with wood, that is," said Tuck. "It's just that he was there and I had the shaft in my hand, and, well, it just *happened.*"

"Yet had you not acted, then it is we who would be crow bait, and not the other way around," said Aurion, placing a hand upon the shoulder of the Waerling. "You are a fine knight, Small One."

"But I was de-ponied!" exclaimed Tuck. "No knight am I."

"Ar, well," said Hogarth, "you just need to learn how to lean into your stirrups and clamp your thighs to your mount."

"No thank you! From now on I'll just stick to what I know." Tuck flourished his bow, and the Men upon the wall shouted another great cheer for the wee warrior. But this hail was cut short by the enemy: *Boom! Doom! Doom!* The great Rūcken drum took up a pounding beat, and harsh horns blatted.

"Sire, they move the trebuchets forward," called Hogarth.

"They begin the attack," said Aurion. "Signal our own catapults to prepare."

Rahn! Hogarth blew upon his oxen horn, and a signal flag was raised.

Out upon the field, Tuck could see the great Ogrus wheel forth one of the catapults. This one slowly approached the north gate. Word came from the east and west that the other two trebuchets were drawing toward the first wall, too. Behind came more Ogrus, towing waggons. As the Trolls hauled the great engine into position, a sense of dread came upon Tuck, for he knew by Vidron's words earlier that these were terrible weapons.

"Lor, look where they stop," breathed Hogarth.

"What is it?" cried Tuck, alarmed but not knowing why.

"Our mangonels have not that range," answered Hogarth, pointing up the mount toward the King's own catapults between the first and second walls. "We cannot return their fire, for we cannot reach them." *Doom! Boom! Doom! Doom!* The Rūcken drum pounded on.

Through the pulsing drum beats, a distant clatter of gears sounded, and the throwing arm of the catapult was hauled down and loaded with a black sphere from one of the waggons. A Rūck with a torch set fire to the missile, and at a cry from a Hlōk, *Thuk! Whoosh!* the arm flew up, hurling a flaring pitch-and-sulphur ball sputtering through the sky and over the wall, to smash and explode upon one of the buildings. Fire splashed outward, and smoke rose up into the air. Warriors rushed to quench the blaze, but another burning ball burst nearby, and flames raged. Again and again the blazing missiles burst upon the city, crashing down upon the tile roofs and wooden walls, and flaming liquid splashed and dripped. Soldiers rushed thither and yon, trying to extinguish the fires, to beat out the flames. But the burning sulphur and pitch clung tenaciously to the blazing wood and ran in rivers of fire beyond reach, spreading in swift strokes. And where quenched, flames would burst forth anew as fire ran back to spring up again.

Missile after missile crashed down to add to the fires, and raging flames grew and fed upon the shops and houses lining the streets, and swept across the town. Away to the south and west rose the smoke of other fires as the great trebuchet there flung its hideous cargo of holocaust upon that part of Challerain Keep. And the third catapult of the enemy hurled fire upon the eastern flank of the city. *Thwok! Thock!* The fuming balls hurled forth, sailing down to blast apart. *Thock! Thack!* Time and again the enemy catapults sounded, hurtling a fiery rain upon the open Keep. All around the mount the flames raged wildly, springing from building to building and street to street, the fires from the north racing toward those raging forth from east and west. Black smoke billowed up and sent warriors reeling and coughing. The heat choked off breath, for the very air seared the lungs, and many collapsed. The fallen were borne forth from the inferno by their exhausted comrades, yet others perished, trapped in the fire storm.

Hours passed, and still the siege engines of Modru hurled sputtering Death, the *thwok!* of the great arms now unheard in the roar of the flames. The answering shots of the King's mangonels fell short, and the Men on the wall wept and raged in frustration, for the city burned and they could do nought to save it. Unchecked, the missiles crashed, and red and orange columns of roaring flames cast writhing shadows out into the Dimmendark. The works of centuries of man's existence upon Mont Challerain fell victim to the ravening fire. And Tuck recalled Vidron's words; and now the Warrow knew that these indeed were terrible machines, for the ancient city of Challerain Keep was being razed to the ground.

And thus the city burned, the great engines casting holocaust nearly unto the fourth wall. When it became apparent to the King that nought could be done to quench the raging flames, he ordered that the fires be let to run their course unchecked, for the warriors must needs save themselves for the coming battle. And so for two 'Darkdays they watched the burning of much they held to be precious and wept to see such destruction. The Horde beyond the walls jeered in revelment and brandished their weapons, but they made no move to assault the battlements. They knew that the fires sapped at the strength and spirit of the Kingsmen, and they waited for the moment when the defenders' will would be at its lowest ebb. And all through the burning, and finally unto the time that black char and ashes and thin tendrils of acrid smoke were all that remained where once stood a proud city, the great drum knelled: *Doom!*

The sharp ring of swift steps upon polished stone jolted Tuck awake. A lanthorn-bearing warrior of the Kingsguard strode hard past the Warrow's couch and into the King's chamber. Muzzy with sleep, Tuck sat up and rubbed his eyes, wanting nothing more than to fall again into exhausted slumber. But what he heard next jarred him fully awake.

"Sire," the warrior's voice was grim, "they stir as if to attack!"

Quickly, Tuck donned the underpadding and then the silveron armor, and he slipped into his boots and down overclothing. As he flung on his Elven cloak and took up his bow and quiver, the King strode out, girting his sword and helming himself.

"Come!" commanded Aurion, and he paced away, following the warrior with the lanthorn, while Tuck ran behind, clapping his simple steel cap upon his own head.

In the stables, as Tuck saddled his pony, Danner and Patrel came with Vidron and Gildor, but there was not time to say other than "Good fortune!" Then the King and Tuck mounted and hurriedly clattered out and across the courtyard.

Down through the charred ruins they rode, and by the twisting route they took, Tuck's grey was as quick as Aurion's Wildwind. Unto the north gate of the first wall the King and Warrow came, riding amid soldiery running toward the bulwark. Whence came these warriors, where quartered, Tuck did not know, for most of the buildings had burned. Yet here they were, streaming to the defense of the first wall, as Captains among them cried out orders. Yet above the shouts Tuck heard the blare of Rūcken horn and the beat of enemy drum: *Doom! Doom!* The advance had begun.

Mounting up to the battlement, the King looked grimly out upon the swarming Horde, and Tuck caught his breath to see them seething forward: Slowly they came, a black tide surging through the pallid Shadowlight and over the land. In the fore the great Troll-drawn siege tower trundled toward the wall, the giant wheels creaking, the Ogrus beneath an ironclad fire shield. To the rear came the Ghûls, riding to and fro behind the files of the Swarm. In boiling ranks came the Rūcks and Hlōks, and to Tuck's unpracticed eye they looked to be without number, stretching beyond his view in a great arc that encircled the mount entire. But Tuck's sight was drawn directly ahead, where aimed square at the north gate came the clenched iron fist of the great ram, Whelm.

With trembling hands, Tuck fumbled among his arrows, ashamed that others might see his fright; yet if the High King or anyone else noticed aught, they did not speak of it.

"What lies beyond my vision?" asked Aurion, turning to Tuck.

The Warrow had to take a deep breath and let it out before he could speak. "Nothing, Sire, to the limit of my sight." And they turned to watch the advance.

Occasionally, lone arrows were loosed from the wall, gauging the Horde's range. At last a signal was given, and the mangonels of Challerain flung flaming missiles at the oncoming Swarm. The flaring trajectiles burst upon the ground before the advance, and great gouts of fire splattered and ran among the teeming Horde. Rūcks quailed back, but the snarling Hlōks amid them lashed with whips and drove them forward again.

Onward creaked the tower and great ram, now the targets of the King's catapults, yet the fire splashed without effect upon the brass and iron cladding. And forward they trundled.

With Tuck in his wake, Aurion Redeye strode up and down the battlement, saying words of encouragement to the defenders. As to the Warrows, scattered as they were among all of the King's companies, only a few were here along this part of the first wall. Yet to these Tuck said a few words of his own, wondering if they were as frightened as he, receiving grim smiles in return. *If Danner were here, he'd be yelling insults at the Rūcks,* thought Tuck, *and Patrel would know exactly what to tell the buccoes.* But those two Warrows had duties elsewhere, with Vidron and Gildor, repelling the attack east and west; hence Tuck alone was left with the task of bucking up the courage of the young buccen near the north gate.

Doom! Doom! Doom! Doom! Now the Horde was too close to the wall for the King's catapults to strike at them. Like maggots, the Swarm seethed and boiled onward, and scaling ladders were borne among them. Forward trundled the mighty ram, forward creaked the great tower. Now the massive Ogrus could be seen in all their awesome power, and Tuck caught his breath to look at them, for they were huge.

The King gave another signal, and hissing flights

of arrows were loosed, streaking down upon the enemy. Rūcks threw up shields to ward against the deadly shafts. Yet many found their marks, and Rūcks fell screaming. But the arrows pierced not the stone hides of the mighty Ogrus, and the tower and ram came on.

Now Rūcken horns blatted, and the Horde cried out with an endless wordless yell. They broke for the wall, and their own black-shafted arrows hissed among the defenders; Men fell, pierced through. At last the howling running Swarm reached the first wall. Scaling ladders were flung up and mounted, while rope-bearing grapnels chanked upon the crenels and Rūcks swarmed up. Shouting Men sprang forward to dislodge the ladders and hooks, braving arrows to cast them down. The great tower trundled forward, now almost to the wall, and the ram came unto the north gate. *Boom! Boom!* The iron fist was driven upon the portal, and the iron gates shuddered under its mighty blows. Burning oil was loosed through the machicolations above to splash down upon the Ogrus, but the fire shield fended the flaming liquid, splashing it aside. Calthrops, too, rained through the slots, yet Rūcks with besoms swept the dire spikes aside and Trolls stepped not upon them.

At last Tuck stood upon the weapons shelf, and through a crenel he took deadly aim, loosing bolt after bolt upon the enemy, driving the shafts down upon Rūcken archers; and he did not miss. *The arrow as strays might well'er been throwed away*: Old Barlo's words ran through Tuck's mind. And as he strung arrow and took aim and loosed each fatal quarrel, Tuck realized that he was deadly calm, his fright gone now that the waiting was over.

Finally the great tower came unto the wall, and a ramp thudded down upon the merlons. With hoarse shouts and grating snarls, swart Rūcks and Hlōks rushed upon it toward the battlements, swinging cudgels and scimitars, War-hammers and curved sickles. They were met by shouting Men with long pikes and gleaming swords, pole axes and brutal maces. Battle cries and oaths and death screams rent the air. Rūcks were slain and Hlōks, and Kingsmen, too, hurtling from the ramp and falling down the face of the bulwark. Here Aurion Redeye battled, his sword wreaking havoc among the enemy, raging fiercely, and no enemy had as yet set foot upon the stone of the wall.

Boom! Boom! whelmed ram upon gate, and Tuck's arrows hissed true. Suddenly the Warrow's eye was caught by a flicker of movement in the Dimmendark, and Tuck looked up to see a force of horsemen, twenty strong, riding at full gallop toward the wall. How they had gotten this close without Tuck seeing them, he did not know. Yet here they were and here they charged, and the horses were swift. Those in front raced after one upon a jet-black steed, and they bore clay pots tied with ropes, while in the rear sped others, carrying flaming torches. Toward the tower they streaked, and the Enemy knew not they came until they thundered past, whirling the vessels overhead. Unto the tower they clove, and the pots were hurled through the open back to smash within the siege frame, and a clinging dark liquid splashed upon the timbers and ran down the wooden walls. The riders that raced behind flung their burning brands after, and a great blaze *whooshed* up within the tower. Wildfire flared, and Tuck shouted with fierce joy, *"Hai warriors!"* Rūcks and Hlōks within screamed in the agony of a fiery death, and some leapt forth flaming and ran amok like living burning shrieking torches.

The Men on horses wheeled back through the ranks of the enemy, but many fell to the black-shafted Rūck barbs. Tuck rained bolt after bolt upon the foe, yet still the Rūcks slew the horsemen, and Tuck wept to see them fall. Yet ten or so broke free and raced toward the darkness, pursued by Ghûls upon Hèlsteeds. Then Tuck could no longer watch, for more scaling ladders thudded up against the wall. Enemy archers slew Men, and the great ram whelmed: *Boom! Boom!*

Tuck drew, aimed, and released, again and again, while Men struggled and cursed and used long poles to push away the ladders. Yet others hurled rocks and rained calthrops and fire and arrows down upon the Horde. And all the while the flames of the burning siege tower roared up into the darkling sky.

Yet the numbers of the Horde were many while those of the defenders were few, and here and there pockets of Rūcks and Hlōks o'ertopped the wall and fierce battles raged. And driven by the mighty Trolls, the great ram battered the gate: *Boom! Boom!* First one hinge shattered, and then another gave way under the juddering iron fist of Whelm. The outer gates began to buckle and sag, and word came from elsewhere that the foe was pouring over the rampart.

"Withdraw!" commanded the King, and the order echoed up and down the line. Tuck followed Aurion down the ramp, where they mounted and rode among the defenders streaming back to the second wall. And the battle plan of Challerain Keep moved toward the next stage.

As they went, Tuck looked back to see jeering Rūcks and Hlōks clamber upon the stone bulwark, and the gates at last shattered under the mighty impact of Whelm. And pallid Ghûls upon Hèlsteeds rode through before the dark tide of the Horde to claim this first battle. And the Sun-Death standard of Modru was raised upon the wall above the sundered north gate.

"Upon a black steed, you say?" The King stood on the second wall and watched as the siege tower continued to flame, a fierce grin upon his face.

"Yes, Sire," answered Tuck, fletching another arrow. "Swift he was and all the Men brave, and he led them upon a horse darker than night, the color of jet."

"Hai! You have named it well, for Jet it was: no horse is blacker." Aurion smote fist into palm. "Ah me, would that I had seen it myself. It would have done my heart good to have witnessed that brave dash. But I was at swords, hewing foes upon the tower's ramp."

"Who rides the black?" asked Tuck, sighting down another shaft, believing he now knew the King's answer but awaiting Aurion's confirmation.

" 'Tis Galen rides Jet." Pride washed over the King's features. "No warrior can fight better."

So that was Lord Galen, thought Tuck. *My Lady Laurelin's Lord Galen.* Tuck's hand strayed to the silver locket at his throat, and for long moments he sat lost in quiet thought.

"See now, they lift Whelm over the first wall."

The King's voice brought Tuck back to the present, and he stood and looked beyond the charred ruins of the lower city to see the massive Ogrus hauling upon thick ropes to raise the great ram over the first bulwark. The huge maul was too long to bring it through the twisting passageway of the north gate—or any other portal for that matter.

Tuck watched for a moment, then his eyes turned to the burning tower. "What about the other towers, Sire, will they be hauled across the wall, too?"

"Nay, Tuck, for they are too massive, even for the Troll Folk," answered the King. "And, too, the word has come that but one tower remains; all others are in flames, as is this one. They were set upon at one and the same time by Galen's band; my son divided his force to do so." Aurion's face turned grave. "They paid a high price to put them to the torch, for perhaps no more than forty Men escaped, all told, and even then they were pursued by Ghola. As to their fate, none here knows. Yet Galen is wily and will best them yet."

Tuck was glad to hear that the towers would no longer be a factor in the struggles to come, yet he fretted over the fate of the Men of Lord Galen. Tuck stepped down and again took up the shafts to work on, sitting with his back to the wall.

"You should rest now, Wee One," said Aurion, "for soon they will have Whelm reassembled and the battle for this wall will commence."

"Yes, Sire," answered Tuck, "but I must needs fletch a few more shafts first, for I spent nearly all my others, and, as I've said before, the arrows of Men are too long for Warrows, though in a pinch they would do."

As the King strode away, Tuck's fingers flew, and shaft after shaft was trimmed and fletched. Iron points were affixed, and the pile at his side grew. Back at the castle was a hoard of arrows feathered and tipped in past days by the Warrows. But Tuck knew that they would be needed later, and so he now made more. And he lost track of time in the crafting of bolts. Hence he did not know how long he had been working when he heard the distant *thwack!* of the enemy's trebuchet. Twice more it sounded, yet he did not look away from his work. But then he heard the anguished cries of Men, and at last he glanced up to see a grisly sight: the Rūcken Horde had decapitated the slain bodies of the fallen Men and dismembered them, and now the catapult flung the mutilated remains to rain down upon the defenders. *Thwack! Thwack!* Again and again the throwing arm of the great trebuchet swept upward, and weeping warriors stumbled through the char and ash of the burned city to gather up all that was left of their slain comrades, horribly disfigured, lidless eyes staring, lipless mouths grinning in the rictus of death.

Tuck turned his face to the stone wall and wept the hopeless tears of a lost child, and still the catapult threw.

"Stand ready; they come." Aurion's vocie was grim as the Horde swept through the burned ruins of the lower city and toward the second rampart. And the howl of Ghûls sounded, and then the wordless shout of Rūcks and Hlōks. Again Whelm creaked toward a gate—the north portal of the second wall—and again the King and Tuck stood where the ram came. Once more the Swarm drew within range of arrow, but the defenders withheld their shafts, for they knew that every shot had to count.

Slowly the iron ring of encircling foe squeezed shut, and finally the Rūcken forces charged, ululating cries bursting forth. From the crenellations arrows were loosed at last, and the black shafts of Rūcks answered. Scaling ladders slapped up against the wall, and grapnels bit the stone, and foe mounted up. Men shoved with poles and chopped with axes to send the scalers down, and Rūcks fell screaming to land with sodden thuds upon the frozen stony ground.

Boom! Boom! Mighty Whelm rammed upon the portal. A whoosh of burning oil gushed out under the gate, but the flaming liquid was shunted aside by a barrier of iron plates set in mud spread by Rūcks upon the cobbles before the ram for just this purpose. And the Ogrus drove the great iron fist again and again into the portal.

Here and there atop the wall Rūcks and Hlōks swarmed, and sword met scimitar, pike drove at spear, hammers and axes clashed, and the clangor of steel striking steel sounded among War-cries and oaths and grunts and gasps of fierce battle. The sound of Death screamed forth.

Grimly, Tuck loosed arrow after arrow, and where each bolt flew Rūck fell dead, pierced through. The number of those he had slain mounted; yet how many he slew, he did not know, for he had not counted. But he had not missed once, and now he had spent nearly sixty arrows—thirty-five at the first wall. But he did not stop to think of this, for if he had he would have been filled to gagging with sick horror. Instead, he nocked arrow, aimed, and loosed, nocked arrow, aimed, and loosed—time after time, with machinelike precision. By the count of his victims, Tuck was by far the most effective warrior upon his part of the wall, this tiny Warrow, but a hand or so more than half the height of Man. Yet had more of the Wee Folk been present than a mere forty scattered thinly upon the battlements, the outcome of the struggle at this wall might well have been different. But more were not there, and soon the dark Rūcken tide swept over this rampart, too, and through the shattered gate, and the defenders withdrew unto the third bulwark.

Exhausted, Tuck slumped against the castle wall. He was weary beyond measure, for he had not slept over a span of two 'Darkdays. Four times the defenders had battled the Horde, and each time the Enemy had won, for their numbers were too many and the Kingsforce too few. Four gates lay shattered behind them, four walls had been o'ertopped. Thousands of Rūcks had fallen, yet tens of thousands remained. Each battle had been fierce, the fighting more intense upon succeeding walls, for General Gann's strategy was correct: the higher up the mount they had come, the less perimeter there was to defend, and the more concentrated became the King's forces. Yet whether they could hold out, they knew not, for the Kingsmen now numbered less than three thousand, and they faced a Horde ten times their strength. And now that Swarm stood before the last wall, Whelm's iron fist aimed at the west gate, and the defenders inside girded for a final assault.

Tuck had caught a brief glimpse of Danner, and later Patrel, and he was glad to see they still lived, for twelve of the Wee Folk had fallen, and he knew not who yet survived. They smiled wanly at one another, their features pinched by fatigue, but then they were swept apart again as the tides of War demanded.

Again came the blat of horns, once more the *Doom!* of drum; now the dark Horde strode forward: the fifth assault began. Tuck leaned wearily upon the merlon and watched grimly as they came, the wheels of Whelm rumbling on the cobbles as mighty Trolls pressed forth this bane. As before, the tactics of the Horde did not vary: slowly they advanced until they came into arrow range, then the Ghûls voiced howling cries, and shouting Rûcks and Hlôks, bearing scaling ladders and grapnels, charged through a hail of arrows, and the ram bore upon the gate.

Again ladders thudded against stone, and the hooks bit upon merlons and crenels. The air was filled with hissing death as arrow after arrow *thocked!* into flesh, and Rûck and Man fell dead or wounded. Tuck moved slowly along the wall, seeking out enemy archers, for they threw death at long range, and Tuck could stay their hand.

Boom! Boom! Whelm smashed against the west gate, iron fist pounding for entry upon the great iron door. But this time the Men had set an Ogru trap: the cobbles before the gate had been soaked with oil, and it was now set ablaze. *Whoosh!* Fire erupted upward and black smoke billowed as flames raged up under the fire shield canopy. The Trolls ran forth roaring in pain, slapping at the fire clinging to their scales, Whelm forgotten. And many stepped upon the calthrop spikes and howled in great agony and could but barely limp thereafter. Great boulders were flung down from the gate towers and fell upon the Ogrus, slaying three of the twelve-foot-high monsters and breaking the bones of two others.

In fury, the Ghûls rode forth upon their Hèlsteeds and lashed at the Ogrus, and they drove the creatures back to haul Whelm forth from the blaze. But the fire upon the ram was too fierce, the massive wooden driver burned with raging flames, and the Trolls could not come near. The ram was abandoned; no more would Whelm's iron fist knock for entry in this strife.

Atop the walls desperate battle raged. Man, Hlōk, Warrow, Rūck, and Elf: all strove weapon to weapon and hand to hand, fighting to the death, slashing, kicking, stabbing, gouging, hacking, smashing, biting, piercing, hurling one another from the battlements. War-cries and screams alike rent the air, as well as unheeded shouts of warning. There, too, was the skirl of steel upon steel, and the crunch of sundered bone, and the chang of iron striking stone, and the chop of blade into meat. Yet Tuck heard nought of it. For him there was only the sound of arrow loosed upon target; he paid little heed to the sounds of War. Nor did he see Young Brill rage past, swinging wide his great sword, cleaving a mighty swath, slaying Rūcks by the score, the battle madness upon him.

And at last the Horde was hurled back! For the first time their swarming failed to take the walls! With harsh blats of Rūcken horns, the Swarm withdrew down and away from the fifth bulwark.

And the defenders slumped down upon the castle battlements, exhausted beyond telling with this "victory." King Aurion called for a tally, and it showed that fewer than a thousand Men survived, and many of these were wounded, and only nine-

teen Warrows yet lived. Unto the west battlement
the War-council was summoned. And among the
Council, too, few survivors remained: Vidron, Gildor, and Young Brill yet lived; Gann, Medwyn, Hagan, and Overn had all fallen. Danner lived and so,
too, did Patrel, though he was wounded in the hand.

"We cannot withstand the next assault," said Aurion. "They are too many and we too few. I ask for
guidance, though our hope is scant."

Vidron spoke what was in his heart: "Sire, we
cannot let you fall. Yet I deem there is but one
course to prevent such an end: we must burst through
Modru's ring of iron and leave the Keep behind.
Aye, we had hoped to hold this fortress and pin the
Horde here until the Host arrives, yet that hope has
gone aglimmering, swallowed by the darkness. But
though that plan has failed, there is yet a way to
slow the enemy's march south: we need but adopt
the tactics of Prince Galen: strike hard into a weakness and melt away into the shadow ere the enemy
can strike back. But first we must break free of this
trap ere we can bait the enemy."

Vidron fell silent and Aurion looked to his advi-
sors, and they nodded in agreement with Vidron's
words. The King turned back to his General. "Say
on, Fieldmarshal."

"This is what I think we must do: when next the
Horde begins to scale the walls, we must burst forth
from the west gate, cleaving through their ranks,
and hie down the mountain and out into the distant
shadow upon the far plains." Vidron looked into
each of their faces. "And this shall be the way of it:
there are enough horses within these walls to mount
the force needed for all of us to win through to the

west stables, where the Men on foot can secure steeds of their own. Then with horses for all we will fly into the enemy's own darkness."

"But, Hrosmarshal," objected Young Brill, "we are not certain that any of the coursers at the west stable yet live. The foul Rukha may have slain them all in malice."

"Nay, Brill," answered Vidron, "the Rutcha will not kill them in malice. *Zlye pozhiately koneny!* They are vile eaters of horseflesh! and would save the steeds for that evil glut." Vidron's eyes flashed in anger, for there is a special bond between the Men of Valon and their steeds, and the thought of Rutcha rending horses brought rage into Vidron's heart.

Gildor spoke: "Whether or no the steeds live or are slain, there is little to choose from in this matter. Either we defend these walls one last time and die in the effort, or we attempt to break through the ring of *Rûpt*. If the horses at the west stable survive and we reach them, then some of us will live on to fight again. If the steeds are slain or if we do not reach them, then again we will die fighting, but many of the *Spaunen* will fall, too." Gildor fell silent, and all eyes turned to the King.

Aurion Redeye searched the features of each one there. "These then are the fates before us: to die upon the walls, to die at empty stables, or to win free upon horses. Of these three, only one lets us continue against Modru, and that is the fate we will seek. *Maeg Adoni laenan strengthu to üre earms!*" (May Adon lend strength to our arms!) "Vidron, we will try your desperate plan."

Upon hearing these words, Tuck exhaled, discovering he had been holding his breath.

"Aye, it's a desperate plan, I know," answered Vidron, "but I see no other way to succeed. Upon the steeds stabled within these walls, those of us mounted must battle to hold back the Foul Folk, the Wrg, until all our comrades are horsed. Then we must fly, down the north slope through the sundered gates and away."

"Why the north slope?" asked Danner. "Why not down the south slope and straight away toward friendly Lands?"

"Because only the broken gates are certain to be open," answered Vidron. "The others may be closed and guarded. Yet you have given me pause to think more deeply. Should we get separated, we must choose a rendezvous. Where say you?"

"How about south to the Battle Downs?" offered Patrel. "Or even Stonehill."

"Aye!" agreed King Aurion. "Battle Downs first and then Stonehill, for that is the direction we must bear to gather allies."

"Wait a moment!" cried Tuck. "Warrows can't ride horses! But hold, our ponies are here in the castle stables, and they are swift—swifter than the maggot-folk on foot."

"But not swifter than Hèlsteeds," said Young Brill. "You'll have to ride horses, mounted behind warriors."

"Then you won't be able to fight," snapped Danner, "and neither will we."

"Let us at least ride our ponies down to the first wall," said Patrel. "Through the rubble they are as quick as horses. Then we will mount up behind Men on fleet steeds to be borne away when the fighting is done."

"Better still," said Aurion, "when we break out, it will be you, the Wee Folk, who race ahead and secure the stables while we stay the foe long enough for the Men on foot to come to you." The King looked about. "Is there aught else? Lord Gildor, you have spoken sagely but now seem troubled."

"Aye, King Aurion," said the Elf, "indeed I am troubled, but for nothing I can see, only for that which I feel. A dark foreboding casts a deep pall upon my spirit, yet I cannot say what this feeling augers. Only this: Beware, Aurion King, for past yon gate I sense a great Evil lurks, an Evil beyond the Horde at our door, and I deem it bodes ill for you."

A dread chill clutched at Tuck's heart upon hearing Gildor's words, for the Warrow, too, sensed that a fell fate awaited them. But except for a vague presentment, he could not pin down the cause of his unease.

"So be it," said Aurion. "Fortune now chooses our fate."

And so it was decided: Vidron's plan would be tried, for to do otherwise led only to death. The word was sent forth, and all the surviving defenders prepared for the escape, quietly withdrawing into the courtyard at the west gate. And as the forces of the King gathered, orders were passed among the ranks as the last-minute planning went on. Word was spread to " 'Ware the calthrops" and "Watch out for poisoned blades," as was other such advice, while they girded for the desperate chance.

All the horses in the castle stables had been bridled and saddled—perhaps a hundred steeds, no more—and warriors stood at their sides, Men of

Valon for the most part, said to be the best riders
in all the Realms. Other Men were afoot, filling the
courtyard, holding their weapons ready for the bold
charge. Among them came the Warrows, now but
nineteen strong, each of them leading a pony. Other
ponies wandered loose, mounts of slain young buccen, and they would run with the rest, adding to
the enemy's confusion.

Outside the gate Whelm still blazed, but the flames
that once raged upon the cobbles were now gone, for
the oil had burned away. Downslope the vast Horde
ringed the castle. Thus all stood for what seemed an
eternity—the grim-faced warriors of the King within,
the foul Rücken Horde of Modru without.

At last the raucous blare of horns could be heard,
as well as the *Doom!* of drum, and Men upon the
battlements signalled that the enemy advance had
begun. Warriors manned the west gate, ready to
throw wide the portal. Men mounted up into saddles, and spears were couched in stirrup cups, a
thicket of lances stirring to and fro. Now the horse
column stood ready with King Aurion and Hrosmarshal Vidron at the point, and Lord Gildor, with
Bale ablaze, just behind, Young Brill at his side. At
the very back sat the Warrows astride their ponies,
bows now strung with precious arrows, their quivers nearly empty. And Men upon foot fingered swords
and pikes, though a few here and there bore axes
and fewer yet held longbows. And all could hear
the knell of the great drum as the Horde came forth:
Doom! Doom! Doom!

Now came the howls of the Ghûls, followed by
the harsh yells of Rücks and Hlôks, and in his mind's
eye Tuck could see the dark Horde running toward

the walls. Black-shafted Rūcken arrows hissed through the air to shatter upon the stone merlons or to fly through the crenels atop the battlements. *Thock! Thud!* They heard the scaling ladders strike stone. *Clink! Chank!* Grapnels bit the castellations. Yet the King stayed his hand, watching the sentries in the gate towers. Tuck watched, too, waiting for the signal, and his heart was pounding. Crawling Rūcks swarmed up the ladder rungs and up the knotted ropes; swart fingers grasped over the lip of the battlements; and iron-helmed heads followed.

Now! At last the sign was given, and the sentries scrambled down as the gates were flung wide. And then with fierce cries the warriors swept forward, horses charging, spears lowered, ponies dashing after, Men sprinting and yelling, free ponies running madly in confusion. And as Tuck burst through the gate and past flaming Whelm, he looked to see startled Rūcken faces snarling, and then he was beyond them, his pony running full tilt downslope toward the distant stables.

Ahead of Tuck the column divided, horses wheeling right and left, curling back toward the flanks of the Men on foot. The Warrows charged straight ahead, galloping downhill, for it was their mission to secure the stables until those on foot arrived. Above the pounding sound of running ponies, Tuck could hear the enraged cries of the mounted Ghûls, but then his steed came again to a road, and he plunged along it and down the face of a craggy bluff, and all noise was drowned out but for the ring and clatter of hooves upon cobbles.

Below was another slope on which were the great western stables, and beyond them the land fell

sharply unto the fourth wall. Now they thundered
out and toward the stall barns and horse pens. As
they ran, Tuck threw a fleeting glance back over his
shoulder and saw that Men afoot were beginning
to come down the road behind, and atop the butte,
silhouetted against the Shadowlight sky, were the
guarding warriors on horseback, wheeling about to
meet the foe, some even now engaged in battle.
Amid them Tuck could see the flash of Gildor's
burning sword flaring red.

Tuck now looked ahead where lay the stables, and
young buccen clapped heels to pony flanks, dashing
cross-slope toward them. Some few horses could be
seen in the outer pens, but carcasses could be seen
there, too, and Tuck thought, *Oh, Lor, let there be
live horses in the stalls!*

To the low horse barns they came, hauling the
ponies up short and leaping to the snow. In pairs
and triplets the Warrows spread out, running silently among the stables, jewel-eyes alert, arrows
set to string, flitting through the Shadowlight to
mew doors blackly ajar.

Through a portal leapt Tuck, with Wilrow swift
upon his heels, dodging quickly around the door
frame and ducking into deep shadow, eyes scanning
darkened stalls, ready to slay lurking Spawn. Silence. Blackness. *Is nothing here?* Slowly they crept
down the aisle. *Blam! Blam!* Two thunderous sounds
shocked forth from the left, and Tuck's heart leapt
to his throat as he dropped to one knee, his bow
drawn to the full, arrow aimed into darkness where
surged a frightened horse. In its fear it had lashed
at the wall; now it backed into a corner and stood
trembling. The steed's eyes rolled white in terror,

and it heaved and snorted as if to blow its nostrils free of a dread odor. Slowly Tuck and Wilrow relaxed their aim and wondered at the creature's fear.

"Hst!" Wilrow motioned Tuck to him. He whispered, "There," and pointed into another stall. Tuck looked and then averted his eyes, for the sight was grisly—mangled remains of horse, scattered in sodden blood-soaked straw, with haunches rent from the carcass and gaping holes torn in the flesh, as if fangs and claws had ripped it asunder.

"Vidron was right," breathed Tuck to Wilrow. "This is Rūck work. They eat horseflesh. We must go on, and quickly. The Men will soon arrive."

Forward they pressed, passing down the row of stalls, some empty, most with frightened horses, and others reeking with the bloody carnage of mangled steeds partly consumed.

They had come nearly to the end of the barn when ahead they heard a hideous rending and tearing and a foul smacking of lips. And there, too, came a harsh laugh and the low sounds of grating words:

"Guk klur gog bleagh," came a guttural voice, speaking in the Slûk tongue, a foul speech common among the maggot-folk.

"Yar. Let them stupid grunts crack the High King's crib whilst we enjoys a bloody meal," came another voice, this one using a distorted form of the Common Tongue that Tuck could but barely recognize.

Again there was a rending sound and a smack of lips. Tuck and Wilrow slid forward to see two Rūcks hunkered down at the side of a slain horse, great gobbets of torn flesh clutched in their grasping hands, their blood-slathered faces buried in the dangling meat as they bit and chewed and gulped the raw flesh down their gullets, pausing only long enough to lap at the blood dripping from their fingers and running down their arms.

Th-thuun! Sssth-thok! Tuck's arrow struck the Rūck on the left, Wilrow's drove into the one on the right, and the maggot-folk were driven backwards, dead before they thudded into the wall and sprawled down lifeless.

As Wilrow stepped into the dark stall to make certain that the two were slain, a third Rūck leapt from behind a hay bin, where he had been squatting unseen. With a harsh cry he brought an iron cudgel smashing down upon Wilrow's helm, and the young buccan fell. Tuck shouted in rage and sprang forward and stabbed an arrow like a dagger into the Rūck's back. Spinning, the Rūck lashed out at Tuck, knocking the Warrow to the straw, and stepped forward snarling, cudgel raised; but then a look of surprise came upon his swart features, and he clawed at his back, trying to reach the shaft as he toppled dead at Tuck's side.

Tuck scrambled over to Wilrow's fallen form, but the young buccan was slain, too, killed by Rūck cudgel. And at that moment the Warrow heard the steps of running Men enter the stables and the shout of their voices. Sick at heart, Tuck closed Wilrow's golden eyes in final sleep and arranged his hands over his breast, and whispered, *"Thuna glath, Fral Wilrow"* (Go in peace, Friend Wilrow), speaking in the ancient Warrow Tongue. Then he stood and went to meet the Men, for the ruthless brunt of battle leaves no time to mourn the dead.

"Swift! Mount up! The King is hard-pressed!" Tuck heard a voice cry, and he ran through Men saddling and bridling horses and back outside unto his pony.

Tuck looked to the cobbled road along the face of the bluff. Halfway down, a fierce battle raged between the mounted Kingsmen and Ghûls upon Hèlsteed. As Tuck's sapphire eyes sought out the King, more Ghûls came to the top of the cliff and rode to the fray, while above on the lip, dark Rūcken forces hurled rocks upon the Men, and black-shafted arrows rained downward. Slowly the horsemen backed down, fighting for every inch yielded, and the King upon Wildwind was among the last to come. And the mêlée was furious, for they fought to the death; even as Tuck looked on, a Ghûl and Man, Hèlsteed and horse, locked in battle, plunged from the road and hurtled down. And boulders smashed among the Men from the cliffs above.

"Ya hoi! Ya hoi!" Tuck cried an ancient call to arms and sprang into the saddle and clapped his heels into his pony's flanks. As he raced back cross-slope he was joined by Danner and Patrel and other Warrows riding to the call.

They sped to the foot of the cliff and leapt to the snow. "The archers above!" cried Patrel. "The rock hurlers, too!" And the Warrows sped their deadly arrows toward the Rūcks upon the bluff above, taking careful aim, for the shot was a long one—eighty feet or more—and their shafts were few. Yet Patrel had directed their aim aright, for the black-shafted arrows and hurled rocks were taking a deadly toll among the Men, and Patrel knew that only the Warrows could slow the fatal rain from above.

Shaft after shaft hissed upward, and even at this distance they sped true. Rūcks quailed back from the cliff edge above the Men, and the fall of stone and arrow ebbed greatly. But snarling Hlōks lashed about with whips, and once more Rūcks came to the fore. They were joined by the Great Ogrus, who hurled huge boulders, and the deadly rain of rocks fell anew. Now the black arrows struck among the young buccen; some bolts found their marks, and Warrows fell. Tuck's arrows now were spent, but he scooped up the quiver of a slain comrade and sped six more quarrels into the enemy before these, too, were gone. He began plucking the black Rūck shafts from the earth, and these he winged into the foe. And then he was surrounded by thundering horses and yelling Men as those from the stables at last charged to the battle, and horns sounded their presence.

Now the Kingsmen upon the narrow cobbled road turned their steeds and sped down, for all the Men, the five hundred or so that yet survived, now were mounted, and the dash down the mount through the sundered gates could begin. Tuck sprang again into his saddle, and all the Warrows, now but twelve strong, sped their ponies to the north and down, down through a gauntlet of Rūcken archers; and four more of the Wee Folk were felled. Tuck and Danner and Patrel yet lived, and together past the gauntlet and through the broken north gate of the fourth wall and among the char and rubble of the burned city they ran along the steep twisting streets and down. And behind came the Men on horses, and in back of them thundered Ghûls on Hèlsteeds, overhauling riders from behind and felling them with spears and tulwars as Men turned to make a stand.

Veering down through the black spars of the burned ruin they dashed, through the third gate and the second, and ash flew up from the pounding hooves. Now they ran for the first gate, the last before they would be free upon the foothills and the plains beyond. Tuck thought, *Here we must mount up behind Men, for the ponies will not be swift enough once we leave the twisting path.* And then the north gate of the first wall hove into view, and Tuck gasped in dismay and hauled his pony up short; for there, massed upon Hèlsteeds, stood row upon row of leering Ghûls.

Now the King rode up and checked Wildwind's gallop, bringing the courser to a standstill. Even in his despair, Tuck was glad to see that the King yet lived. Then came Gildor and Vidron, and Young Brill, and three hundred more, and all clattered to a stop, the steeds blowing plumes of white breath into the cold air. And behind them the pursuing Ghûls harshly reined up and jeered in victory—for the Men were trapped.

At the gate, among the stark Ghûls, sat the vacant-eyed emissary upon a Hèlsteed. Now he was led forth by a pallid Ghûl to face the High King. Once again the messenger's face *writhed*, and then Evil stared out upon the assembly. Suddenly the jeers stopped, and Tuck heard Gildor gasp. The Elf spurred Fleetfoot to the fore, and then he raised Bale on high. Ruby fire blasted forth upon the blade, and the Ghûls quailed back from its light. Yet the emissary snarled a harsh command—*"Slath!"*—and now the lines held firm.

Then the ghastly pit-adder voice hissed forth and

carried over the ruins: "You were given a choice, Aurion Redeye, yet you spurned my mercy. You have sought to stand against me and win, but the prize you have earned is death!"

Young Brill began to shake, and spittle foamed upon his mouth, and his eyes rolled white, then wide, as the battle madness seized him; and with an inarticulate cry of rage he spurred his horse forward, springing down the slope toward the emissary.

"*Gluktu!*" cried the ghastly voice, and the Ghûl at the messenger's side drove his Hèlsteed up, and Ghûl and Man raced at one another, and the sound of horse hoof and cloven hoof rang out upon the cobble. And Young Brill lashed his great sword out and down with unmatched fury. Sparks flew as blade met helm, and he clove the Ghûl from crown to crotch; yet the Ghûl had struck, too, and his tulwar chopped through Young Brill's neck; and they both fell dead unto the stone.

It was if a dam had burst, for Men and Ghûls alike vented cries of rage and spurred forward at one another to come together in a mighty clash of arms, and Tuck's pony was swept forth in the charge. Yet even as he surged forward, Tuck heard Danner shout in hatred, and an arrow hissed through the air to strike the emissary full in the forehead, crashing into the Man's brain and hurling him backward over the saddle and onto the frozen ground. And then Tuck was borne away, and all about him battle swirled and cries of death and fury filled the air. Tuck was without weapons, and he tried to ride toward the gate, but Ghûls there barred the way and fought with the King's forces. Tulwars and sabers skirled upon one another, and meaty chops sounded as blade met flesh. Only Gildor's sword, Bale, seemed to have effect, for where it slashed Ghûls fell, spewing black blood. But the swords of Men hacked into the pallid flesh, and great gashes opened; yet they bled not, and the Ghûls fought on unaffected, felling Men.

Beheading! Wood through the heart! Fire! Silver blade! Tuck's mind raged. *These are the ways to kill Ghûls. Not simple sword wounds or knife cuts. We stand no chance if we cannot flee.* Again he pressed through the mêlée, but still the gate was barred . . . yet wait! The Ghûlen force was turning, as if to meet a new foe. It *was* a new threat! For bursting through the ranks warding the north gate and scattering them asunder came a force of men, thirty strong, shouting and casting oil and torches upon the enemy. Flames sprang up and Ghûls howled, Hèlsteeds bolted, afire. And leading the Men was a grey-clad warrior upon a jet-black steed: Lord Galen!

"Now!" he cried. "The way is open!" and wheeled the black to meet Ghûl tulwar with steel sword.

Tuck spurred his pony forward, ducking a sweep of enemy iron. Through the gate he dashed, others speeding behind.

Danner also galloped into the passage, but a wild-running Hèlsteed slammed into his mount, and the young buccan was hurled to the cobbles, his pony fleeing from the stench of the beast. The Warrow scrambled to his feet. He heard a cry—*"Danner!"*—and looked back to see Patrel bearing down upon him, leaning out to catch him up. Danner reached high and grasped Patrel's hand, the wounded one, and swung up behind him, and they thundered out beyond the gate. Then others poured through behind.

When Tuck emerged outside the walls his steed ran but a short way north before the battle again caught up and swirled about him. Back he was pressed, and then forth, and he looked and saw . . . "My King! My King!" Aurion was besieged on all sides by Ghûls and Hèlsteeds. Wildwind reared and lashed out, belling challenges. Gildor spurred Fleet-foot toward the fray, Red Bale felling foe before him as he went.

Tuck, too, attempted to ride to the King, though the Warrow had no weapon. Yet Aurion Redeye was swept away by the combat, and Tuck's pony was buffeted by horse and Hèlsteed alike, and cursing Men and howling Ghûls drove him aside and to the edge of a ravine. And ere he could spur to the King, one of the foul, white, corpse-people slashed at Tuck with whistling blade, missing the Warrow but chopping into the pony's neck. The steed stumbled forward and fell slain, pitching with Tuck down into the blackness of the steep-sided ravine. Tuck was thrown free of the dead pony as down they tumbled, hurtling into scrub and rock, snow slithering behind. Then he struck his head and all consciousness left him, and the shout of battle above him went unheard.

When Tuck came to, he did not know how long it had been since he had fallen, yet now there were no sounds of combat. Instead, he could hear the distant yammering of Rûcks, using the foul Slûk speech, coming along the ravine bottom, and from afar he could see the light of torches held high. He could hear another sound, too, nearer—hooves! *Ghûl!* he thought, floundering to his feet. *They search for survivors. Hide! I must hide!* Frantically his eyes sought concealment, yet nought did he see but the heap of his slain pony and his bow lying in the snow nearby. Snatching up the bow, he fled silently north along the ravine bottom, while behind came the sound of hooves and Rūcks.

Now the ravine narrowed and rose, and up Tuck ran, to come out into the Shadowlight. Around him were the rounded barrow mounds of Challerain Keep. He fled a short way among the grave mounds and came to a great tumbled ring of stone. *Orthran's Crypt!* his mind cried, and he ran to ring's center. There before him stood a low stone ruin; snow-laden brittle vines covered it. The door had been torn asunder and flung aside by plundering Rūcks. Inward Tuck fled, stumbling down three steps inside. There, in the center of a smooth marble floor, by the Shadowlight shining through the doorway, Tuck could see a tomb; it, too, had been defiled by the Foul Folk. The stone lid was cast off, and nearby urns and boxes had been smashed as if by War-hammer.

Outside, the sound of shouting Rūcks drew closer. Tuck's sapphirine eyes frantically searched the shadowed strewn rubble, but nought did he find to defend himself. *Yet wait! The tomb!* Quickly he stepped to the sarcophagus, sundered by the looters. The Shadowlight of the Dimmendark fell pale inward and illumed the bier. Lying in the dust of ages were the yellowed bones of the long-dead seer, smashed as if by Rūck cudgel, and vacant eyes stared from grinning skull into Tuck's own. Ancient remnants of sacerdotal raiments clung to the skeleton, and a plain but empty knife scabbard was girt at the waist. The fleshless arms were folded across ribs, as if in repose, but clutched in skeletal fingers were two weapons, one in each hand. Ceremonial they seemed, yet weapons naytheless: One was a Man's long-knife, gleaming and sharp though entombed ages agone, golden runes inlaid along silvery blade—unplundered by the defilers, for it was a blade of lost Atala and Rūcks could not abide its touch. But it was the other weapon that Tuck snatched to his bosom: an arrow, small and straight, dull red it was, and made of a strange light metal—yet it fit the Wee One's bow as if waiting ages to do so.

Now the shouting drew closer, and Tuck set shaft to string. *If they find me, at least one will die ere I do*. And Tuck slipped into the shadows behind the sarcophagus. There came a soft clatter of hooves, and the Shadowlight was blotted out as a form came through the entrance leading a steed. *Ghûl!* Tuck drew the metal shaft to the full, aiming at the dark figure, waiting for him to move into the spectral light, waiting to make certain of the shot.

Now the harsh voices grew loud as the Rūcks tramped past outside, and light flickered from the burning brands they bore, torches to search the darkness. Firelight guttered and shone into the crypt, and by its light Tuck centered his quivering aim, ready to loose hissing death into the shadows near the entrance. For there in the light Tuck could see a white hand gripping the hilt of a broken sword as the figure leaned forward to peer out at the passing Rūcks, and from his neck dangled a golden locket glittering in the receding torchlight, and behind him stood a jet-black steed.

CHAPTER 6

THE LONG PURSUIT

"Lord Galen!" gasped Tuck, and the Man spun and crouched, holding out his shattered sword before him like a knife. Tuck turned his aim aside and down, letting the tension from his bow. "Lord Galen," he breathed, "I am a friend."

Long moments fled, and outside the Rūcks tramped away, their sounds growing faint. At last the Man spoke: "Friend, you say, yet you are Rukh-height. Can you prove this no trick of the Evil One?"

"Trick!" hissed Tuck in ire. "I am Tuckerby Underbank, a Warrow of the Boskydells, and no Rūck!" spat the young buccan, stepping forward into the pale Shadowlight, his sapphire-jewelled eyes flashing in anger.

"A *Waerling!*" Galen lowered the shard of his sword at last. "Forgive me, Sir Tuckerby, but these are suspicious times."

Jet, too, wondered at this small tomb-mate, and he shifted his stance and lowered his head and snuffled at the Wee One and seemed satisfied with the young buccan in spite of Tuck's anger.

"Oh, Lor!" cried Tuck, his mood shifting like

quicksilver as he slumped to the floor, appalled.

"Sir Tuckerby, are you wounded?" The Prince swiftly knelt at the Warrow's side.

"Nay, Sire, not wounded," said the young buccan, a shaken look upon his face, his voice hushed, "but I just realized, I nearly shot you for a Ghûl."

"Ho, then, we are even," smiled Galen, "for I mistook you for a Rukh. Not the best of ways to start an acquaintance, I would say."

"Nay, Sire, not the best of ways." Tuck managed a weak grin, and then gestured at Jet. "Were it not for this black steed of yours, and the golden locket at your heart bearing a snippet of Laurelin's hair—"

"Laurelin!" Galen reached out and roughly grasped Tuck by the shoulders. "Is she safe?" The tension in Galen's voice fairly crackled the air.

Pain laced Tuck's voice as he spoke: "Sire, in the company of Prince Igon and Captain Jarriel and a mounted escort, she left the Keep bearing south in a waggon bound for Stonehill and beyond; that was one week agone, if my reckoning is right—one day ere the Dimmendark came upon Mont Challerain."

The Prince released Tuck's arms and stood, and the Warrow shrugged gingerly. "Forgive me, Sir Tuckerby," said Galen, wearily. "I meant no harm to you, and I have treated you rudely, yet this is the first word I've had of my love." Lord Galen extended his hand down, and Tuck took it and was raised to his feet. "I am fortunate to have met someone who could tell me of her," said Galen.

"Sire, more fortunate than you realize," answered Tuck, taking up his bow, "for had I not known your Lady, who told me of the locket you wear, and your sire, who spoke of your black horse, Jet, then surely you would have been pierced through with this arrow I found in yon bier." Tuck held out the bolt for Galen to see.

"Is that the only shaft you have?" asked the Prince. At Tuck's nod, Galen took up his shattered sword, blade snapped near the hilt. "Then we have not much to meet the foe with, you and I: a broken blade and a lone arrow."

"Nay, Lord Galen, there is another weapon here," said Tuck, stepping to the sarcophagus. "This bright edge." The young buccan drew forth the rune-marked blade from the long-dead grasp of Othran the Seer. In Tuck's hand it was long enough to be a Warrow's sword, but given over to Lord Galen, it became a Man's long-knife.

"Hai, but it has a sharp edge!" said Galen, testing it with his thumb. "These runes of power, I read them not, yet they look to be Atalain, the forgotten language of a drowned Realm. This, then, is an Atalar blade: these are renowned for their power to combat evil." He held the long-knife back out to Tuck.

"Nay, Lord Galen." Tuck refused to take it again. "Keep the blade, and take the sheath, too, that lies in the bier, for I know nothing of swords and would most likely end up cutting myself. This is my weapon, the bow. Besides, now we are each armed—though if I were given a choice, your steel would be longer and my quiver full."

Galen stepped to the shattered tomb and took up the plain scabbard at Othran's side. As the Prince girted himself, Tuck saw the resemblance Galen held to both Aurion, his sire, and Igon, his brother. In his middle twenties was Galen, with all the endurance and speed of youth matured into the fullness of strength. Tall he was, like his sire, six feet or an inch more. Dark brown was his hair, like that of Igon, and his eyes were steel-grey, too, though in the Shadowlight they seemed black. Grey quilted goose-down winter garments he wore, and his cloak was grey, too. A leather and steel helm was upon his head, and now a long-knife was at his waist. He tied his sword scabbard to Jet's saddle and turned to face Tuck and spoke: "Did you hear aught of plans where the Kingsmen gather?"

"The Battle Downs, and Stonehill after that," answered Tuck. A troubled frown came upon the Warrow's features. "Lord Galen, the King, is he safe? Did he win free? When last I saw him, he was beset. But I know nought of the battle's outcome, for I was thrown down into yon ravine."

The look upon Galen's face was grim to behold. "Sir Tuckerby, I know not the fate of my sire. We were sundered in the fight, and I saw him not again. Yet my heart is ever hopeful, though what I know bodes ill. They were too many, the Ghola. I was forced aside, and my sword was broken as it clove through Ghol helm. But ere I could take up another weapon, one from a slain hand, the remaining force of Men broke free; many were scattered, though most rode hard to the east. Yet my eyes saw not Wildwind, running with the King astride, though he could have been among the larger band. I turned Jet into the ravine, to wait until I, too, could ride away. But then the Rukha came searching, and I led Jet to the crypt, where now we stand. Yet as to my sire, I cannot say else."

Tuck's heart plummeted at this uncertain news.

"Though I have been the King's far-seeing eyes but a short while, I love him well, for although he is a great leader, in many ways he is like unto my own sire."

"Far-seeing eyes?" Galen's look was puzzled. "There is a tale here for the telling, yet you can speak of it as we ride south, for we must leave this place: Rukha abound, and may come again."

And so they peered out into the Shadowlight, and led Jet among the deserted barrow mounds. Mounting up, they rode forth quietly to the north and west, Warrow bestride horse behind the Man, armed with but a single arrow and a blade of Atala and nought else save their courage. In secret and by wending ways known unto Lord Galen, they slowly worked their way through the margins of the foothills and around Mont Challerain, turning west and finally south. Then, at last, away from the gutted, burned hulk of Challerain Keep they rode—Prince and Thornwalker—heading for the Battle Downs, leaving the sundered city behind.

"Hai, then, by my tally you with your small bow have slain seventy, eighty, or perhaps even more of the Yrm!" Lord Galen tilted his chair back from the table and gazed in wonder at his jewel-eyed companion. Flickering candlelight cast writhing shadows as Tuck mutely nodded, stricken by the very numbers. The Prince leaned forward and broke off another hunk of stale bread and ravenously bit into it.

They had ridden for hours, southward across the prairie, drifting westward, too, following alongside the Post Road. After reaching the plains, Tuck had ridden mounted before Galen, the Warrow's sharp sight ever on the alert for enemy movement. But they had seen no one, though Tuck once thought he had heard a distant cry above the hammer of Jet's hooves. Yet his searching eyes saw only rolling plains and dark thickets in the gloomy Shadowlight, and the call, if it was that, was not repeated as the black steed drove on. Swift was Jet, and strong, but even the best of coursers needs must rest and be fed and watered. At last they had come to an abandoned farmstead, and there they found grain and water and a stable with hay.

Tuck and Galen had entered the house. Small it was, with but two rooms—a kitchen and one other— and beds were in the loft above. Closing the shutters so that no light would shine out, they had lighted a candle and had found a scant store of food—stale bread, dried beans, a tin of tea, nought else. They had then kindled a small fire on the kitchen hearth and had set a pot of water to boil, from which tea had been brewed and the beans cooked. Now the travellers avidly consumed the meager meal as if it were a sumptuous banquet. And their talk was of the Winter War, as this struggle with Modru now was called.

"When Igon and I first came unto the Dimmendark, sent by Father to see what was this wall, we knew nought of what the darkness held. Outside it was a midsummer's day, and in the company of four Kingsmen we rode through the winds along the Black Wall and into the Shadowlight." Galen sopped up the last of his beans with a piece of bread. "Like riding into a winter night, it was, and snow lay upon the land and our eyes were filled with amaze. Back we rode into warm day, and Igon and I took the cloaks and jerkins and breeks from the Men of our escort, fairly stripping them bare ere we sent them home. Now, bundled against the cold, once more Igon and I pierced the Black Wall into the Winternight, this time determined to explore.

"Two 'Darkdays we rode within the black grasp and saw nought of any other living thing. But on the third 'Darkday, while riding through a twisting defile, we turned a corner, and there facing us stood a squad of startled Yrm. Without hesitation, Igon couched his lance and spitted a Rukh ere any could move even one step. Hai! But he will be a mighty warrior when he comes full into his years.

"It was a short fierce battle, Igon felling three Rukha in all, while I slew but one Rukh and one Lōkh. The other Yrm turned and ran, scrambling up the ravine walls and away; six or seven fled beyond our reach.

"Straightaway we rode to warn the King, for this was news of import: Rukha and Lōkha bestrode the land within the 'Dark. Not an hour after the battle, we came out through the Black Wall and the Sun rode high in the sky. Then we knew that in the Dimmendark, Adon's Ban ruled not, and the fell creatures of the night—Modru's minions—were free of the Covenant.

"Although my sire was ired at me for sending the Kingsmen back and taking Igon—'A mere lad!'—into what proved to be mortal danger, still the King was proud of what we had done and bade me to lead a force of warriors back into the Winternight to watch for sign of the gathering of Modru's Horde of old. A hundred Men came with me, yet Igon was not one of them, and bitter was his spirit, for he would ride at my side. Yet perhaps my sire was right in keeping him from the Dimmendark, for seventy of my Men had fallen ere the last battle with the Ghola at the Keep, and half or more of those remaining were slain in that final combat. And for what did all those who perished yield up their lives? Mayhap for nought, for Challerain Keep has fallen, and the Horde is now free to rave south." The Prince bitterly swirled the dregs of his drink in the bottom of his cup and then tossed the tea into the hearth, where it hissed and sputtered. "Ah me, but I am weary. Let us get some rest."

"You sleep, Lord Galen, I'll stand the first watch, for there is something I must do," said Tuck, taking his diary from his jerkin pocket.

"Ah, yes," Galen smiled, "the journal you spoke of. Perhaps some day I will ask you to scribe it into a Waerling history of the Winter War, some day when the fighting is done. But now, it's me for bed."

The Prince clambered up into the loft and fell asleep watching the Wee One's pencil slowly crawling through the candlelight and across a page in the diary, leaving a track of words behind it.

The next 'Darkday, south and west they pressed, taking with them the last of the bread and beans, as well as grain for Jet. Later they came upon another abandoned stead; this one was bestrewn with wreckage, as if a fight had occurred, and Tuck was reminded of the Vulg-shatter in Arlo and Willa Huggs' farmhouse along Two Fords Road in the Boskydells; it seemed so long ago, and yet it was just seven weeks past, when Hob and Tarpy were still alive, and Danner and Patrel, too. *Stop that!* Tuck angrily berated himself. *For all you know, Danner and Patrel yet live.*

In the wrack Galen found food—dried venison and some turnips.

Onward they rode for many hours, bearing ever south and west. Finally they stopped to camp in the lee of a thicket, huddled beside a small fire, its light shielded by brush.

Early after resuming their way, the margins of the Battle Downs hove first into Tuck's view and then into Galen's. And they rode alongside the hills, going upon the Post Road now as it swung to the west. Miles passed under Jet's hooves, and Man and Warrow often dismounted and walked to rest the steed, feeding him grain when they took their own meal, as was their practice.

They had ridden some six hours, covering nearly twenty miles, when they rounded the flank of a hill and Tuck saw shapes ahead.

"Lord Galen, something stands upon the road," he quietly said.

Galen reined Jet to a stop. "Say on, Sir Tuck."

"It moves not, and appears to be . . . a waggon." Tuck peered intently. "I see no team, nor Folk of any kind."

"Mount behind me, Tuck, for we may meet the foe." At the Prince's command, Tuck swung to the rear of the cantle, removing his bow from across his shoulders and leaning out to see. Galen flicked the reins, and Jet stepped forward, moving at a walk. "Remember, Tuck," said Galen, "we will fight or flee if there be enemy. If we fight, you will slip straight back and drop to the ground and use that deadly bow of yours where it will do the most good. But recall, we have but a long-knife and a single arrow between us; thus it may be best to run. If we flee, hang on tightly, for Jet will veer and leap as he flies o'er the 'scape."

Along the road they went; now more waggons came into view, as Jet rounded the curve of the hill. Now Tuck could see that they were in disarray, some on the road, some off, and all were abandoned; many were burnt while others lay upon their sides.

Now Galen, too, could see them, and his voice was grim. "It's a waggon train." Tuck's heart pounded loudly in his ears.

Closer they drew, and other shapes could be seen lying in the snow—horses, Men . . . dead, felled. Tuck gasped, "Lord Galen! There! A slain Hèl-steed!"

Galen spurred Jet to a canter and swiftly closed the distance. They came unto the first of the be-strewn and burned wains. Dismounting, they walked among the slain, hacked by blades, pierced by spears, and frost and rime covered all.

"Lord Galen." Tuck's voice was filled with anguish, and he stood by a spear-pierced warrior, dead eyes staring up through icy glaze, broken shaft pointing at the darkling sky. "Lord Galen, it is Captain Jarriel, and there lies your messenger, Haddon. Lord, this is the caravan of the Lady Laurelin!" And Tuck burst into tears.

Long they searched and much horror they saw as they moved up and down the grim train. Tuck's faltering steps carried him along in a benumbed state as he saw the savage slaughter that had occurred when the caravan had been overrun: Men were slain, and Women, too, as well as the oldsters; but worst of all were the children, some but babes in arms. Even the steeds were slaughtered, cut down in their very traces.

As to who had done the deed, there was no doubt, for Ghûls had been felled, as well as Hèlsteeds.

Yet neither the Lady Laurelin nor Prince Igon was found among the dead.

Galen had rearmed himself, taking up Jarriel's steel. And he filled Tuck's quiver with arrows found in one of the waggons. Now they stood at mid train, where a great track beat eastward through the snow.

"Five 'Darkdays agone," gritted Prince Galen, bale in his eyes, "and there lies their wake. East they fled from this butchery."

"But, Lord Galen," asked Tuck, "where is the Lady Laurelin, and Prince Igon?"

"I know not, Tuck," answered Galen, his eyes locked upon the Ghûlen track. "Igon may have won free with the Lady Laurelin and galloped south for Stonehill, for Rust is not among the slain steeds. Or they could, one or both, be captives of Modru's butchers." Galen struck a fist into palm and ground his teeth in rage. "Yet free or captive, the only trace lies there in the snow before us, and even though the trail is old we shall pursue these slayers. If they hold Laurelin or Igon, we will find a way to free them. And then there shall be another slaughter—only this time it will be the Ghola who fall."

Galen spun and headed for a waggon. "Come, Tuck, we must find provisions for a long pursuit, for they have a lead of five 'Darkdays upon us, and if they continue to run, the chase will be a lasting one." Galen wheeled and looked in the direction of the trail. "Yet we will follow these ravers, even unto Modru's Iron Tower if need be: this I swear as a Prince of the Realm!" Galen turned once more and made for the waggons.

Thus it was that in less than an hour the black horse thundered forth upon the eastward track of the Ghûls, saddlebags filled with grain for Jet and biscuits of crue waybread for Galen and Tuck. They bore no other food, for as Galen said, "We needs must make Jet's load a light one, for our chase may be long, and food such as venison or even beans carries more bulk and weight and less nourishment than these bland biscuits. Finding water for Jet will be our main concern, yet if we melt enough snow, then that, too, will be resolved."

East they went, following the swath in the snow made by the cloven hooves of many Hèlsteeds, the path curving to and fro among the Battle Downs but ever bearing eastward. Some hours Galen and Tuck rode, at times cantering, at times trotting, and occasionally walking, the Prince varying the gait of Jet but ever conserving the black steed's strength.

At last they stopped to camp in a sheltered dell. Jet was fed some grain as Tuck bolted down a crue biscuit. Although it tasted like nothing more than lightly seasoned flour, the Warrow's hunger disappeared, for as he said, "It certainly fills up the hollow spots."

"Fear not, Wee One, we'll not starve on this ration," said Galen, melting snow in a copper pan over the fire, chewing upon a biscuit of his own.

"In fact, we may thrive on the diet, but this food will swiftly grow wearisome upon our tongues."

Soon Galen bedded down as Tuck took the first watch. And as the buccan melted snow for Jet, he trimmed the Man-sized arrows down in length to suit his Warrow bow. And when Galen awoke to take his turn, he found Tuck scribing in his diary.

Again they went upon the eastward track, moving through the Shadowlight of the Dimmendark, Tuck's jewel-hued eyes scanning to their limits. Yet nought did he see but the bleak 'scape of Winternight, and onward they pressed. And though he did not remark upon it, Tuck knew that this 'Darkday was Year's End day; tomorrow would be Twelfth Yule, Merrilee's age-name birthday, the first day of a new year—and Mithgar was in chaos.

The next 'Darkday, Year's Start Day, a snow began to fall, and Galen raged at the darkling sky, for the Ghûlen track before them began to fade 'neath the new fall. Eastward they rode for many hours, and the snow swirled thickly. Now at last they could no longer see the Ghûlen wake, yet Lord Galen continued onward; but what track he followed or what sign he used to guide him east, Tuck did not know. Yet the young buccan sensed that eastward they went, for Warrows are wise in such matters.

Then before them, through the swirling snow, dark shapes loomed. *Trees! Thickly wooded!* "Lord Galen, a forest lies ahead," said Tuck, his voice muffled by his hood drawn tight.

"Aye, I see it," answered Galen, for in the thick

snow the Warrow's sight was no better than the Man's. "It is the Weiunwood, I deem."

Weiunwood! An ancient homeland of the Warrows. Settled before the Boskydells. Steaded in the last days of the *Wanderjahre*, near the end of the long journey of Homecoming. Weiunwood, a shaggy forest in the Wilderland north of Harth and south of Rian. Weiunwood, now stark in winter dress.

"Slip behind me, Tuck," said Galen, "for we know not what we may meet therein."

Into the barren woods they rode, and still the snow eddied down. Now Jet was slowed to a walk, picking his way through the trees. They came among a stand of ancient oaks and rode through into a glade. Across the open space they went, but ere they entered the oaks again:

"Chelga!" came a sharp cry, and Tuck was astounded, for it was a command in the ancient Warrow tongue and meant "stand still and speak your name."

"Ellil!" (Friend!) cried Tuck, and urgently whispered, "Stop Jet, Prince Galen, for we are under the eyes and arrows of my kindred." And the black horse was reined to a halt.

"Chelga!" came the command again, and Tuck slipped over the tail of the steed and to the ground. He stepped to the fore, casting back his hood, and called out, "I am Tuckerby Underbank, Thornwalker of the Boskydells, and my companion is Prince Galen, son of High King Aurion."

"Welladay now! Why didn't ye say so in the first place?" came the voice from on high, and Tuck looked up to see a golden-eyed young buccan step out along one of the great limbs of an oak. In one hand he bore a bow, string nocked with arrow. "From the Bosky, are ye now? And ye, my Laird, is yer sire Redeye himself?"

Tuck nodded and Galen laughed, the first merry sound Tuck had heard in many a day.

"Well, then, I am called Baskin, and I come from the Westglade, south of here," said the young buccan. "Where be ye bound?"

"Sir Baskin," answered Galen, "we are on the track of a large force of Ghola. East they fled from a slaughter of innocents, perhaps with a hostage or two. They would have passed through here perhaps five 'Darkdays agone. Have you seen aught?"

"Nay, Laird Galen," responded Baskin. "But five 'Darkdays past we were locked in great struggle with Modru's Spawn. Whipped 'em, too, we did now, striking hard and melting back, and they couldn't get their grips on us. Three 'Darkdays we fought—the Warrows of Weiunwood, the Men of Stonehill, and the Elves from Arden—and a fine Alliance it is, for now the Spawn march east, lickin' their wounds, passin' us by.

"Yet as to the ones ye're chasin', they could have come here and none may know the better for they could have passed through unseen. Perhaps they joined the struggle, though I'm sure I can't say." Baskin paused in thought. "But wait, if perchance someone spied them then they would have sent word to Captain Arbagon. When my relief comes in an hour or so then I'll take ye to my squad's camp and get ye a guide to haul ye to the Captain."

And so they waited while snow fell to earth from the Dimmendark sky above. And while Baskin stood guard, both Tuck and Galen sat with their backs to the great oak and dozed, for they were weary. An hour passed and then another, and at last Baskin's relief came riding a small brown pony. Wide were the Warrow's emerald-green eyes to see Tuck and Galen, and he was but barely introduced—Twillin was his name—before Baskin fetched his own hidden steed and led the strangers away.

"Aye, it's Captain Arbagon yer lookin' for, and he's to the east, followin' the progress of the nasty Spawn, makin' sure they're pullin' no tricks whilst they run away." The speaker was Lieutenant Pibb, leader of the squad assigned to keep watch in this area of the Weiunwood. "After ye've had yerselves a good rest, Baskin'll lead ye to him, and if anyone has reported sight of them that ye're after, then he'll have the word."

"Ye'll like Arbagon," said Baskin, "for a great buccan warrior is he. They call him Rūckslayer, now, for he slew many in battle. And once he even rode a horse to combat—one that was runnin' free, its own master felled. Arbagon got so mad, he got on that horse and rode it to the fight; and it was a real horse, too, and not a pony like Pudge there. Ah, ol' Arbagon must've been a terrible sight upon that great beastie."

Tuck looked at Jet tethered nearby and wondered how a small Warrow could ride in command of such a large creature.

With his stomach full of the first hot meal he'd had in more than a week, and with a Warrow squad standing guard close by, Tuck slept the sleep of the dead. Yet he did vaguely recall having a bodeful

dream, one filled with visions of pursuit and dread—
but whether he was chasing or being chased, he
could not say.

Sometime during the hours they slept, the snow
stopped. Yet the track of the Ghûls had long been
hopelessly lost, and when Tuck awakened, his spirit
was at a low ebb; for if Laurelin or Igon *had* been
captured, Tuck did not see how they could be found,
even with Arbagon's advice.

After breakfast, Baskin led them away through
the winter forest, following unmarked Weiunwood
trails. Tuck was again mounted before Galen upon
Jet, for Pibb's squad had no ponies to spare for
Tuck's use.

As they went they varied the pace of the steeds,
at times dismounting and walking, for the trek to
Arbagon's camp was a long one. During one of these
walks, Baskin told them of the Battle of Weiunwood, at times his voice chanting like that of a
skald's: "Three 'Darkdays we fought and had many
battles, the first one bein' where the Elves led the
Rûcks and the Hlôks headlong into a trap. Right
into the gorge they ran, and we hurled rocks and
boulders down upon them and set great logs to rolling, smashing them flat.

"But they were too many, and so we slipped away
into the forest, Warrows leading Men and Elves
alike. By the hidden pathways we went, brushing
the snow behind to hide our tracks except where
we wanted them to follow.

"In a great loop they chased us, to come runnin' out of the trees where they'd started. Oh, ye
should've heard them howl in rage.

"Back into the 'Wood they ran, right into another trap, can ye believe? This time we fought with sword and pike and arrow, and a great slaughter befell the Rūckish Spawn.

"Out we drove them screamin', runnin' for their safety, for they didn't know how to fight among the trees, how to use them for shields and wards.

"And that was the end of the first 'Darkday.

"Now they licked their wounds for hours, but then the Ghûls came. Oh they howled in anger, made my blood chill to hear it.

"Once more into the woods they came, this time creeping forward in caution. Before them we faded like smoke, drawing them into deadfalls and staked pits, flying arrows at them from hiding, felling at a distance. Still they came on as we drew back.

"And that was the end of the second 'Darkday.

"At last, toward the great oak maze we led them, and into it they walked unsuspecting. Now their great force divided as they became confused, wandering among this wood.

"Split, they were, into several factions, and we came upon them one at a time, slaying one group, then falling upon another, till they ran forth shrieking in terror.

"Now the Ghûls became enraged, and to the woods they thundered in wild fury, upon Hèlsteeds swift and dark. A hundred raced in among the trees, where Men with long pikes lay in hiding. Now the pikemen leapt up to their feet, the lances braced well upon the ground. It was too late for the Ghûls to turn, and into the great spears they rode full tilt, impaling themselves upon the wood. Elves with bright swords sprang among the fallen; snick snack, they cut them into pieces. A hundred Ghûls had charged in fury; less than thirty fled in fear.

"And that was the end of the third 'Darkday.

"Toward the east they withdrew, marching for the Signal Mountains, skirting the Weiunwood, passing us by.

"Hundreds upon hundreds we had felled, but we escaped not unscathed, for many of our brethren had fallen—Men, Elves, and Warrows alike. And whether or no we can fight like that again, I know it not, for the tally of our slain was considerable.

"Yet this I say: Evil Modru will think twice before comin' at the Weiunwood again, for it'll cost him dear to conquer these glades."

With that, Baskin leapt upon his pony, while Tuck and Galen remounted Jet, and through the woods once more they rode. And Tuck could not but marvel at the victory won by the Alliance of Weiunwood.

Baskin's steed, Pudge, was quick through the woods, and they covered nearly thirty miles before making camp. And all the time they rode they saw neither Warrow, Man, nor Elf, though Tuck felt that they were safe, as if well watched by the shaggy Weiunwood itself.

Early after breaking camp, they rode into the site of the Weiunwood Alliance. Men, Elves, and Warrows were there, and all looked curiously at Tuck and Galen upon Jet as the black horse followed Baskin's pony to camp's center.

Arbagon Fenner, buccan, Captain of the Warrows, was at the main fire. Small he was, three inches short of Tuck's height, sapphire-eyed, brown-haired.

When he learned of Lord Galen's identity, heralds were dispatched, and soon a rotund Man, Bockleman Brewster of Stonehill, arrived and knelt unto the Prince. Shortly thereafter came a tall Elf, Inarion by name, one of the Lian Guardians from Arden. These three—Arbagon, Bockleman, and Inarion—captained the Weiunwood Alliance.

"Well now, that's a bad piece of news that I never thought to hear," said Bockleman Brewster, wringing his hands in front as if wiping them upon the apron he customarily had worn as proprietor of the White Unicorn, the inn in Stonehill. "The Keep burnt and abandoned. What will Modru do next, I wonder?"

"Whatever it is, I'm thinkin' he'll steer clear of the Weiunwood, after the drubbin' we've dealt him." Arbagon stood up to his full three-foot three-inch height and fetched another cup of tea for Tuck.

"Be not certain of that, Small One," said Inarion, softly, "for we are a thorn in Modru's side that he will want to pluck forth once he can bring his full weight to bear upon us. We met but a tithe of his strength, and then it was all we could do to fend them aside." The Elf turned to Tuck. "Those we met in battle must have been but a splinter of the Horde that brought down the Keep."

"Perhaps you fought that distant force we saw from afar marching to the south," said Tuck, harking back to the first 'Darkday the Horde had come to Challerain Keep.

"Well, splinter or Horde, they'll not root us out of these deep woods," responded Arbagon, "no matter how many they send against us."

"But, Arb," objected Bockleman, "they won't have to come in and get us. Modru'll just starve us out. You can't grow crops in Winternight, and that's a fact. All he has to do is wait till our food runs out, and then we're done for."

"Ye may be right, Bockleman," answered Arbagon, "and ye may be wrong. But, thinkin' like Modru, what's the good of conquerin' Mithgar if ye don't bag a bunch o' slaves to do yer biddin'? And how can ye keep a crop o' slaves if ye don't raise a crop o' food to nourish their bodies? I say this: Modru has some trick up his sleeve to banish the cold once he's brought Mithgar to its knees. Then we'll have crops aplenty to sustain us in our fight."

Inarion shook his head and smiled at Galen. "The debate goes on, and neither knows the mind of the Evil One. Bockleman is right, I think, in that Modru will take vile glee in starving many of us, warrior and innocent alike. As long as his power holds icy Winternight o'er the Land, crops will not grow, for there will be no spring nor summer, and no autumn harvest. Yet I think canny Arbagon has a strong point upon his side, too: Modru must have some plan for bending us all unto his will and tormenting us in the endless years of slavery thereafter; and this he cannot do if there is nought to keep us alive."

"Ar, you're right as rain about one thing, Lord Inarion: none of us knows the mind of Modru," said Bockleman. Then he turned to the Warrow Captain. "Arb, we don't need to inflict ourselves on our visitors." Now Bockleman turned his gaze upon Prince Galen. "Baskin tells us you and Master Tuck ride on a quest, m'Lord."

"Yes, Squire Brewster," answered Galen. "We

follow a force of Ghola, perhaps one hundred strong. They butchered the folk of a waggon train upon the Post Road, on the north margins of the Battle Downs. The Ghola left the slaughter behind, their track beating east. This path in the snow we followed, but the storm of two 'Darkdays past has covered their wake, and we know not their destination. And my betrothed, Princess Laurelin, as well as my brother, Prince Igon, may be hostage of the ravers."

"Hostage?" Bockleman and Arbagon burst out together. Inarion shook his head in regret.

"Such a force did pass eastward," said the Elf, "on the first 'Darkday of battle with the *Spaunen.* We were just out on the plains, my company from Arden, horse-borne, ready to flee before the great force of *Rûpt,* to lure them into the trap we had set within the woods. From the west came the band of Ghûlka you name, to the east they went. Ah, but we did not think they may have had hostages among them, and so we did nought to stop them. Yet even as they went by, our plan was already in motion, and we were running south toward the forest, drawing the *Spaunen* behind." Inarion fell silent.

"Aye," continued Arbagon, "Warrow sentries elsewhere saw them, too. Our eyes followed them as they skirted east. When last we sighted them, five 'Darkdays past, they had swung a bit south as east they bore."

"What lies east and south?" asked Tuck. "What goal?"

Arbagon looked to Inarion, then said, "Many things: the Wilderness Hills, Drear Ford, Drearwood, Arden, all of Rhone, the Grimwall. *Pah!* I

name but a small part of where they could be bound.
Who knows their goal?"

Inarion pondered. "Drear Ford and Drearwood
beyond, I would say. It was a fell place before the
Purging. Perhaps they seek to make it a dread region
as of old."

Arbagon pointed to a trail between two great pines.
"Then that's the way to follow, for it runs through
these woods to the Signal Mountains, and beyond
them lies the open plain to Drear Ford on the River
Caire."

"Hoy!" Bockleman interrupted, "didn't the north
lookouts also tell of a lone rider on the same course,
a 'Darkday or so behind?"

"Man or Ghol?" Lord Galen's voice was tense.

"That I cannot say," answered Arbagon. "Ghûl
we thought, but Man it might have been."

Lord Galen turned to Tuck. "Sir Tuck, I must ride
on, and soon. It would be better for you to stay with
your kith in Weiunwood. Here you have food and
shelter and companions to aid you, a safe haven.
Whereas I ride after one hundred enemies, and—"

"Nay!" Tuck sprang to his feet, his denial vehe-
ment. "You cannot leave me behind, for I love Laurelin as a sister, and Igon as a brother. If they are
captive, then you will need my bow." Tears welled
in the young buccan's eyes. "Lord Galen, if you tell
me that Jet cannot bear my weight, then I will take
a pony and follow after. And if a pony I cannot have,
then I will run on foot. But afoot or on pony, I will
follow, even though I come days late. *Hlafor Galen,
tuon nid legan mi hinda!*" (Lord Galen, do not leave
me behind!) Tuck started to kneel to the Prince, but
Galen raised him up ere he could do so.

"Nay, Tuck," answered Galen, "Jet can bear thy weight as well as mine. That is not why I would have thee stay. Tuck, I follow a hundred Ghola, to who knows what end? It will be dangerous beyond compare, and I would not have thee fare 'gainst such ill odds."

"I remind you, Lord Galen," Tuck held his bow on high, his voice grim, "I have slain more than eighty Rūcks with this. Know you another warrior who can say the same?"

"Eighty?" Arbagon's jewel-blue eyes went wide with wonder, and Bockleman put his hand to his mouth in astonishment.

"And I thought I had done well to slay eight," breathed Arbagon.

"And I nine," added Bockleman.

"Hai, Warrior!" cried Inarion, leaping to his feet and flashing his sword on high, then bowing to Tuck to the wonder of those nearby in the camp. Inarion then turned to the Prince. "Lord Galen, you forget one thing: you *must* take Sir Tuck, for you will need sharp Warrow eyes for vantage o'er the foe."

Before Inarion could say on, there was a great hubbub from the south, and into the camp an Elf on horseback thundered, hauling the steed short. "Alor Inarion!" cried the rider from the back of the rearing horse. "The *Spaunen* turn! South of here they attack the Weiunwood along the east flank, from the Signal Mountains!"

Horns sounded, and Man, Warrow, and Elf alike sprang to their feet. Pikes were hefted, and bows and swords sprang to hand. Ponies and horses were mounted, and quickly the force gathered to sprint southward to meet the enemy's thrust.

Inarion came leading a grey steed. "Prince Galen, come with us to fight the foe, or stay till we return. Then I and others will join you on your quest."

"Nay, Lord Inarion," answered Galen, "we cannot spare the time to stay, nor can you spend warriors upon a quest to follow Ghola who may hold no hostages at all. You will need all the strength at your command to repulse this foe that besets you now. And even more are at Challerain Keep, and they will march south to join their foul brethren, perhaps to fall upon this strongholt. Nay, I'll not wait, nor should you send warriors to aid. There shall come a time when we will stand shoulder to shoulder 'gainst Modru, but this is not the day." Galen drew his sword from scabbard and raised it on high. *"Poeir bē in thyne earms"* (Power be in thine arms!)

Inarion briefly clasped Galen's forearm and then leapt into the grey's saddle, and the horse reared, pawing at the air. "Should you need help, strike for Arden," called the Elf Lord, and he wheeled the horse to join a mounted troop of Elvenkind.

Arbagon Fenner came near upon a pony, and Baskin, too, rode nigh. "Good fortune!" cried the Warrow Captain, and Bockleman Brewster upon a horse hefted a pike in salute.

Lord Inarion turned one last time to Galen and Tuck, and the Elf scribed a rune in the air and called out, *"Fian nath dairia!"* (May your path be ever straight!)

And then there was another call of horns, and the frozen earth shuddered as hooves thundered forth. In moments the camp stood empty of all but Galen and Tuck and Jet, the black horse tossing his head in his desire to ride with the others to combat, as receding horn calls echoed among the ancient trees. Soon even these distant sounds faded into silence.

At last Galen turned to Tuck. "Come, Wee One, east and south we go, with nought but slim hope that we will find the Gholen tracks again."

And so they mounted upon Jet, turning the black steed toward the far Drearwood, leaving behind the abandoned camp, silent now but for coals sputtering 'neath the quenching snow.

Hours they rode, passing among the hoary trees of eld Weiunwood, following the trail pointed out by Arbagon. At last the forest came to an end, and they rode into the chain of the ancient Signal Mountains, running south of Rian to Harth below, a range so timeworn by wind and water that it was but a set of lofty craggy hills. Atop the tallest of these tors were laid the beacon towers of old, now but tumbled ruins of stonework, remnants of a bygone era. From the towers had flared the balefires, signalling the march of War, back when Gyphon strove with Adon, four thousand years agone. Now, again, Mithgar was beset by an evil foe; indeed, Modru, the servant of Gyphon, once more harried a beleaguered world. But the beacon fires of old burned not: they did not signal the calamity now upon the Land. And even were the ancient fires kindled once again, the Dimmendark would muffle the call to muster, the black Shadowlight snuffing the warning cry ere it could be relayed on. Those thoughts Tuck scribed in his diary as he sat his watch by the small campblaze in the hills of the Signal Mountains.

Galen wakened Tuck to a bland breakfast of crue and water; now the Warrow knew what the Prince had meant when he had said that they would soon grow weary of the taste of the waybread. Still he ate it, thoughtfully chewing as he gazed through the Shadowlight at the flanks of the nearby tors. Jet, too, seemed tired of the unchanging grain of his diet, and Galen smiled at both of them.

"I know not which of you finds the taste of your food the more wearisome," said the Prince. "Yet it is all we'll see for many a day, and neither of you will have aught else to sustain you but this food and memories of sumptuous meals apast. So bite into your tasteless biscuit, Tuck, chew upon your constant grain, Jet, and dream of savory roasts and sweet clover."

Tuck growled, "Right now, I'd settle for the clover."

Lord Galen burst into broad laughter, and Tuck joined him. In a merry mood they broke camp and set forth upon their grim mission.

East they rode, veering south, coming through the Signal Mountains and out upon the snowy plains far north of the Wilderness Hills. All around them Shadowlight fell, and Tuck saw nought but bleak Winternight to the limits of his vision.

"Were Patrel here then we'd have a happy tune to help us on our way," said Tuck, and then his face darkened, a frown upon his features. "Oh, I do hope that he got away, and Danner, too, as well as the others from the Bosky. Not many of us made it to that last battle at the gate, you know —just eight—and I suspect that even fewer escaped."

"I cannot say that I saw any Wee Folk mounted behind any in the force that broke free, nor did I note others scattering to the four winds," said Galen. "But I was engaged in battle and had no time to look about."

"Oh, Lor! I don't think I could take it if I were the only one to survive." Tuck's eyes brimmed with tears, and neither he nor Galen spoke for many miles.

At last, they again made camp, this time in a coppice upon a rolling hilltop, some fifty miles from Drear Ford.

Once more they continued eastward, the land falling gently toward the valley of the River Caire. Long they rode, down the sloping land, and when at last they made camp, they had not reached the river banks, stopping some fifteen miles shy. Tuck was impatient to be there, but they needs must save Jet's strength, for they knew not how long the chase would last. As yet they had seen no sign of the Ghûlen track, but Lord Galen said, "If they were bound for Drear Ford, then that is where we'll find their wake, for I deem the snowfall covered their tracks to the river, and perhaps some beyond. In any case, even had they passed nearby, leaving tracks for all to see, still we know not which way to turn to find them, north or south. And so, it is at the ford where lies our best hope to find their spoor and take up the pursuit once more."

Three hours after breaking camp, Tuck's eyes espied the trees of the border woodland along the banks of the River Caire.

"Look for a break in the tree line," said Galen, "for there will lie Drear Ford."

Long Tuck scanned as Jet cantered forth. "There! Far to the left," he said at last, pointing.

Down the fall of the land they rode, and now Galen's eyes could see the woodland as they bore north. Tuck continued to search the limits of his seeing for signs of life, yet nought moved upon the land but the black horse and his riders.

Suddenly, Galen reined Jet to a halt and sprang to the ground and knelt upon one knee. Tuck looked and leapt down, too, for there in the snow was the track of a lone steed, runing in a line to the west and east.

"Pah! It is a track 'Darkdays old," said Galen, "so wind-worn that I cannot say whether it was made by horse or Hèlsteed, nor even whether it was ridden to the east or to the west, or if it was ridden at all. Were I to guess, I would deem it ran east, down toward the ford."

Tuck looked at the smooth shallow depressions and did not see how Galen chose east for the steed to be running.

Back upon Jet, they followed the track through the snow, coming at last to the ford. Here the approach to the river was low and gentle, but both upstream and down the banks fell steeply to the frozen river. Across the hard windswept surface went the black horse, hooves knelling upon the river ice, and Tuck could not help but remember the herald's steed at Spindle Ford, the slaying of the Vulg, and poor drowned Tarpy. And Tuck's heart thudded while Jet's hooves rang on the ice, a sense of relief washing over him when the horse reached the far shore.

Again Galen dismounted, gazing intently at the snow. The lone steed's track drifted leftward, east swinging slightly north. Long Galen looked, then grunted. "Here, Tuck, see the faint dimples in the snow? Widespread they are, and swing north, too. I think we see the track of the Ghola, and it was still snowing when they passed this way."

Again Jet paced forward, and every mile east the wake grew more pronounced. Now the lone steed's track they had followed could be pointed out no longer, for it was lost among the spoor of the others. Yet even though that trace was lost, Tuck's heart soared, for again they were on the track of the Ghûls.

"The trees of another forest lie ahead, Lord Galen," said Tuck, peering through the Dimmendark, "and the Ghûlen spoor runs into it."

"It is Drearwood, Tuck," answered Lord Galen. "We will camp there when we come to it."

Camp in Drearwood? Tuck felt a vague sense of foreboding at the thought of staying in this dread wood, for in days of old this dark-forested hill country was a region most dire. Hearthtales abounded of lone travellers or small bands who had passed into the dark woods never to be seen again. And stories came of large caravans and groups of armed warriors who had beaten off grim monsters half seen in the night, and many had lost their lives to the grisly creatures. This Land had been shunned by all except those who had no choice but to cross it, or by those adventurers who sought fame, most of whom did not live to grasp their glory. Yet seventy years past there had been the Great Purging of the 'Wood by the Lian Guardians, and no fell creatures had been seen in the area since. But now that the Shadowlight pressed darkly upon the Land, Tuck wondered if Modru had caused the dire monsters to return.

Now they came among the trees, and Galen stopped to camp. All that night during Tuck's watch, the slightest sound caused him to jerk up from his diary and peer this way and that for sign of danger. But in spite of his foreboding, when it came his turn to sleep, he immediately fell into a deep, dreamless slumber.

It seemed to Tuck that he had no more than put his head down ere the Prince was shaking him by the shoulder.

"Come, Tuck, we must away," said Galen, fetching the Warrow a biscuit and handing him one of the leathern water bottles.

Stumpily, his joints creaking, Tuck hunkered down by the fire and ate his crue while watching Jet at his grain. "Hmph!" grunted the buccan, "not enough warmth, drink, food, or rest. And we are surrounded on all sides by a wood reputed to be full of monsters." Then his mouth turned up in a wry smile. "Ah, but this is the life, eh Jet?"

The black horse rolled his eyes at the Warrow and tossed his head, and Tuck and Galen burst out in laughter. And while Tuck bundled the blankets and quenched the campfire with snow, Galen removed Jet's feed-bag and saddled the steed. The blanket rolls were tied behind the cantle, and then the warriors mounted up, and once more the long chase resumed.

Into Drearwood the track led, and among the dark trees went the three—Warrow, Man, and horse. Tuck now rode behind the Prince, for here the buccan's sight was no better than Galen's, and in these close quarters there could come an unexpected need to fight.

Now the Ghûlen wake turned straight to the east, and as they went it came sharp and clear; for here the wind did not reach, and no new snow had fallen since the Hèlsteeds had trod this way.

On they went, through the grim woods, and the Shadowlight fell dim among the clutching branches. Hours they rode, and at times walked, ever following the eastward trek. At last they came into the open, leaving the trees behind.

Ten miles or more they travelled across a great clearing where the trees grew not, and Tuck now rode on Jet's withers. Then ahead the Warrow again saw a line of trees as they came once more to the Drearwood.

"Lord Galen! Something lies in the snow ahead." Tuck strained to see what it was, but he could not discern its form. "Nought else is there near, only a crumpled bundle on the ground, just at the edge of the woods."

Jet was spurred forward, and his canter swiftly closed the distance. Now Galen's sight saw it, too. "A body, I think."

Now they came to it, and Tuck could see that the Prince was right. Galen reined Jet to a halt, and

Tuck sprang down, his heart racing, and ran to the form lying face down in the snow. Tuck dropped to his knees and reached forth with trembling hands, reaching across and taking hold of a shoulder, fearful of what he would see, and he rolled the body toward him, the face coming into view.

"Waugh!" he cried, scrambling backwards, *for he was staring into the dead black eyes of one of the corpse-people.*

"He's dead, Tuck, the Ghol is dead, yet he is unmarked by weapon." Galen stood and looked at the Warrow. "How he was slain, I cannot say."

"Lor, but he gave me a fright," said Tuck. "My heart is still pounding at a gallop. I don't know what I expected, but it certainly was no Ghûl." Tuck looked down at the pallid flesh and the blood-red slash of a mouth, and he shuddered. "Why is he here? What was he doing?" asked the Warrow, but the Man shook his head and said nought.

Now Lord Galen examined the tracks leading east. Just beyond the tree line he found the ashened remains of a burnt-out fire, and all around the blanket of snow was beaten down.

"Here they made camp," said Galen, and he took up a charred limb from the dead fire and held it to his nose. *"Rach!"* he cursed, flinging the wood aside. "Tuck, we have not gained more than one 'Darkday upon them, if that, for this fire is four or even five 'Darkdays old." Galen strode away a few paces and stood long in thought. At last he turned to Tuck. "If we but had more steeds, then we could ride apace. Yet here we must make camp, too, for Jet alone cannot run forever. He is not made of iron as was

Durgan's fabled steed. Even so, Jet has borne us nearly four hundred miles these past twelve 'Dark-days, from Challerain Keep to this dismal place, and he may need to go four hundred more ere we are done with this chase."

And so they made camp; but ere Lord Galen settled down for his rest, he took up his sword and strode past the trees and out to where the Ghûl lay. When he came back, his sword was black with gore. "I have made certain that he is dead beyond recall," said Galen, and Tuck shuddered but understood.

East they rode, soon emerging from the woods, and the track began swinging northward. "They are striking for the mountains," said Galen, "but whether the Rigga, the Grimwall, or the Gronfangs, I cannot say, for north they come together, north those three dread ranges join. There, too, is the frozen Grūwen Pass, known to the Elves as Kregyn, and it leads down into the Land of Gron, Modru's Realm of old."

Onward they paced, and the miles glided by 'neath Jet's steady hooves. The land began to rise around them, for they were coming into the fringes of the foothills of the unseen mountain range ahead.

Eleven leagues they rode—thirty-three miles—before they again stopped to make camp, this time in a sparse coppice set against the granite side of a craggy loom running north and south beyond seeing.

Lord Galen was asleep and Tuck sat scribing in his diary when the Warrow looked up from his journal to see two Elves standing across the fire from him, bright swords gleaming in the flickering light.

"Wha—" cried the Warrow, springing to his feet,

and the sound of his call brought Lord Galen up, sword in hand.

"Kest!" (Stop!) barked one of the strangers, holding his blade at guard, but Galen had seen that they were Elves and lowered the tip of his sword to the snow. "Take warning," spoke the Elf, "you are under the arrows of the Lian."

"But wait!" cried Tuck, stepping closer to the firelight. "We are friends!"

"Waerling!" gasped the second Elf, astonished.

Their stances relaxed a bit, yet still they did not lower their swords. "Your names and your mission."

Lord Galen spoke: "My companion is Sir Tuckerby Underbank, Waerling of the Boskydells, Land of the Thornwall. He is a Thornwalker and a Rukh slayer and serves in the Company of High King Aurion, and now rides with me as my trusted companion. We are on the track of a band of foul Ghola, slayers of innocents ten 'Darkdays past."

"And your name?" One Elf had now lowered his sword.

"I am Galen, son of Aurion," said the Prince, softly.

"Hai!" The Elves now sheathed their blades, and one turned and signalled to the crags above. "I am Duorn and this is Tillaron, and we were sent to slay you if you served the Evil One, or to fetch you if you be friends, for you are camped upon our very doorstep."

"But . . . how . . . I did not hear you approach," stammered Tuck, then his voice turned to self-disgust: "Hmph! This rock would make a better sentry than I."

"Blame not yourself, Wee One," said Tillaron,

"for at times we can move as softly as even the Waerlinga." And his tilted eyes twinkled as Tuck's rueful laugh sounded quietly among the crags.

"If you are to fetch us, then who sent you, and where are we to go?" Lord Galen asked.

"Captain Elaria sent us," answered Duorn, "and as to where we will go, why, to Arden Vale."

"Arden?" blurted Tuck. "That's where Lord Inarion bade us seek help if aught was needed. Lord Gildor spoke of it, too. But I thought Arden lay to the south, down near the Crossland Road."

"Aye, it is in the south, Wee One," answered Tillaron, "yet Arden reaches far north, too, and is but a few steps from here—less than a league to shelter and warm food."

And so they broke camp, scattering the fire, quenching the embers with snow. Then toward the craggy bluff they went on foot, Galen leading Jet. Straight at the sheer stone they strode, and Tuck wondered at their course. Through close-set pines they pressed, and into a hidden cleft in the rock. Jet's hooves rang upon rock as into an arched granite cavern they were led, hands outstretched before them, for they could see nought in the dark. "Trail your hand along the wall on your left," Duorn's voice came, echoing softly, "and fear not for your toes or your crown, for the floor is smooth and the ceiling high. Five hundred paces we will go in the dark, for a light might be seen by unfriendly eyes."

It was nearly nine hundred paces by Tuck's count ere they came out of the tunnel, yet he had expected it to be so, for his stride could not match that of the tall Lian. When they emerged into the Shadowlight, Tuck could see a deep craggy gorge lying before him, a gorge lined by tall pines growing thickly in the soil that lay on either side of the river below, now frozen in the winter cold.

A steep narrow path fell down the gorge wall to come among the pines. And Tuck could see several long low buildings nestled in the trees below.

Along the path they went, and as they strode down they heard the horn of a sentry signalling the arrival of strangers into the gorge. Down the path and among the pines they went, to come at last to the central shelter. An Elf took Jet and led him away as Tuck and Galen were ushered inside. Vivid colors and warmth and the smell of food assaulted Tuck's senses as they entered the great hall, lambent with yellow lamps glowing in cressets and fires burning on the hearths. Bright Elves turned as the strangers entered, and silence reigned as the Elven leader stood to greet them, his consort at his side.

Tuck and Galen doffed their cloaks; their quilted goose-down outer clothing was shed, too. And there before the assembly came two bright warriors, Tuck's armor silveron and Galen's bright red. And Galen looked at the Warrow "Princeling" and smiled a broad grin, receiving a smile in return, for neither had seen the other in aught but bulky down, and now they both looked the part of warriors.

And as they strode to the dais, Elves murmured in amaze, for visits to Arden by Men were rare, but here come among them was a jewel-eyed Waerling.

"My Lord Talarin," said Duorn in a voice all could hear, "I bring you Prince Galen, son of Aurion King, and Sir Tuckerby Underbank, Waerling of the Boskydells."

Talarin bowed, a tall slim figure with golden hair

and green eyes, dressed in soft grey. He turned to his consort. "Prince Galen, Sir Tuckerby, this is the fair Rael."

Tuck raised his eyes, and his heart was filled with wonder, for here was a beauty like unto that of the Lady Laurelin. Fair was Rael, and graceful, too, yet where Laurelin's hair was wheaten and her eyes pale grey, Rael's locks were golden and her eyes deep blue. Dressed in green, she was, with her hair bound in ribbons. And she smiled down at Tuck, and his sapphire eyes sparkled.

"You must eat and drink and spend some days with us," said the Elfess, "and rest from your journey."

"Ah, my Lady, much as we would like, we cannot," responded Galen. "Yes, tonight, perhaps, we will eat and drink and be warm, and rest under your guard—"

"And take a bath, too, please," interrupted Tuck, his head bobbing.

"Aye, and bathe, too, if we may," continued Galen, smiling. "But on the morrow we must leave at haste, for we are on the track of Ghola, and north we ride."

"On the track of Ghûlka?" exclaimed Talarin. "Prince Galen, ere you set at our board, there is someone you must see, for it may bear upon your mission. Follow me."

Talarin strode quickly down the length of the hall and out the doors and across the snow with Galen and Tuck in his wake. As they crossed toward another building, Tuck heard the sentry's horn announcing another arrival, and he looked up at the gorge wall to see a horse bearing an Elf clattering swiftly down the distant path.

But Tuck's attention was drawn to Lord Talarin's words: "He was found three 'Darkdays past," Talarin said as they walked, "lying in the snow, wounded and fevered, cut upon the brow, perhaps by poisoned blade. He would have frozen had my patrol not happened upon him. His horse had bore him toward the entrance to the gorge, and he was not far away. But he had fallen from the saddle and lay among the rocks—for how long, I cannot say—and he was nearly dead.

"But he, too, mumbled of Ghûlka, and now at times he rages, fevered. Even so, he might bear you news, though he has not awakened."

Into the building Talarin led them, and down a central hall of doorways. Tuck's heart was racing, and a great sense of foreboding filled his being. Ahead, a door opened, and an Elven healer stepped into the corridor. "Alor Talarin," the Elf greeted the Lian leader.

"How fares the youth?" asked Talarin.

"His face is flush with heat, yet I deem the fever has begun to break, for he is at times no longer racked with chills, and he will waken soon." The Elf's eyes slid over Tuck and Galen, wonder in his gaze, but he spoke on to Talarin: "Yet he has been near death, and trembles with weakness. His strength will not return for a fortnight or two, and then only if the herbs the Dara Rael used can throw off the poison of the *Rûpt* blade."

"I would that Lord Galen sees him, for it may bear upon the Prince's quest," said Lord Talarin, and the healer stepped aside, opening the door.

With Tuck's pulse thudding in his ears, into the candlelit room they quietly stepped. There in a bed lay a young Man, his face to the wall, and he was weeping.

Galen spoke softly to him, anguish in his voice: "Igon."

And as Tuck's hopes crashed down around his heart, Prince Igon turned his face to that of his brother. "Galen, oh, Galen," he wept, "they've got Laurelin."

Tuck sat numbly on a bench against the wall as Lord Galen held Igon to him, and tears streamed down the faces of all three. Yet the look upon Galen's visage was grim to behold. The candles cast a soft yellow glow over the room, and Lord Talarin stood by the door, his eyes glittering in the light. But then Galen gently lowered Igon unto the bed and called for the healer, for the youth's fever had flared again, and the young Prince had swooned.

As the healer stepped to the bedside, there came the muffled steps of someone striding hard down the hall, and Talarin stepped into the corridor. Tuck heard the faint sound of hushed voices, muted by the door, and then into the room came Talarin, and another Elf was with him, dressed in stained riding garb. Tuck looked up. *"Lord Gildor!"*

Galen turned his bleak face to Lord Gildor's, and the Elf gripped something tight in his fist.

"I come bearing woeful news, Galen King." Lord Gildor held out his hand, closed upon a token, and

Galen reached forth to take what was offered—a scarlet eye-patch. "Aurion Redeye is dead."

Tuck sat stunned. He could not seem to get enough air to breathe, and he no longer could see through his tears.

Galen spoke at last: "My sire is slain, and my betrothed is taken captive, and my brother lies wounded by poisoned blade. And Modru's dark tide drowns the Land. These are evil days for Mithgar, and evil choices am I given."

"Galen King," said Lord Gildor next, "for all of Mithgar, you must ride south to lead the Host against vile Modru's Horde."

"North! Ride north!" Igon cried, starting up from a fevered dream, his wild eyes unseeing. "Save the Lady Laurelin!"

Here ends the first part of the tale of The Iron Tower.

The second part is called Shadows of Doom. *It continues the stories of Tuck and Galen, of Laurelin, and of other companions in beleaguered Mithgar.*

The third part, The Darkest Day, *tells of the last desperate gamble of the Alliance to thwart Modru's evil plan.*

About the Author

Dennis L. McKiernan was born April 4, 1932, in Moberly, Missouri, where he lived until age eighteen, when he joined the U.S. Air Force, serving four years during the Korean War. He received a B.S. in Electrical Engineering from the University of Missouri in 1958 and, similarly, an M.S. from Duke University in 1964. Employed by a leading research and development laboratory, he resides with his family in Westerville, Ohio. Though he has freelanced articles for magazines, *The Iron Tower* marks his debut as a novelist.